CORRODE

ELLA FIELDS

DEDICATION

To those who seek forgiveness,
may you one day be granted a second chance.

When your heart and mind are at war,
it's hard to tell which lie holds the most truth.

PROLOGUE

Felix

Sunshine has never felt so good. Sure, I've been outside plenty of times in the past eighteen months and felt its warmth. But sunshine feels different now that I'm finally walking away from the pen that's confined me for so damn long. Tastes different, even. The feeling of freedom blankets my body and I let it soak into every part of me.

"What are you doing?"

Tilting my head back down, I squint to find Sam leaning against the back of her car. A tiny smile tugs at her pursed lips as she gazes at me from behind her sunglasses.

Shrugging, I say, "Just taking a moment to let it sink in."

She nods as if she understands. No one can really understand what it's like to be in prison unless they've been there themselves. But I don't hold it against her, considering she's one of the only people besides my brother who came to visit me.

The reminder makes my teeth grit together.

I won't lie. At first, her visits made me mad, but Sam didn't care. She kept coming. After a few months of her visiting once every four weeks, I gave in and decided that having someone give a shit about me wasn't something I should feel annoyed or gripe about. She said I could use a friend, and though I didn't care too much for friends at the time, I guess she had a point.

Especially seeing as a certain brown-eyed woman never bothered to put a stop to my endless waiting. She never showed. Not once.

Anger scorches a blazing trail through my body. My spine steels; my fists clench. The sound of the bag in my hand crinkling and Sam's voice have me taking a deep breath as I try to let some of the tension go.

"How's it feel, being out?" She holds a hand over her head, trying to block the sun from creeping in between her sunglasses and eyes.

That ever-present sting won't let up, but I give Sam my best attempt at a smile. "Surreal, and like it's about damn time."

She straightens from the car and walks over to me with her hips swaying. I swallow and glance away. "I thought I told you that Jared was picking me up." Surveying the lot, I find scattered cars, but none of them familiar.

She stops in front of me, the smell of her perfume traveling into my nose. "I know, but I wanted to see you just in case you changed your mind."

Her softer tone has me looking back down at her. I know why she's really here. And even though going to find them is all I've been thinking about doing for the past three weeks, now that I'm actually free, I'm not so sure I can. For fear of what I'll find, or what I'll do.

But the fact Sam wants to prolong it? Yeah, that grates something fierce.

She knows. Damn it, she fucking knows I'm not cut out for anything with her or anyone else. Yet she keeps putting herself in front of me once a month to tempt me, trying to make me cave.

A part of me wants to just say fuck it and give in. That angry, hurt, starving part of me.

But the rest of me is too busy longing for the other half of my heart, so I never do.

Tires crunching over the gravel lot have my eyes swinging away from Sam and landing on a beat-up truck. Good thing, too. A guy can only ignore a broken heart for so long before the temptation to put a Band-Aid over it starts looking good. Even if it is only for a couple of hours.

"Sam …" I start.

"It's fine." She holds up a hand. "Go with him. I'll come see you later?"

"I have no idea what I'll be doing."

Her shoulders lift. "That's okay. I'll come find you soon, Lix."

She's always called me that. I've never had the heart to tell her that I fucking hate the nickname.

"Yo, felon!" Jared hollers, slamming the truck door and walking over. A huge grin is plastered on his face, but it slowly falls when he sees who I'm standing with. He stops, looks at me, then looks at Sam.

Sam clears her throat. "I'll see you later." After giving Jared a wave, she walks back to her car.

Jared waits until she's driving out of the lot before starting in with the questions. "What the actual fuck, man?"

"Don't give me shit, kid. Let's just get out of here." I start walking to the truck, noticing that he left the spitfire at home.

When he first brought her to see me, I couldn't believe he'd landed some rich, snotty socialite and managed to make her his. But she makes him happier than I've ever seen him, so I don't particularly give a fuck if she's a bit of a bitch.

"Hang on a damn minute." Jared catches up to me while I'm opening the door. I don't wait; I want away from this shithole as soon as possible, so I dump my bag on the floor of the truck and close the door.

He curses, climbing back in the driver's seat and starting the truck. "Sam? Why the hell was she here?" He lights a cigarette and heads out of the lot. I snatch his pack from the dash, lighting one for myself. I quit years ago, but fuck it, I feel like one.

I cough as soon as I inhale the first drag, winding down the window and ignoring the chuckle from the shithead next to me.

"She visited me," I finally say. "Every month."

Jared's silent for a while, then hums. "I see." He flicks some ash out the window. "And Maggie didn't."

Fucker. He's right, but that doesn't mean anything's going on. I tell him as much, and he just laughs. "Yeah, for now. Stay away from her, man; she's like a rash you've had for over a decade. Time to take a bath and swipe some lotion over that shit. Get rid of it once and for all."

That makes me laugh. I start coughing again, smoke leaving my mouth and stinging my eyes.

"You're a dickhead."

He shrugs, taking a drag of his cigarette. "You know I'm right, though. You've got other shit to focus on; you don't need her messing anything up for you."

Again, he's right. I've got so much shit to focus on that I can almost feel it strangling me. I run a hand over my scruff, wondering where the fuck I'm gonna start.

"The shop need me?"

He guffaws. "Your shop too, dude. Of course, it does."

That makes me feel marginally better. Getting a job is hard enough, but getting one after doing time could prove impossible.

"Can't believe you're finally out. Fuck, you must feel so relieved."

I do. But I don't. At least behind bars, I had a way of dodging the mess I'd left behind. Now, not so much. It's time to try to fix it. The only problem is, I don't know how I'll ever get past what she's done. Or what to even do about it all. I know I messed up in a fucking spectacular way, but damn, to keep my son from me? I just don't understand how she could hate me that much.

Anger fuels the words that leave my mouth next. "Relieved isn't exactly how I'm feeling right now." I sigh, trying to rein it in. "But yeah, I'm not fucking mad about being out. I think the sound of old Barry's snoring and him jerking off in the bunk above me will take years to wipe from my memory."

Jared laughs. "At least he never tried any funny shit." He glances over at me. "Though you're not exactly an easy target."

"Shut the fuck up." I huff out a laugh of my own and finish my cigarette before flicking it out the window.

Being locked up wasn't exactly a cakewalk. Those first few months were spent with my eyes constantly open, and it took three fights for a few assholes to finally see I wouldn't be taking any shit. People left me alone after that. It was boring and depressing as fuck, but I'd rather be bored than get in trouble and have my parole denied.

Which reminds me. "I'm going to need to see my parole officer before I can do anything."

Jared nods. "Well, we'll get you sorted out. Then you can

go find that nephew of mine."

Right. My son. I have a son I've never met. Only a worn-out picture of a wrinkle-faced newborn that I've looked at so many times, it's imprinted on my brain for life. Jared said the picture was left in an unmarked envelope in our mailbox, and he brought it to me months ago.

He'd look much different now. If I'm guessing right, he's gotta be at least twelve or thirteen months old.

I stare out the window, one tree joining the next in a myriad of brown and green. But all I can see is my kid's face and the face of the woman who not only broke my fucking heart but also kept him from me.

What the hell is she thinking?

My Little Doe should know better than to think she can hide from me.

CHAPTER ONE

Ten Years Ago
Maggie

"Come on, Maggie," Lucy groaned. "You're acting like the police are about to throw your ass to the lawn and arrest you at any moment."

Untucking my arms from around my waist, I tore my gaze from the dilapidated house. I was kind of worried it would collapse in on itself from the vibrations of the music and the number of people that appeared to be inside it. "You don't know how much trouble I could get in for this," I hissed at her. "Why couldn't we just stay at your place like you originally said we were going to?"

She rolled her eyes, flicked her brown hair over her shoulder, and marched toward the door. "No one is going to find out," she said with a grin. "Besides, you could've stayed behind if you really didn't want to come."

Damn it, that was true. I could've stayed at her place and

read my book or watched a movie. But, well, I was curious. My embarrassment over never having been to a party that involved illicit things such as alcohol and maybe drugs had my feet stuffing themselves into my Chucks and marching me out the door. Only now that I was here, I was suddenly extremely nervous.

What if I drank too much? Oh, God. What if I threw up?

"Maggie, come on!"

Sighing, I shuffled over the jungle of weeds and walked in behind Lucy before pulling the door closed behind me.

The noise had my ears immediately screaming in outrage. The smell of tobacco and other acrid scents drifted down the dingy hallway to greet me.

Grabbing Lucy's arm, I whisper-yelled into her ear, "Who are these people again?"

She shrugged my hand off. "It's some kid's house from the public school; he always throws these parties."

"But where are his parents?" I asked as we nudged past a group of guys laughing around the entry to the kitchen.

She threw me a glare. "Who cares? Dean said they're okay."

Her new boyfriend. Right. Okay.

Straightening my shoulders, I followed her into the kitchen and stood by the old fridge as Lucy rummaged through it.

Her head appeared above the door a moment later, a huge smile making her blue eyes twinkle mischievously. "Beer." She shoved one at my chest, and I barely caught it in time to stop it from dropping to the sticky linoleum floor.

The pop and hiss of Lucy opening her can snapped my attention back to her. Closing the fridge with her ass, she tipped the can back and took a lengthy pull. "Go on, then." She wiped her mouth with the back of her hand.

Fumbling with the tab, I opened it and brought the cool

metal to my lips. My nose crinkled at the foul taste, but one look at Lucy, who was chugging back most of her own, had me holding my breath and attempting to do the same.

"Let's go find Dean," she said, walking out the other doorway of the kitchen to the small living room. I followed, of course. What else was I supposed to do? The beer sloshed around in my belly in a weird, fizzing way. I needed to burp but kept the urge at bay even though the likelihood of anyone hearing it in that room with the loud music was very slim.

"Lucy!" I called, but she waved me off when some guy wearing a backward facing baseball cap and a sweat-stained band t-shirt walked over and grabbed her hips. That must be Dean.

Damn it.

Leaning against the wall, I decided that if I couldn't at least muster up the courage to dance and mingle, then I might as well try not to look like any more of a loser. I finished half my beer but couldn't bring myself to drink any more.

Feeling awkward just standing around, I decided to go for a walk. I dumped my beer on a side table and left the room. Maybe my father was right about one thing at least. Maybe I wasn't missing out on a lot by staying away from this kind of fun.

Shimmying past a couple of girls making out, I slid open the back door near the kitchen and stepped out onto the small deck.

The cool air was a welcome respite from the noisy crowd polluting the stale air inside. I closed the door and walked down a set of cracked concrete steps, thinking I'd just sit out here and play snake on my phone for a while before going to find Lucy.

Then I heard something.

"Lix, you always say that. Why? Why can't you just give me a chance?"

"Sam, Christ. Don't do this now. Let's just go back inside."

I froze with my ass halfway to the step when who I'm guessing was Sam let out a frustrated cry. "I've given you everything, and I'm starting to get sick and tired of feeling used."

Male laughter hit my ears, dark and raspy. "I've never lied to you, Sam. And I never told you that you had to. In fact …" He lowered his voice as I lowered my butt to the step, straining to hear what he said next. "You throw yourself at me every fucking time. I don't want to hurt you; you're my friend. But fucking hell, I'm not interested in being anything more, and I've always told you that."

"Throw myself at you?" she almost screamed. "You know what? Find someone else to warm your dick, Felix. Fuck you."

Then she was rounding the corner of the house, the dark of night unfolding around her like it was making way for her turbulent feelings. I shrank down, trying to look interested in my phone and not like I'd just heard the poor girl have her heart broken.

She paused just before she reached the steps, and I lifted my gaze to find her looking at me, but she only sniffed before continuing past me up the stairs and then heading inside. The noise escaped the house for a moment before the door slammed shut.

Well, crap. Maybe parties were interesting after all.

I hated to soak in other people's misery, but I'd never had my heart broken by a boy before. I'd only been kissed a few times, had a boob grab or two, but it was over the clothing, so I didn't know if that even counted. I was often living vicariously through other people's experiences. Couldn't help it if I found them interesting. A girl took what she could get when she was never allowed to partake in the usual adolescent fun that her friends did.

"What are you doing?"

Crap. Turning my gaze to the left again, I found the guy who broke hearts.

Felix—half shrouded in the shadows, half shining in the moonlight.

He sat down across from me on a plastic chair near a burned-out drum, which I guessed was used as a fire pit.

"You got a voice, Little Doe?"

"Uh." I cleared my throat. "Little doe?"

He shrugged, tipping a beer can to his mouth and draining the contents. He then crushed it and chucked it at the drum. "You got that whole deer caught in the headlights look about you."

My eyes widened. "I do?"

He chuckled and the sound was like an old, rough, well-loved blanket that wrapped around me, making me want to inch closer to him. To see what it might've felt like to press my palm against his chest while he laughed.

Jabbing a finger at me, he said, "Right there, Little Doe."

"Oh." I tried to school my features.

"What are you doing out here? Party's in there." He tilted his head, peering at me curiously. "Wait, you even from around here?"

Busted. "Yeah, no. My, um … my friend's boyfriend told her to come, and I tagged along." I fidgeted with the plastic casing on my phone. "I guess."

His lips tilted to one side. "You guess?"

Heat infused my cheeks, but I nodded.

"Where do you go to school?"

Picking at a thread on my jeans, I murmured, "Bonnet's

Bay High."

He whistled, diverting my attention back to him. "A Bay bitch."

My head snapped back. "A *what?*"

"A Bay bitch." He reclined in his chair, the plastic creaking with his weight. "Rich girls."

I tore my eyes away from the sliver of skin peeking out from between his jeans and his black long-sleeved shirt. "I'm not rich." It was all I could think to say.

Because my family was definitely not rich. They owned a bakery, worked hard, and sometimes struggled to pay tuition to keep us in school. Well, it was a bit easier since my sister graduated two years ago and there was only me, but still.

His eyes roamed over me, and it took everything in me to sit still under his intense inspection. He scratched at the stubble coating his jaw. "While that may be so … you definitely don't look like a lot of the girls who hang around here."

I glanced down at my off-the-shoulder peach sweater. "So?"

He grinned, looking like a wolf gnashing his teeth together before he pounced on his prey. "Why don't you come sit over here, Little Doe?" He kicked his leg out, catching the chair next to his and dragging it closer with his booted foot.

I shivered. "I think I'm good where I am, thanks."

"Scared?"

Was I? I guess I was. Something about him had my instincts screaming to run. But in which direction, I wasn't sure. To him or away from him?

Trying to act aloof, I scoffed, "No."

"Prove it then." He nudged his head toward the chair.

Oh, what the hell. I rose from the step, my butt a little numb from having sat on the hard concrete, and dumped myself into the chair next to him. "There, satisfied?"

He leaned his chin on his fist, staring at me.

I swallowed as I took in his dark brown eyes and the even darker lashes that framed them. Handsome wasn't an adequate word to use for this Felix guy. Roguish was what came to mind. He couldn't be much older than I was, but the hard lines and deep cut of his cheekbones made him appear much older. The two-day-old scruff that peppered his square jaw and surrounded those full lips didn't exactly help matters either. And his hair—oh God, his hair. It stood in every direction, dark brown and thick. I had the sudden urge to lift my hand to see for myself just how thick it was, but thankfully, his voice stopped me from humiliating myself. "I'll be satisfied when you tell me your name."

"Why do you want to know?" I didn't know where my bravado had come from, but I wasn't going to complain.

"So when I go home, climb into bed, and wrap my hand around my cock, I know whose name I'll be whispering into the dark."

Wow. That should have had me running. Away from him. Definitely away from him.

But I didn't.

Tingles ignited over the skin of my neck, dancing down my spine as I puffed out a nervous breath in response.

He chuckled again, reaching out to wrap a thick finger in a strand of my long auburn hair. "Shit, Little Doe. You're fun to play with." He leaned in and sniffed the strand wrapped tight around his finger, causing my stomach to clench. "Strawberries."

"My shampoo." This guy … this guy named Felix was sniffing my hair. And as if that night couldn't get any weirder, I realized that I liked it. I liked it way too much.

He hummed. "Where's your friend?"

"Inside with her boyfriend, Dean."

He sat back a little, letting my hair drop. I think I might have sighed in disappointment. "Dean Trellot?"

I nodded. "Yeah." Then frowned. "Why?"

He shook his head with a snicker. "That dickhead's got his hands full."

I didn't know what he meant, though I'd find out later.

"Do, ah, you go to school here in the city?" I asked quietly.

"I do." He sucked on his lip for a second. "How old are you?"

"I just turned eighteen," I said, glad that I could now ask him the same. "How old are you?"

He reached into his pocket and pulled out what looked like a cigarette. "Eighteen, too."

I watched as he lit it; the way his eyes narrowed and the way he cupped the flame with his large hand. He tucked his lighter away and inhaled.

That was when the weird smell hit me that I'd noticed inside. "What is that?"

He passed it over to me. "A blunt."

I took it from him, staring at it. "You mean … weed?"

He laughed, and I tried not to drop the smelly thing. "Yes. Weed. You've never had any?"

Not wanting to look like an idiot in front of him, I shook my head and brought the blunt to my lips, instantly coughing when I inhaled.

My lungs felt like they were on fire, and my throat burned.

"Whoa, Little Doe." He reached over and took it from me, then to my horror, he started rubbing my back. "You okay? Small drags for a beginner."

He moved his chair right next to mine, his arm looping around my shoulders as he showed me how to do it. I tried again, taking a few short drags and only coughing once. "No more for you," he said, finishing off the blunt. "Otherwise, you'll be high as a kite."

I think I already was. "So was that your girlfriend?" I asked when he finished, then laughed at my own audacity and covered my mouth.

He grinned and my eyes narrowed, trying to get a good look at his straight white teeth. "What are you doing?"

"Nothing." I sat back in my chair.

He chuckled. The clouds moved past the moon, and seeing his face in the light again, I noticed his eyes looked a little bloodshot. I wondered if mine did, too. I reached up as if I could check by touching them.

He nudged my hand down. "Trying to poke your eyeball out?"

I laughed, loud and crazy sounding. "Of course, not."

He kept my hand in his, and I let him. It felt warm, large, a little rough, and a whole lot nice. "You heard that earlier conversation, did you?"

"Sure did, if that's what you call it." I threw him a smirk. "Though I didn't mean to. I was just trying to play some snake and then bam." I tossed my free hand into the air. "Heard you break some poor girl's heart into itty-bitty pieces."

Laughing under his breath, he never moved his keen eyes from my face. "We weren't together. She's a friend."

"You usually let a friend keep your *you know what* warm?" I snorted, and he grinned, shaking his head.

He brought my hand to his lips, softly rubbing them over the back of it. "I did. But it seems it was a mistake."

My breath hitched loudly, which made him groan against my hand. He lowered it to his thigh. "You're really fucking cute."

What? *Cute?* My nose crinkled with annoyance. "Cute?" I

asked as though he'd called me a toad instead.

"Yeah. I mean, you're beautiful. But you won't even say the word *dick*."

"Dick," I blurted out, then promptly dropped my head down and started howling with laughter.

He waited for me to get my crap together before saying, "You're definitely high."

I lifted my head, which kind of felt like it was spinning. "You've corrupted me, big guy."

"Big guy, huh?" He huffed. "And I guess I should feel bad about that?"

Sniffing, I flopped my head to the side, and stared at his lips. "But you don't." My voice was all breathy; I'm surprised he even heard me.

He shook his head again, his tone low and husky, sending shivers skating over my skin. "I really don't."

Then he was leaning in, his other hand grasping my chin while his lips hovered over mine. "Are you …" I swallowed hard. "Are you going to kiss me?"

"Do you want me to, Little Doe?" His breath washed over my lips. It smelled like beer with a slight hint of spearmint.

"I think I need to ask you a question first."

His lashes fluttered half closed, his eyes hooding. "Ask."

"Did you kiss your friend earlier?"

He exhaled before answering. "Not tonight, no."

"Okay," I whispered with my heart banging against my chest. "You can kiss me now."

"Thank fucking Christ." His lips landed on mine, and I didn't know what I expected, but it wasn't the gentleness I received.

He kissed me softly, as if he was planning to memorize the feel of my lips pressed against his to recall long after the night was over.

Dragging them up and down, he hesitantly parted them, fusing his bottom lip between both of mine. I freed my hand from his and lifted it to the side of his face, feeling the coarse stubble over his jaw before discovering just how thick his hair really was. My other hand joined in, sinking in and tugging gently, trying to pull him closer, deeper, *everywhere*.

He groaned. Then I was on his lap, sitting sideways.

Just as his tongue touched mine, the noise from inside grew louder from the back door sliding open. "Maggie?" Lucy's voice had my head snapping back. "Shit, Maggie, is that you? How much did you have to drink?"

I jumped up, wobbling on my feet a little, and Felix steadied me with a hand on my hip.

"What's up?" I tried to act cool, but one look at my face had Lucy asking, "Holy shit, are you stoned?"

"Ah, I think so. Maybe." I shrugged and tried for a smile.

Laughing, she shook her head. "Come on. Let's go."

I frowned at her. "What, why?"

She sighed loudly. "Because Dean's a two-timing asshole who was just kissing some other chick in the laundry room while I was on the stinking toilet, that's why."

"Shit." My eyes bugged. "But …" I glanced back at Felix, wishing I could stay.

Lucy turned around and marched down the side of the house. "Sorry, dude, she's coming with me. Hurry up, Maggie. I need to get out of here before the sleaze finds me."

"Maggie." The sound of my name from Felix's mouth had me giving my attention back to him. "You dropped this." He held out my long-forgotten phone. I took it, only to have him grab my wrist and bring my hand to his mouth once again. "Text me when you get home."

I nodded, still wondering when I'd dropped my phone, but then I realized I didn't even have his number. "I don't have your nu—"

His crooked grin had my stomach fluttering as I realized what he'd done. I tucked some hair behind my ear, giving him a small and probably dopey smile before removing my hand and following Lucy out the side gate to the street where we waited for a cab.

I didn't wait until we were back at Lucy's place to text him. I did it on the way there.

Me: Felix. Like the cat. I love cats!

Felix: I hate the reminder, but from you? It's not so bad. ;)

CHAPTER TWO

Ten Years Ago

My parents didn't always fight. But when they did, you could guarantee it would end in tears. My mother's tears.

"You didn't need to pay it yet, you fucking idiot!" my father roared.

I sometimes wondered if my mom truly loved my dad and that was why she put up with the way he treated her.

My mom's family lived in France. She came here on an exchange program in high school, met my dad, and never went home. She's estranged from her family because of it. It wouldn't have surprised me if her parents didn't even know about me or my sister, Genevieve.

My father's loud voice had me cringing and desperately trying to lose myself in the words I was looking at on my lap. I crossed my legs, leaning back against the headboard, and squeezed my favorite cat pillow to my chest.

Eventually, the shouting stopped, and the only sound was

the branches tapping against my bedroom window from the gentle breeze outside.

Glancing over at my little white alarm clock, I bit my lip and took my phone off charge before dialing his number. We'd talked almost every night since the party last weekend, but I always waited until my father had gone to bed before I called.

"Mags?"

My lips tilted at the sound of his voice. He had started calling me Mags almost instantly, but I didn't mind.

"Hey, did I wake you?" It was almost ten thirty at night.

"Nah." His voice was gravelly, as though he'd been lying in bed. "You know I was waiting for you to call."

My smile turned into a gigantic grin. After moving my book to the nightstand, I laid down and climbed under the covers of my bed. "Did you work this afternoon?"

He'd told me about working for his foster dad, and how he and his brother had ended up going to live with him. My heart broke when he told me about the way his own parents used to forget him and his brother. Choosing drugs and alcohol over making sure their kids were okay. And for the first time in my life, I felt grateful for my own.

Something I never thought I'd feel.

"Yeah, Darren's decided it's time I learn how to weld. One of the guys who works there is gonna teach me."

I knew without asking that he didn't plan to go to college. But I didn't think any less of him. In fact, the more I learned about him, the more I admired the way he was paving his own path, especially after the cards he'd been dealt. "Welding? So you'll be able to build bikes all by yourself in no time then, right?"

He chuckled. "Not for a while, but I gotta start somewhere I guess." He yawned. "And with graduation right around the corner, I don't wanna be a shit kicker at the shop when I'm done."

Staring at the ceiling, I hesitated for a moment, then decided to just ask. "What are you doing this weekend?"

He didn't hesitate. "Taking you out."

My heart bottomed out. "Taking me out?"

"Yeah."

I cleared my throat, thinking back to the weekend. To Sam. "Do you, um, normally take girls out?"

"Never." He sighed. "Look, what you saw? Or heard. That's not, okay, no ... that is what I'm like. *Was* like." He paused. "But with you, I kind of want to see what it'd be like not to be like that for a change."

"Really?" I asked a lot more breathy than I'd intended. With my cheeks flaming, I closed my eyes, feeling like an idiot.

But he only chuckled. "Really. I don't think I could be any other way with you. I kinda think I might wanna keep you."

His words didn't scare me. No, the pounding of my heart scared me. It was racing, echoing in my ears in a way that made me wonder if he could somehow hear it too. "I kinda like that." Was all I could think to say in response.

"Yeah?"

"Yeah." Then my eyes widened. My parents. My dad. *Crap.*

"Um, but my parents. Well, you know how I've told you they can be kind of ..."

"Protective? Overbearing?" he supplied. "You may have mentioned it once or twice. But I think I got that after last weekend."

Chewing on my lip for a second, I released it and muttered, "So I'll probably have to work something out. Maybe we'll have to hang out during the day." I winced. "How lame. I'm sorry. I'll totally understand if you want to change your mind right now. I'll completely—"

"Mags."

My mouth closed, and I drew in a shaky breath. "Yes?"

He let out another chuckle. "You're cute."

My nose crinkled. He knew it, too. "You scrunching up that little nose of yours?"

I scoffed. "No."

He laughed deeply, and my whole body relaxed at the sound of it. "Right. Meet me in the city tomorrow morning?"

Thinking it over for a moment, I decided I could probably swing that. "Sure. I'll think of something to tell them. What time?"

"Ten. I want as much time with you as I can get."

He told me to meet him in the first parking lot at the beach, then listened to me murmur the details of my day to him. I fell asleep with the phone on the pillow next to my cheek and a smile etched on my face.

My dad was thankfully already at work when I got up to get ready that morning. I had breakfast with my mom, who looked so damn tired that I doubt she knew I was even asking her a question. But nevertheless, I told her I was going into the city to look for a graduation dress with Lucy. She said to be home before my dad was and that was it.

Some might say my mother was a weak woman—a stupid one even—for staying with a man who used her as his own verbal punching bag. I wouldn't blame them because some part of me resented her for exactly that reason.

But I was mostly just disappointed. Disheartened that she allowed it to continue. They never used to fight in front of us, and rarely let us hear it happen. But after my sister left for college, it was as if my father lost his reasons for giving a damn.

I'd spoken to her about it, begging her to look at the situation and see it for what it was. Wrong.

But she wouldn't hear it. She would just pat my hand and tell me I was too young to understand.

How could I not understand what was so plainly obvious? But I let it go. My dad's temper could scare the pants off a man twice his size. Even I had come to fear him.

Sighing, I parked my Honda Accord and flipped down the visor to check my reflection. I opted for a charcoal gray sundress, pantyhose, boots, and a cream cardigan, praying I didn't look too dressed up. I fluffed my auburn hair and quickly swiped on some lip balm before climbing out of the car.

My stomach sunk as I looked around the half full parking lot and found no sign of Felix. Then the sound of a motorcycle hit my ears and had me turning around.

A guy rode in and parked right next to my car. My eyes bugged out as I watched him turn the bike off and grin at me.

I felt silly. I mean, he'd told me he had one, but I just assumed he meant a dirt bike. Or a quad bike. Or I don't know, the kind of bike you'd expect a teenage boy to play around on.

Not a Harley Davidson.

Felix climbed off, hung his helmet, and walked straight to me.

"H-hi," I stuttered dumbly.

He just grinned further, then swung his arm around my waist and tugged me to him. Tucking some hair behind my ear, he said, "Hi, Little Doe."

Damn it. "I'm doing it again, aren't I?"

He nodded. "Beautiful."

Flushing down to my toes, I blurted, "You actually ride a motorcycle?"

He glanced behind him at said motorcycle, then brought those dark eyes back to me. "I do. Darren got it for me for my eighteenth birthday. We're still fixing it up, but it runs well."

"Wow." Yeah. That's what I said. Like a girl who'd thought she'd seen all the bad boys there were to see in her fancy prep school, only to discover she was wrong. And was now feeling a little bit—okay, *a lot*—in over her head.

"You okay?" His arm tightened around my waist. I then realized my own arms were hanging like limp spaghetti noodles. I cleared my throat and lifted them, placing my hands tentatively on his hoodie covered chest, as I nodded.

He stared at me for a moment, then leaned forward. I thought he would kiss me, and my heart kick-started, but he only slid his nose along my cheek. My blood turned to lava at the gentle touch, my skin prickling with goose bumps when he placed a kiss on my cheekbone.

He inhaled deeply, then let it out, his warm breath stirring my hair and ghosting over my ear. "Strawberries." That was all he said before grabbing my hand and dragging my liquefied body out of the parking lot and down the street.

We walked down the main street that ran parallel to the beach until I finally managed to ask, "Where are we going?"

"Nowhere, anywhere."

"Sounds good." I laughed.

We walked to nowhere and talked about anything and everything. From my sucky prom date to Felix's brother's latest suspension from school after someone caught him with a girl in the sports equipment room.

"He sounds like he might break more hearts than you," I remarked.

Felix huffed, squeezing my hand playfully. "Well, yeah. I tend to stick with the same chick for a while, whereas Jared wouldn't be caught dead with anything that resembled a fleck of commitment."

I briefly wondered how long he'd stick with me but kept those thoughts to myself. "He sounds like trouble, this Jared."

He laughed at that. "That's one way to describe him."

We stopped for hot dogs at a stand set up near the beach, then walked over to a picnic table that overlooked the water. I went to sit down opposite Felix until he said, "No, here."

And so I sat down next to him without question or thought; it was what I wanted to do anyway.

He popped open the can of Coke, then offered it to me. I took it and drank a big mouthful before putting it down and starting on my hot dog. We'd been walking around the city for ages, and I was kind of starving by that point.

We ate in silence. It seemed like Felix only took three bites of his hotdog, and then it was gone, so I offered him the last bite of mine. "I'm full anyway." I wasn't, but I suddenly wasn't that hungry either.

He grabbed my wrist and lifted my hand to his mouth. His lips wrapped around both the hot dog and my fingers holding it. I swallowed, though there was no food in my mouth, at the warmth and soft tickle of his tongue sliding over my skin. He kissed my hand, releasing it to swallow the bite, and then took a huge gulp of Coke while keeping his eyes trained on me.

I nervously reached out to toy with my purse on the table. His gaze moved to my fidgeting hand, and he huffed out a low chuckle. "When you said you loved cats, I didn't think it would extend this far." He flicked my purse, which was small and had a cat face covering the front of it.

I pretended to be offended for a second but realized I didn't really care. "My sister thinks it's childish." I twisted my lips, trying not to laugh at my weird obsession. "But I'm nowhere near as bad as I used to be."

"You got a cat?"

Shaking my head, I murmured, "Not anymore. We had one growing up, but he got sick and died a few years ago." I didn't tell him that my dad refused to help poor Wilfred, no matter how much I begged. He just had him put down to save the expense of treating him.

"He was ginger. Huge, fluffy, and fat." I smiled fondly, remembering him. "Kind of grumpy at times, but I loved him."

Felix stared at me for a moment, then took my hand in his, squeezing it gently.

"So tell me about this sister of yours." He released my hand and turned, straddling the bench. I did the same.

"She's two years older than I am, and in New York, attending college." I shrugged. "We're not really all that close." Which was true. We kind of just co-existed as team players in the same family.

Felix's dark brows knitted. "Why's that? You guys don't get along?"

"We get along fine. Just different people, I guess. She wants a life free of struggle, has her heart set on marrying some fancy doctor wannabe she's met. All her hopes and dreams seem to revolve around getting away from Rayleigh and bagging someone who'll take care of her."

Felix continued to watch me carefully. "And you don't want the same?"

"I got accepted to NYU, too. But I don't know." I glanced around at the beach, at the families playing together on the sand. "This is home. I like it here."

He blew out a loud breath, and my eyes slid back to him. "You're leaving?" he asked.

I tucked my hair behind my ear, suddenly feeling nervous. "I think so."

"You think so?"

My stomach clenched. "I don't know if I want to, but that's the only college offering me a full scholarship."

His eyes shuttered momentarily, and my ringing ears drowned out the sound of the gulls and the people surrounding us.

"Yeah, right." He glanced away, rubbing a hand roughly over his jaw. "You can't go turning something like that down, can you?"

No, I couldn't. It'd be a huge mistake, and I knew that. But it didn't change the fact that I didn't really have any desire to move to New York, and right then, the new possibility sitting across from me only had me more confused. Maybe I shouldn't have mentioned it, but he should know. "Sorry, I should've told you—"

"Mags." He cut me off with a sharp, gruff laugh. "Don't sweat it. That sounds like an awesome opportunity, and I'm fucking thrilled for you."

I sensed a *but*, yet I didn't get one. We just sat there, silently staring at each other, until my nerves had me changing the subject. "So, um, are you going out with your friends again tonight?"

He shrugged, a shadow moving over his face. "Not sure, maybe. If I don't, I'll give you a call."

"Okay." I sucked my lips into my mouth, glancing down at our legs but not really seeing much.

"Come on, we should probably go."

We'd only been hanging out for a few hours—which really, should've been plenty of time—but I wanted more. He said he wanted as much time as he could get. I realized then that telling him I was leaving at the end of summer had probably changed that.

Who wanted to get attached to some girl he'd just met, only to be forced into a long-distance relationship with her? At our age? I might have been young, naïve, and had my head stuck in the clouds a lot of the time, but even I knew the likelihood of that working out was very slim.

He stood and held out his hand to help me up. I took it with a tremulous smile playing on my lips and butterflies roaring back to life in my stomach. But they dropped dead when he released my hand and silently walked beside me back over the grass to the parking lot.

"You'll call me?" I asked hesitantly when we reached my car. "If you don't go out, that is." A nervous laugh bubbled out of me.

"Sure."

I nodded, frowning as I turned to open my door to climb inside. It felt like I'd shared so much of who I was with a guy who was now not interested in me.

It stung badly. I now had a whole new respect for the poor girl who'd had her own heart crushed by him last weekend.

I'd just closed the door and was about to start the car when the door opened and he pulled me out. "Wha—"

His lips slammed into mine, kissing me forcefully and effectively cutting me off. My back was flush with the rear passenger door of my car, and his breath was coming in harsh pants as he pulled his lips away and rested his forehead on mine.

His hands ran up my arms until he was cupping my cheeks. "I'm sorry, I shouldn't …" He swallowed audibly. "Not when you're only going to be moving away. But fuck, I want you anyway."

"You do?" My heart soared.

"More than anything I've ever fucking wanted in my life."

A laugh burst free of me, happiness causing my hands to shake as I lifted them to his cheeks and brought his lips back to mine. But that time felt different. I was stone cold sober for one, yet I'd never felt so adrift. As if I could look outside myself and see the way my hands still shook as they moved up his cheeks and sunk into his hair. As if I could see the way both of our eyes fluttered closed and the breath whooshed out of our chests at the same moment. That very moment when our lips touched and our hearts became twin flames that ignited instantly, that glowed so brightly—I could see it all through the layers of clothing and flesh and bone.

I'd had first kisses, but I'd labelled them incorrectly. Because that kiss? That was a real first kiss. The gentle glide of his lips on mine. The hesitant touching of our tongues. And the soft sounds of our breath escaping us both.

And it felt like the only kiss that would ever matter.

CHAPTER THREE

Ten Years Ago

We graduated two months later on a sweltering day at the end of May. Well, I did. I think Felix did too. Except he wasn't there for his graduation.

Because he was at mine.

I bit my lip as I walked off the stage, spying Felix in the back of the crowd. Sitting in the front row, my mom was smiling and dabbing at her eyes while my father sat stoically and looked off at the sky beyond the stage. My parents didn't notice Felix, but a few of the other students did, judging by the murmurs and whispers that reached my ears when I sat back down. I impatiently counted down the minutes until this was over and I could see him.

As soon as the clapping and cheering ensued, I stood and made a beeline for my parents, hoping to wave them off somehow so I could get to Felix. They still had no idea he was my boyfriend.

Boyfriend. The word made me feel stupid amounts of giddy.

I'd had boyfriends before, but none that lasted more than a few weeks. Once they realized I wasn't so easy to date, or maybe sleep with, they lost interest. Felix didn't even ask me; it was never a question of whether I was his anyway. The first time I went to his house and met Darren and his brother, he introduced me as his girl, and that was that.

Girlfriend seemed too insignificant a word for how I felt about him. Hell, the word love felt insignificant. I never thought I'd be that girl. The one who falls before realizing it was happening. But I started falling the night I met him and never stopped. He'd stolen pieces of my heart since that night, unrelenting until he had them all. And I'd be a liar if I said I knew when that happened. I just knew that it had. I think he knew it, too, despite never having told him.

My parents stood when I reached them. "I'm so proud, baby girl." My mom hugged me tightly and started murmuring to me in French, as she usually did when she got all emotional. My father simply patted my shoulder. "Let's get out of here, Elodie."

"I'm, um, I'm going to hang out with Lucy for a while, if that's okay?"

My dad frowned. Lucy chose then to thankfully appear at my side, swinging an arm around my shoulder. "Please, Mr. Ross."

My dad grunted. "Fine; be home by six for dinner."

"Martin." My mother touched his arm. "She's just graduated high school; let the poor girl go have some fun."

He sniffed, clearly annoyed, and kept us waiting for a full thirty seconds before speaking. "She'll stay at your place then?" he asked Lucy.

Lucy's eyes widened a fraction. "Uh, sure. If that's okay with you, of course."

He gave a firm nod. "Your mother will call you before bed; make sure you answer."

Taking my mother's hand, he led her off the football field and toward the parking lot.

"Holy shit, thank you," I breathed, hugging Lucy tightly.

She squeezed me back. "Lose that v-card and tell me all about it tomorrow, or I'm never covering for you again." Her brow quirked when she pulled back, giving me a stern look. "And though it's totally sweet of him to be here and all, you need to get him out of here before someone gives him away."

I laughed, nodding and saying goodbye so I could go do just that.

Felix was leaning against the bleachers near the back where he was more out of sight.

He stepped forward, and I ran the distance between us, jumping into his outstretched arms. He swung me around, then placed me on my feet, flicking the tassel on top of my graduation cap. "How's it feel, Little Doe?"

His arms constricted around me as I stared up into his face. "Like I'm free for the night to do whatever I please."

His brown eyes widened, the gold specks glinting under the sunlight. "Seriously?" I nodded, biting my lip. "Fuck me; let's get out of here then."

He grabbed my hand, and we got my stuff before hurrying out of the school to where he'd parked on the street. I climbed into the white truck he shared with his brother and closed the door with a sigh.

I should've felt nervous. We could finally do more, go all the way, instead of fleeting touches and rushed orgasms gifted by our hands. But I wasn't.

I was so ready and at peace with the knowledge that he'd be taking something no one else had. He was the guy who drove to my school almost every day, leaving his own early to see me for a brief ten minutes before going back to the city and working all afternoon. The guy who sent me good night text messages even after we'd been on the phone for hours. The guy who snuck me into the movies on the weekend, where we'd make out and feed each other popcorn in the dark, dusty corner. The guy who waited and never complained about the constraints my parents put on our relationship.

The guy who owned more and more of my heart with every small thing he did for me.

Because they weren't small at all. Not to me. They all added up, becoming too much in their entirety, until they became something no one else could ever measure up to.

Felix brought my hand to his lips to place a kiss on top of my palm, then rested it on his thigh to change gears. We sat in silence for most of the drive back to the city.

I'd come to learn that, except for with me—even though he never filled the silence with unnecessary talk even with me— he wasn't much of a conversationalist. Not unless he knew you or felt comfortable.

"You didn't even go to your graduation?"

I knew his was today, too. We'd spoken about it all week on the phone.

He shrugged. "Got Jared to get my diploma for me."

"Darren isn't going to be happy about that."

Felix just laughed. "Fuck no, he's not. But he'll get over it."

We were quiet for another few moments. Then I grabbed his hand and brought it to my lips, brushing them softly over his warm, rough skin. "Thank you."

He gave me a tiny smile as he pulled into his driveway.

Darren was waiting in the kitchen, leaning against the sink with his arms crossed over his meaty chest and wearing a scowl on his face. I smiled meekly at him, and his face softened marginally.

Darren was a big guy who had long gray hair, a matching beard and moustache, and was covered in old tattoos. He'd be extremely intimidating if it weren't for his kind blue eyes.

"Boy," he grunted. "Care to explain why I took half the day away from the garage to attend your graduation when you didn't even plan on showing up to it your damn self?"

Felix pulled me to his side. "Because I wanted to see Mags graduate instead." He then forced out a mumbled, "Sorry."

Darren looked at us and huffed out a husky laugh. "God damned smitten fools, you two are." He smiled then, waving his hand around. "Whatever. I'll be at Kenny's for beers tonight. So no funny shit; the last thing we need is Miss Magdaline's parents abusing the shit out of me for letting you corrupt their daughter under my watch."

Felix tightened his hand around my waist. I looked up to find a grin curling his lips to one side. "Corrupt?"

Darren straightened from the counter, stabbing a finger at him. "Don't give me that shit. You know damn well what I'm talking about, boy." He stepped closer to us, chucking me under the chin and causing a big smile to bloom on my face. "Congrats, you two. I'd say welcome to the real world, but it's all downhill from here." He chuckled, mussing Felix's hair before walking off.

I dumped my bag in Felix's room, shrugging my arms out of my robe and tossing it to the floor. He grabbed me from behind, picking me up and tossing me onto his bed. Laughing, I rolled over onto my back, looking up at him when he climbed on top of me. "No funny shit, big guy."

He grinned, all wolfish and all consuming. "Nothing about what I'm going to do to you will be funny."

My breathing sped up. "Is that right?"

His head lowered, his nose rubbing a path up the column of my throat and forcing my head to tilt back. His tongue then followed the same path his nose took, running over my racing pulse and licking a torturously slow trail to my mouth. "That's definitely right."

My hands grabbed his head, forcing his lips to mine. I licked the seam, parting them, then teased him by touching my tongue to his, only to retreat. He knew my game well and played along, his tongue creeping into my mouth, searching out mine. He bit my bottom lip, tugging it into his mouth and groaning when my hips started rocking into him.

He was hard, and I felt deliciously soft in comparison. Pliable and wanting him to meld me to his strong body until we couldn't tell whether we were two people or one.

"What's up, graduates!" Jared bounced on the bed behind us.

Felix tore his lips from mine, then grabbed his pillow, throwing it at his brother. "Fuck off."

I was still trying to catch my breath and tilted my head back to find Jared smiling down at me. "Nah, I kinda like hanging out right here." He winked at me, and I couldn't help but giggle. The guy was a serial flirt who had no shame.

Felix growled, and I sat up, grabbing his arm and tugging him back to the bed before he could move to the other side and likely haul his brother out by the scruff of his shirt. As he'd done a few times before.

"Chill, it's okay."

"Yeah, listen to Mags here. Besides …" He pulled out a sheet of paper from behind his back. "Didn't I get this for you?"

I grabbed it from Jared and traced my fingers over Felix's name on his high school diploma. I looked up at Felix, beaming.

"Congrats, big guy."

His face softened, and he tilted my head back more to kiss my lips upside down.

Jared cleared his throat. "Yeah, I'll be going now. Just wanted to say congrats." He got up but paused at the door. "And hey, don't go knocking her up with all that pent-up semen you've probably got, bro."

Felix lunged off the bed, and Jared laughed his ass off, running down the hallway.

I knew Felix wasn't a virgin, but that didn't bother me. Much. I mean, one of us should probably know what we're doing. Didn't mean I liked getting any reminders, though.

"How long has it been?" I asked once Jared had slammed his bedroom door closed, and we could hear music blaring through the walls of the small house.

Felix sighed and sat back down on the bed. "You really wanna know the answer to that?"

A lump moved from my chest to my throat, making it hard to breathe. He wouldn't have … "Mags, no." He palmed the side of my face, staring at me intently while he smoothed his thumb in circles over my cheekbone. "You seriously think I could ever do that?"

I let out a huge breath, relief crawling over me in mini waves of warmth, and shook my head. "The last time was the day before the night I met you."

Oh, well, shit. I guess I did ask.

"Hey, come here." He sat back against the headboard, and I climbed on his lap, straddling him. "Don't forget that I had no idea I'd be meeting the girl I'd want to spend the rest of my life with the next day." A soft laugh escaped him, and he shook his head. "How could I have known? You were unexpected. This innocent looking girl in her Chucks, jeans, and pretty sweater who had no business hanging out with scum like me." I frowned at that, but he continued before I could reprimand him for talking so badly about himself. "But unexpected or not, I knew you were meant to be mine the moment I saw those eyes of yours grow huge every time you looked at me."

With my heart pounding throughout my body, I blurted out, "I'm in love with you."

He smiled. "I know."

My head reared back. "You do?"

Tucking some hair behind my ear, he nodded.

"Am I that obvious?" I laughed, feeling heat slide up my neck to settle into my cheeks.

"I'm glad you are 'cause I don't exactly want to be alone in this."

"What? You mean …?" My words trailed off into a tremor.

His lips brushed mine. Those brown eyes burned with intensity when he said, "I'm in love with you, too. Have been for two months now."

A shaky breath left my mouth, and he inhaled it before sinking his hands into my hair and tilting my head to kiss me deeply. Nothing was playful about that kiss. It was both a promise and a changing of the tides.

He was mine already, but hearing those words only cemented it. Made me realize that although we were young, this kind of love, what we shared, was permanent. As if I'd just tattooed his name on my heart and sealed my fate.

The knowledge that came with giving all of yourself, a part of your soul, to someone else evoked a sting. A sense of danger that tried to be heard. But the sweet rapture that wrapped around that knowledge, that suffocated it with an inferno of promise and overwhelming happiness, eclipsed everything.

"Yo, Williams! Get over here and try this shit," one of Felix's friends, Holland I think his name was, yelled out across the crowded living room.

"Nah, I'm good," Felix said, eyeing the white powder on the coffee table.

We spent the rest of the afternoon hanging out at his place and watched a movie before getting ready to come here. Rayleigh public school's graduation party. Well, one of them. I think I'd call it more of a gathering, though, considering probably only twenty people were here. Not that I was an expert, of course, but they weren't doing much partying. Just sitting around, getting high, and talking shit. With the occasional girl dancing on her way to the kitchen to fetch more booze.

But I wasn't uncomfortable. Not with Felix holding me tight to his side on the couch. Plus, Jared was here too, though I didn't know where he'd disappeared to. Last I saw, he was leaving the room with a giggling blonde attached to his hip.

Felix tipped his beer back, swallowing a mouthful and giving me a wink. "You okay?"

I nodded, giving him a smile in return. I kind of just wanted to go home, well, back to his place. Nerves started tap dancing in my stomach at the thought of what might happen once we finally got there. He'd said he felt bad for ditching his friends at graduation and wanted to at least come hang out with them for a little while, which was fine.

Until Sam arrived.

The door slammed closed, and she stumbled into the living room, wearing a huge smile on her face until her eyes fell on me.

To say that we'd talked to each other or had even seen each other since Felix and I started going out would be a lie. This was the first time. And I didn't like the way my chest grew tight when Felix's arm gripped my side harder as he spotted her.

She removed her gaze and sat down with the other guys and a few of the girls, smiling, talking, and laughing.

After sitting rigidly for about ten minutes, I finally decided I needed a drink or something. I went to get up, but Felix tugged my hand until I was bending over him and he could study me intently. "Don't go swimming inside your own head, Little Doe." I nodded, wondering how he knew, but I shouldn't have. He knew me in ways I didn't know myself sometimes. He pressed his lips to mine, and my eyes fluttered closed. "We'll go soon. 'Kay?"

Nodding again, I straightened when he released my hand, moving to the kitchen and grabbing a glass of water. I was leaning against the counter drinking it when Sam strolled into the kitchen. She paused as if unsure whether she should say whatever it was she obviously came in here to say to me.

"Hi, Maggie, right?" she finally settled on, adjusting the bottom of her hot pink tank so that it sat on the waistline of her tiny white boy shorts.

I felt a bit out of place in my yellow sundress that sat mid-thigh, but I offered a polite smile and put my glass down. "Yeah, hi."

"I'm Sam," she said. "Don't know if you've heard of me, but I just wanted to introduce myself."

"Well, ah, hi again, Sam." I laughed nervously and tucked some hair behind my ear.

She laughed, too. "Shit, sorry. How awkward. I guess I should just come out and say it …"

I bit the inside of my cheek and waited as she heaved out a

loud breath, her slim shoulders bobbing down. "Felix and I, we kind of had a thing for a long while."

Blinking, I moved my head up and down, not sure if I should admit I already knew that.

She continued, "I just thought, you know, that I should say hi and let you know there are no hard feelings, I guess."

"You guess?" I couldn't help but ask, though I had no idea where the courage to do so came from.

She smiled thinly. "It's no secret that I've been in deep with the guy for years now, so yeah, it hurts." She stared at me for a drawn-out moment. "I want to hate you, but you seem really sweet, and I think that's going to be hard to do."

"Oh." Another nervous laugh erupted from me. "Well, for what it's worth, I'm sorry. I can't imagine how you must be feeling. He said he wasn't involved with—"

She held up a hand. "Yeah, we weren't serious, no matter how much I tried to change that. So don't sweat it. You have nothing to feel bad about. I just didn't want things to be awkward." She shrugged. "If we ever ran into each other, you know?"

My respect for the girl grew astronomically. I knew it must have been costing her to stand there and say all that to me. To choose to be nice instead of tearing me or Felix down.

I gave her a genuine smile. "Consider it officially non-awkward."

She huffed out a laugh just as Felix walked into the kitchen. His eyes darted from her to me and back again, finally settling on me. He grunted a short hello to Sam before grabbing my hand. "Wanna get going?"

Nodding, I turned to Sam just before we left the kitchen. "It was nice to meet you, Sam. I guess I might see you around?"

Her smile was shaky as she looked from Felix to me. "You too. And I'm sure you will."

CHAPTER FOUR

We made the ten-minute walk down the dark streets to Felix's house. It wasn't a great neighborhood, but having his hand around mine, with the soft breeze battling the humid air, made me feel like we could've been walking anywhere.

I was still thinking about how good it was of Sam to introduce herself to me like that. "She seems pretty nice."

Felix paused in front of his driveway. "Who, Sam?"

"Yeah."

He continued walking, tugging my hand as we climbed the porch steps to his front door. "She is nice." He unlocked the door and held it open for me to walk in ahead of him. I slipped off my flip-flops and waited as he locked it behind him.

"Why couldn't you make things work with her?" I could've slapped myself for saying something so stupid. "I mean, you know, considering she's pretty and she seems kind of cool." My cheeks flamed.

He chuckled quietly, kicking off his boots before grabbing

my warm face. "She may be a cool girl, but she's not you."

With my lashes and heart fluttering, I asked, "What do you mean?"

He pressed his lips to the tip of my nose. "No one could ever have my heart but you. Not in the way you do." His voice was a husky whisper. "So there's no point in worrying over what-ifs. You're my girl, I'm your guy, and that's all you need to wrap your beautiful brain around."

"I love you," I blurted out yet again.

With his lips close to mine, he murmured, "Yeah, you do."

Then I was in his arms, my own looping around his strong neck as he carried me down the hall and kicked the door to his room closed behind him.

He gently placed me on my feet, his hands moving to the hem of my dress. One look at my face was all the permission he needed and it was gone, followed by my bra. His breath stalled when he skated his hands over my b-cup breasts.

"So fucking beautiful." He squeezed them, then moved me back to the bed, laying me down and hooking his fingers into the sides of my cotton panties to drag them down my legs.

I was suddenly glad I'd shaved down there the night before, though I had no idea what had possessed me to do so. Call it equal parts hope and desperation that tonight we'd finally be able to do this..

He groaned, standing and tugging his shirt over his head, then unzipped his jeans before shoving them to the floor. My eyes danced over his solid pecs and the sparse trickle of chest hair that matched the same trail that led into his black briefs. His abs contracted, the muscles on his arms bulging as he clenched his fists at his sides and stared at me. He was all lean muscle and utterly breathtaking.

We'd fooled around before. He'd pulled many orgasms

from me, and I a few from him. Albeit, I fumbled under his direction, but he seemed more than happy to teach me. Whether it be in the back of a movie theatre or in the front cab of his truck.

At that moment, though? I became a squirming, self-conscious mess as I lay buck ass naked on his blue sheets. More exposed than I'd ever been in front of anybody.

"Mags."

My eyes came unglued from the thick bulge in his briefs. Christ, I was spacing out while staring at his junk. Go me.

I lifted my gaze to his, and he gave me that wolfish grin. "Stop freaking out."

He then tucked his thumbs into the waistband of his briefs and chuckled darkly. "Wanna see it, don't you, Little Doe?"

I licked my lips, nodding, and propped myself up on my elbows.

Then the briefs were gone, and his long, thick length was bobbing against his stomach.

My eyes widened, and I had this intense urge to touch it. To wrap my hand around it as I'd already done a few times before. Only, it was never like this. Never just the two of us alone in a room where we were naked and … about to have sex. *Holy crap.*

I sat up, and he stepped forward, knowing what I wanted. He hissed sharply when I gripped it gently in my small hand, smoothing my thumb over the head, rubbing the pre-cum around it in circles.

"God, fuck. Lie down."

I moved my gaze from his cock to his eyes. They were dark and hooded. He blinked, and I let go of him, lying down as he'd told me to.

"Good girl. Now, open your legs."

They opened slowly and almost of their own volition. As if Felix held the strings to my body, and it moved as he willed it to.

He climbed onto the bed, situating himself between my thighs on his stomach then ran his fingers over me softly. "Such a pretty pussy. Want me to eat it?"

My breath hitched in response, and he chuckled again. "Words. Say the words, Mags."

"Y-yes," I croaked. "Please."

He'd done it once before, and I shivered just remembering how amazing it felt.

His finger glided over me, gently parting me with a quiet groan. I closed my eyes, feeling another finger touch me to spread me open for him.

Blowing a gust of warm breath over my sensitive flesh, he cursed gruffly at the way I twitched and shivered in response. "You're dripping. Pink and fucking dripping for me."

I swallowed hard, not knowing how or if I could respond. His tongue fluttered through the wetness at my entrance, then he was lapping up every drop that pooled there with another groan. I whimpered some pitiful sound while my thighs spread wider and my pulse climbed higher. The heat of his tongue and mouth left me, and then a finger was slowly dipping inside.

"Fuck me," he whisper-hissed, pulling his finger out and pausing before thrusting it back in. "I should feel bad about what I'm going to take from you, but I really fucking don't."

I garbled out an incoherent response, and his rough laugh bounced around the otherwise silent room.

His tongue then flitted over my clit while his finger stayed planted inside me.

"Shit," I breathed out, feeling myself slip closer to a blistering orgasm.

He kept at it until I was grinding myself on his face. "That's it. Fuck my finger and my face, Little Doe."

His words had me riding the sharp crest, my hips rolling into the movements of his tongue while he slowly rotated that thick finger inside me. "I'm, oh shit …"

My thighs gripped his head, my body shaking as I let out a long moan. He kept flicking his tongue over me then sucked my clit into his mouth, almost making me scream as the pleasure became too much.

I tried to shove his head off me, laughing breathlessly. But he pushed my hands away and kept at it, licking every drop of wetness from my orgasm while pinning my hands and thighs to the bed. It was too much. The sweetest kind of torture. And he knew it, too.

"Felix, shit, shit … I can't."

He finally stopped, and I felt like I could sleep for a hundred years. My body spent and my head spinning.

He climbed over me. "You on the pill? I've never been with someone bare before."

I tried to catch my breath before replying. "Yeah." My mom had put me on it a year ago and told me not to tell my dad.

His length nudged at my entrance, and he pushed forward. I guess he wasn't wasting any time then.

Breathing became difficult again. I'd never felt so damn full.

He stopped once he hit that barrier, and I squirmed, this time trying to adjust to the sting and the size of the invasion. "You okay?" He heaved out a huge breath. "Shit, I feel like I'm gonna come already."

A small laugh slipped out of me, and I wrapped my legs around his hips. "I'm okay."

He stared at me then, his eyes alight with hunger and

affection. "I don't know much about this shit, being a guy and all, but I know it's probably going to hurt."

"I'll be okay." I moved my hips a little. "Do it."

He nodded, but still, he hesitated before lowering his big body over me. His forearms came to rest beside my head, hands cradling it while my own were smoothing over his back as he rested his forehead against mine. "I'm sorry, and I love you."

"I love you, t—"

I knew it would hurt. I knew that, and still, nothing could've prepared me for the searing pain that lit up my lower body and made me cry out. "Oh. My. God."

He kept going until he was all the way in. "Fuuuuck."

I tried desperately not to cry, but the pain was so fucking bad. It took him a moment to realize that I was barely there. That I was lost within the fire that had taken up residence between my legs. And it wasn't the good kind.

"Shit, fuck. Mags?" His voice was strained.

My eyes were clenched shut. When had I squeezed them closed?

"Look at me, please."

I pried them open, and to my horror, a tear ran down my cheek.

His eyes grew huge at the same time his face seemed to crumple. He leaned down to kiss the tear. "I'm so sorry. Fuck. Want me to stop? We can try again another—"

"No." I wanted this. And I knew from the girls at school it was mainly the first time that hurt like hell. It was supposed to get better after that. "Move. Maybe it'll help." My voice was a raspy, choked whisper as I tried to contain just how badly the pain had ravaged me.

He started raining kisses all over my face, his hands sliding into my hair before his tongue swept into my mouth. It took a few minutes, but the pain started to fade. Oh, it was still there, but his lips on mine, his tongue rubbing against mine, and his teeth gently nibbling my lips all helped to take the edge off.

Then he started moving, his hips slowly rocking while he kept our mouths fused together. It got even better after that. I knew I wouldn't have another orgasm, and I think Felix figured that likelihood was slim too, as he started moving deeper and sped up a little until he was groaning throatily into my mouth. My nails ran up the smooth expanse of his back, running over the dips and ridges of his flexing muscles as I started to move my hips in sync with his.

It didn't feel good yet, but I wanted him to feel good.

And being with him like this, sharing this with him—it felt like everything.

"I'm gonna come, Mags," he rasped against my lips.

"Come inside me." I pressed my mouth firmly to his, reveling in the way his whole body seemed to lock up at my words, then, after thrusting in and out of me three more times, he stilled. I squeezed him to me as he shook and cursed into my mouth.

"I'm so fucking sorry, shit," he said afterward, lifting his head from my neck. "I feel like a selfish bastard."

I ran my hand down the side of his cheek, then moved it up to smooth the crinkle between his brows. "Don't. It was perfect."

His face scrunched up comically. "It was fucking horrible. I thought I was going to kill you; you were in so much pain."

I laughed, and the sting between my legs flared, causing me to wince. He cursed again and went to move off me, but I stopped him with a hand at the back of his head. "No, giving this to you. Being with you like this …" I admitted in a shy whisper. "It was everything"

His face softened marginally, but not enough, so I continued, "Besides, it's supposed to get much better after the first time. And you did take care of me before." I pushed his face to mine, kissing his nose. "So as far as first time's go, I never thought it'd be this perfect."

Which was true. I had no idea when I might finally give up my v-card. I thought it would be at a random party when I started college or something. It probably wouldn't have meant a thing and wouldn't have been anything I'd look back on fondly.

So giving myself to Felix, everything about those mere minutes in time, meant more than anything I could've hoped to dream for.

He seemed appeased with that and helped me clean up in the bathroom. Mortified, I tried to push him out, but he wouldn't have any of it after he saw the blood between my thighs.

He turned the shower on and killed my heart further by cleaning me with a gentleness that no one would ever expect from this gruff, serious, and big man of mine.

Then he took me back to bed, where he rubbed me softly while we made out until I came again.

CHAPTER FIVE

The next morning, I felt warm all over and wore a tiny smile the whole way back to my place. Felix dropped me off at the end of my street with a sweet kiss goodbye, telling me that he'd call me on his lunch break. He had to go into the shop to help Darren out for a few hours.

I noticed my mom's car wasn't in the driveway as I approached and prayed my father had gone to work with her this morning. No such luck. He was sitting at the dining table outside the kitchen. Waiting for me, if the anger that marred his face was any indication.

My happiness died a quick, terrifying death, wretched from my body and thrown to the tiled floor, splattering at my feet.

"Where've you been?"

I shifted my bag over my shoulder, feeling uncomfortable. It didn't help that I was still in yesterday's clothes and could still taste Felix on the tip of my tongue. Crap. I hoped I didn't smell like him.

"You have ten seconds to answer me, and it had better be a good enough answer, Magdaline."

He knew. Despite quickly calling my mom last night, somehow, he knew.

Oh, God.

Yet I tried to keep up the lie anyway. "I was out, at Lucy's place. You know that."

He was out of the chair in an instant, so quickly it fell backward, banging into the wall at the same time he backhanded me hard across the face.

"Do not lie to me, girl!" he shouted over my hunched body.

I lifted my head slowly, pain radiating through my face as I held my cheek.

"What …" I stopped and swallowed. "What do you want me to say?"

He looked like he was about to hit me again, but then the front door opened and my mom walked in.

"Martin!" She gasped, dropping the groceries she was holding. One of the glass jars broke as it smacked against the tiles.

Rushing over to me, she pulled me away from him.

"Stay out of it, Elodie. You knew our daughter was running around with some teenage shmuck in the city, and you didn't say a word about it."

"I didn't know." She glanced from my dad's red face to mine briefly, and I saw it there in her eyes. She *did* know.

Part of me was thankful that even though she knew, she never tried to stop me. But that part was small and swallowed whole by the fear turning and twisting my insides.

He'd never hit me before. He was verbally abusive but never physical.

"Well," my dad said, taking a measured breath and

smoothing his features as though a curtain had dropped over his wrath. I shivered inwardly, never having seen that eerie calm pass over his face quite like that before. "You've got nothing to say for yourself?"

I pulled my hand away from my face, not realizing it was wet, and rubbed it over my chest. "He's a good guy. You'd like him if you'd just—"

His harsh laugh cut me off. "Don't even bother. You want to be with this piece of city scum?"

Blinking dazedly, I didn't know what he expected me to say, so I settled for the truth. "Ah, yes, I do."

He nodded, running a hand over his chin as his brown eyes drifted over me.

"All right." He nodded again. "I can be fair. You're eighteen. So you can do what you like but not while you're living under this roof. Got me?"

"Martin ..."

"Shut up, Elodie, for Christ's sake."

She shut up, but I didn't. "What are you saying? That I'm not allowed to see him if I'm living here?"

He smiled, but there was no warmth in it at all. "That's precisely what I'm saying. You're not tainting this family's reputation. You're going to New York like your sister. You're going to get a good degree and a good job, then you can find yourself a good man. This is why we've been so hard on you." He scoffed. "Always with your head in the clouds. You need direction, and you need to make better decisions. This is what we've tried to prevent you from doing, you know? Making idiotic mistakes like this. But even after all our hard work ..." He threw his hands in the air. "You've found a way to do it anyway. Should've known we couldn't win with both of you." As he left the room, he mumbled under his breath, "Stupid kid. Unbelievable."

My mom took my hand and led me to the bathroom, closing the door behind her. My bag was gently slipped off my arm to the floor, and she directed me to sit on the side of our corner bath.

I was still in a daze, blinking slowly at the shiny cream bathroom tiles.

Mom lifted my chin, gently running a wet washcloth over my cheek. When she pulled it away, I saw not only the sadness in her eyes but some blood. Damn it. I stood and stared at myself in the mirror. There was a deep, small gash on my cheek, probably from where my father's wedding ring had met my skin.

"Ma chérie, you should not anger him like that. You know this." My mom rinsed the cloth next to me, then turned to me.

My face paled further as I stared at her in the mirror, incredulous. "Are you kidding me, Mom?" I shook my head. "How'd he find out, anyway?"

Her eyes moved down to the sink. "He thought it was strange that you didn't come home to get a change of clothes. Then this morning, he saw Lucy's mother when he went to the bakery to check on a few things. She told him that you were probably with your boyfriend. The one who works as a mechanic and lives in the city."

Great. I groaned, dropping my head. "What am I going to do?"

Her hand traveled over my back, rubbing in smooth circles. "You're young, sweetheart." Her accent became thicker with her emotion. She moved my hair aside, gently running her fingers through it. "Very beautiful. You will meet another man."

I stepped back, horrified by the mere thought. "I don't want another man."

She tilted her head, giving me a sad smile. "I know you think that now, but—"

"No." My heart raged at her for even suggesting it. "You don't understand. We might be young, but we're not *that* young. We know what we're doing." My head started shaking again. "It's not a fling or something fleeting, okay? I love him."

Her brown eyes grew wide. "Sweetheart, no. He's not worth giving up your life for."

I scoffed at her. "What life? All I do is go to school, come home, rinse, and repeat. If I'm lucky, I might get to hang out with Lucy somewhere in-between. I'm not a kid anymore. If I want to have a boyfriend, then I'll have one, damn it."

She blew a strand of red hair off her face as she exhaled loudly. "But you know he is serious. I cannot control him when he gets ideas like this in his head." Panic filled her eyes, and her hands shook around the washcloth held tightly in her hands.

I was suddenly enraged. So fucking mad that she could stand there and tell me that I had to live my life by my father's crazy standards. Disappointed that she could still try to get me to do as my father willed after he had smacked me in the face and threatened me.

"Do you hear yourself right now?"

She frowned at my harsh whisper, and I continued, "He's an asshole, Mom. And you know what? You might be fine with putting up with him, but I'm not." I laughed, a little crazy sounding. "So I'll keep my scummy boyfriend and go pack my bag. Thanks for the support." I shouldered past her to the door.

"I hope you know what you're doing, Magdaline." My feet stopped moving in the hall, but I didn't turn to face her. "Love isn't always enough."

I closed my eyes and begged her words not to penetrate my ears, continuing down the hall and packing a duffel bag full of enough clothes and toiletries for a week.

I parked my car on the street and dropped my head back against the headrest. Taking a deep breath, I slowly released it and looked over at the rolled-up garage door.

One of the guys was standing outside, watching me as he smoked a cigarette and talked on his phone.

A sinking feeling in the pit of my stomach had me wondering if I'd made the right decision.

The guy disappeared inside a moment later. But when Felix came running out to my car, worry stamped all over his features as he pulled open my door, my heart cried out in affirmation that this was right. Perhaps the only right thing I had in my life at that point.

"Mags," he breathed, leaning an elbow on the open door. "You okay? What're you …"

His eyes bulged when they stopped on my cheek, then he was pulling me out of the car.

Framing my face with his hands, he caressed the cut with his thumb, growling, "What the fuck happened?"

Sighing, I gave him as reassuring a smile as I could. "My dad. You know how he gets angry sometimes?"

I could almost hear his teeth grinding together. "You mean he did this to you? Getting angry and hurting you are two different things, Mags."

I didn't respond. I didn't know what to say.

"Shit." He ran his thumb over my cheek again and again. "Are you okay?"

My eyes closed, and I shook my head as much as I could

with it in his strong grip. "Um, not really." I opened my eyes. "He found out about us and told me I couldn't live under his roof anymore if I continued to see you."

He cursed, dropping his hands and stepping back to run them through his thick hair. I closed the door, leaning back against my car. "So what? This is it then, and you've come to say goodbye or some fucked up shit like that?"

He stopped fidgeting but wouldn't look at me; he just stared at the weeds below his feet that were creeping out of the sidewalk.

I erased the terrifying distance that was suddenly growing between us and grabbed his face. "Do you really believe that?"

His eyes met mine, his long lashes butting up against the bottom of his thick brows. "You mean, you're …"

I nodded, pressing my lips to his. He crushed me to him, grabbing my face and stuffing it in his neck as his whole body seemed to heave with his sigh of relief. "Thank fuck. You can't go back there anyway. I'm not fucking letting you."

"Everything all right, boy? We've got a car here that still needs its oil changed," Darren's voice yelled from behind us. "When ya feel like it and all, no fucking hurry or anything."

I pulled out of his arms, and Darren smiled at me. "Hi, Miss Maggie."

I gave him a small wave as Felix held me pressed against his side.

Darren's eyes fell on my cheek, the blood smear on my yellow dress, then finally lifted to Felix with a hard look in his eyes. "Care to tell me why the heck Maggie's got a banged-up cheek for, boy?"

Felix tensed beside me, and I quickly rushed in with, "It wasn't him; it was, um …" Darren raised a bushy gray brow, silently telling me to spit it out already. "It was my dad."

Felix growled, leaving my side and rushing back into the garage.

Darren's gaze followed him until he returned outside and opened his truck door. "Where do you think you're going?"

"To make sure her fuck-head of a dad knows that if he ever touches her again, he's gonna fucking regret it."

"Hey, now. Don't you move another muscle," Darren's voice boomed across the parking lot, halting Felix in his tracks and causing Jared to come swaggering out of the garage.

He nodded at me, stopping by their truck. "What's going on?"

Felix gave them a brief rundown of what had happened.

Darren ran his hand over his long beard, shifting on his feet and squinting at the ground. "Well, fuck."

Well, fuck indeed. "It's okay. I'll be fine. I'm going to give my friend Lucy a call and see if she can help me out for a—"

"You're not going any-fucking-where besides our place. Right, Darren?" Felix asked, though it didn't sound like much of a question.

Darren shifted again, tugging up his jeans a bit and sniffing as he looked at Felix, long and hard. He looked back at me, and I shook my head, smiling at him. "It's okay. You don't have to do that … really."

He smirked. "Don't be telling me what I don't have to do, young lady. Right." He turned back to the boys. "Boy one and boy two, get your asses over here so I don't have to keep yelling across this lot like some fucking old cranky bastard."

"But you are an old cranky bastard, Daz." Jared laughed.

Darren cursed at him, and Jared only smirked. Felix's jaw clenched as he walked over and swung an arm around me once again, melding me to his side.

Jared stared at Felix, mouthing the words, "We'll go pay him—"

Darren smacked Jared playfully over the back of the head, causing Jared to scowl at him. "You're not going anywhere until her ass-bag of a dad isn't home. And even then, you'll only go to help pick her shit up and bring it back to our place. Understood?" He looked between Jared and Felix, an eyebrow raised pointedly.

They both nodded, and I tried not to laugh. Darren had a way of being able to get those two seemingly untamable young men to heel.

"Thank you," I whispered. Felix pressed a kiss to the side of my head.

Darren and Jared watched me, and my chest filled with warmth at having their smiling faces directed my way. This might not be ideal, and I couldn't help but feel like I was imposing. I mean, their house was pretty small, and even though it felt otherwise, Felix and I were still kind of new.

But they didn't make me feel like crap for it. They seemed to genuinely want to help, and I was so relieved and too grateful to pay attention to anything else right then.

CHAPTER SIX

Nine Years Ago

"Morning, Miss Maggie," Darren said without looking up from the paper.

"Morning." I smiled, even though he wasn't looking, as I walked into the kitchen to make some coffee. "Where's Felix?"

Despite feeling like I'd invaded their lives, they never made me feel that way. In fact, they seemed almost glad to have a woman in the house. Especially when said woman did a lot of cleaning for them and made dinner sometimes.

My mom had called me relentlessly at first, begging me to come home. She gave up after a few weeks, then only called to check in. My sister didn't give in as easily. Her worry and annoyance over what I was doing with my life evident every time I answered her calls. Yet needing to have someone or something to tether me to my old life, I still answered them.

Darren lowered the paper he was squinting at. He had reading glasses but said the silly things were a nuisance, so he never wore them. "In the garage, I think."

"Here?" I put the milk away and leaned against the counter, blowing on my coffee.

He gave me a short nod, and I moved out the back door to the garage to find Felix staring at his bike. He was still wearing his pajama pants, which hung tantalizingly low on his defined hips. His black t-shirt was sleep rumpled, and the muscles in his arm jumped every time he stroked a hand through his hair.

"Hey." I stopped in the doorway of their small garage.

He looked up, a huge grin crawling over his face. "Come here."

I walked over to him, and he wrapped his arms around me from behind, leaning his chin on my shoulder as he continued to stare at his bike.

"What are you staring at it for?" I shouldn't have asked. Those guys did weird things when it came to things with wheels.

Sipping my coffee, I bumped my ass into him to get a response.

"Don't wiggle that thing near my cock unless you want me to bend you over my bike," he whispered and nipped my ear.

I tried not to shiver or roll my eyes. "Well, answer me."

"I think it's done."

Huh? "The bike?"

He grunted in affirmation.

"Right. That's great news." Though it didn't look much different from the last time I saw it a few days ago. "Does that mean you can finally take me for a ride on it?"

He'd never offered, and I'd only asked once. He'd given me a firm no, and that was that.

Felix chuckled, kissing my cheek and stealing my coffee mug from my hands. I'd have protested, but he did it all the time. Never wanted his own and always drank mine. I offered to make him one many times, but he said he preferred to share. *Tastes better*, he said. I didn't agree with him, but it was sort of sweet, so I let it go.

"I'm serious." I cut my eyes at him. "Wait … am I like, not good enough to get on the back of your bike with you or something?"

He almost choked on his next sip of coffee, turning his head from where he was standing next to me with a glare. "You're kidding, yeah?"

Scrunching my nose, I said, "I'm actually not." I didn't like to feel insecure; that wasn't me. But I'd wondered about it a few times.

He reached over to tweak my nose, and I tried not to slap his hand away. "It's not safe, Little Doe."

I glared up at him. When he didn't say anything else, my mouth fell open. "*What?*"

He shrugged, sipping more coffee and looking back at his bike. "You heard me."

"But, but …" I sputtered and shook my head. "But you get on it all the time!"

He gave me a smirk. "Yeah, keyword there being *me*. Not *you*."

That was so stupid, and I could feel my cheeks heat with indignation. "That's such double standard bullshit, Felix."

"Oh, yeah?" His smirk grew wider, morphing into a mega-watt grin that would usually melt my panties.

Not this time. I crossed my arms. "Yeah."

He lifted a shoulder, walking out of the garage. "Hey! Stop right there. I'm getting on the back of that bike with you, big guy. Or else."

He spun around in the doorway, dark brows rising. "Or

else?" I nodded and he asked, "Or else what?"

Pointing a finger at him, I lowered my voice to as menacing a whisper as I could manage. "Oh, you don't even wanna know what else, mister." Because honestly, I had nothing.

He threw his head back with a loud laugh, and some of the annoyance vacated my body. *Some.* "I mean it, Felix."

He nodded, looking at me like he was trying not to laugh as he sunk those white teeth into his bottom lip. "Oh, I'm sure you do, Little Doe."

I huffed. "Well? Are you going to let me ride with you?"

He walked over to me, lifting my chin and planting his lips on mine for a brief, toe-curling kiss. His tongue swept into my mouth, jumbling my thoughts and making my arms move to his sides. He stepped back, and my arms fell away. "No," he simply said before walking away again.

"Fine. I guess I'll just have to ask Jared or one of the other guys at the garage if they might take me for a ride." I inspected my chipped nail polish as he paused, turning around to look at me once more. "I'm sure one of them would feel bad for me after I explain—"

"Stop right there."

Yeah, I felt petty for stooping that low. But it worked.

Ten minutes later, he was putting Jared's helmet on my head and adjusting the straps. Then he was telling me where to put my hands and legs before we rode away from the house and down to the warehouse district.

"This is awesome!" I yelled over the wind that was slapping me in the face.

He didn't reply, but I could feel him chuckle thanks to how tightly I was holding him.

We got a burger and a shake from Shake N' Burger, and the smile never left my face the whole time. "Seriously." I dunked my straw into my shake, taking a long sip. "So awesome."

He chuckled, shaking his head at me while he ate his burger.

"You're in big trouble tonight, you know." He wiped his hands with a napkin and smiled at Nita, the chef's wife, when she walked by.

"Oh?" I pretended I didn't care, but I kind of liked getting in trouble with Felix.

"Don't o*h* me," he grumbled, "Little bribing Doe."

"It'll be worth it." I winked.

He scoffed and took a sip from my shake. "Fucking right it will be." With his jaw clenching, he then asked, "Would you really have done that, asked them to take you out?"

"No, and you know I wouldn't." I gave him a hard look.

He nodded. "Yeah, but that's still fucked up, Mags."

"Sorry," I murmured, grabbing his hand and bringing it to my lips.

Gifting me a tiny smile, he chucked me under the chin and went back to finishing his food.

"Even after this, you're not going to let me ride with you much, are you?" I asked the table quietly after a few minutes had passed.

"Mags." I looked up, watching his lashes bob up and down over his brown eyes when he blinked. "I was serious when I said it's not safe." He sighed. "So no, not all the time. But I know you like it, so I'll try, 'kay?"

I nodded, biting my lip to hold back a grin. That was as good as I would get from him right then. And it was good enough.

"Now that we've started saving, have you given any thought to where we're going to live?"

Fiddling with the plastic cup in my hands, I tried to think

about it.

Felix chuckled, bopping me on the nose and saying, "Don't think too hard. Just say whatever you see when you close your eyes and imagine it."

Imagine it. Closing my eyes as excitement coursed through my veins, I tried to do exactly that. I could feel the salty breeze and see nothing but flat blue, so I reopened my eyes and scowled. "All I can think of is water."

He sat back in the booth seat, tilting his head as he watched me with humor dancing in his dark eyes. "Then water it is. We'll find a place near the water. Simple."

I was still smiling as we walked outside and he tucked the helmet back on my head, careful to smooth my hair back out of my face first. "I love you." I rose onto my toes to kiss his nose.

Giving me a devilish grin, he took my hand and brought it to his lips. "Right back atcha, Little Doe."

CHAPTER SEVEN

Eight Years Ago

To say that things between Felix and me had only gotten better since I moved in and the months wore on wouldn't exactly be true. They had, and they hadn't. It'd been almost two years since I'd last seen my parents.

Some days, I couldn't help but think that for all my dad's faults, he might've had a point. But whenever I got home from working another long shift at the truck stop diner just off the highway, which followed a day of classes, that tiredness and any doubts I had would evaporate as soon as I saw those dark brown eyes.

Not tonight, though. Tonight, those eyes were full of anger and disbelief as I ran my fingers through my braid, undoing it while walking into our room.

I knew why, and I did care, but I wasn't feeling too remorseful. So I dumped my purse, grabbed my pajamas, and went to the bathroom.

He followed me, locking the door behind him.

I got undressed, keenly aware of those eyes burning holes into my skin while I turned on the water and hopped into the shower. If he wanted to be mad, he'd have to come out and say it. I was too tired to start a fight I had zero energy for. I'd been up since five a.m.

"Mags," he finally hissed, opening the shower door.

I tilted my head back, rinsing out the shampoo with my eyes closed. "Mmmm?"

Once done, I grabbed the conditioner, squirted some onto my palm, and ran it through the ends of my hair.

"Are you fucking kidding me right now?"

I rinsed the conditioner out. "About what?"

He cursed gruffly, and as I was washing, he undressed. Then he came straight for me. I wasn't scared, no, my body still lit up, no matter how angry he got or how tired I was. He had a way of turning me on with just a glance. So naturally, seeing him angry, hard, and naked was bound to really turn me on.

I bit my lip, staring up at him as the water sprayed over the harsh planes of his gorgeous face. "Wanna tell me why ..." His voice was rough like gravel as it grazed over every part of me. "I went to pick up my girl from class this afternoon, only to find out she hasn't attended any for over a week now?"

I closed my eyes. I knew he'd find out, and I'd never planned to keep it from him, but I just didn't know how to tell him I couldn't keep up. I'd always been a good student, but I just didn't have the time with the new hours I'd picked up at work, and we needed the money. We wanted our own place, so we needed to save. And most weeks, we were lucky if we could go out and buy a freaking cheeseburger after payday.

"Working a few hours a week isn't going to cut it, Felix." I turned around, rinsing more soap from my body. "We want our own place, a life of our own. We can't have that if we can't afford it."

Calloused hands slid over my stomach, pulling me back into his wet, hard body.

Lips met my ear, and a whisper rolled into it, harsh and tingle inducing. "You think I'm just gonna let you do this, do you?"

"It's too late. It's already done. I couldn't keep up," I whispered honestly in response. "I'd never catch up, and it's just unnecessary stress right now. I don't want to be stressed. I just want more of you and me."

His breath washed over the side of my face with his sigh, his arm constricting around my stomach. "I don't fucking like that you did this, Mags. You should've talked to me first."

I swallowed. "I know."

He grunted. Moving my hair aside to grip in his fist, he used it to tilt my head back for his tongue to lick a long line over the curve of my throat. "You've really pissed me off, Little Doe. First, giving up going to NYU and now this?" His teeth nipped my chin.

Even after all that time, NYU was still a sore subject. Not for me. I didn't regret not going; I could never regret staying with Felix. The fallout of that was much worse than this, though. He didn't talk to me for two days. It was torture. I knew he was relieved I'd decided to stay, but I knew him. I knew his guilt wouldn't let his anger let up. He felt responsible, which wasn't fair. It was my decision, and I made sure he knew that as I brought him back to me with every touch, kiss, suck, and lick until he finally heard me out and we moved on.

"It's for the best. I can always go back one day when things are more settled." I gasped harshly when he started grinding his cock into my lower back.

"Enough. Hands against the wall." He moved me forward until my palms splayed open against the wet, cold tiles of the shower.

I knew what he was doing. Sometimes when he got angry, especially with me, he'd take it out on me. But in a way I could definitely live with.

"Spread your legs and bend, Little Doe."

I did, and he hooked my right leg over his forearm before slowly sinking inside my body with a throaty groan. Moaning softly, I started swiveling my hips as heat ignited low in my belly.

He smacked my ass, and I almost yelped. His free hand covered my mouth roughly, and he turned my head to the side. "You need to be quiet unless you want Jared to hear you come."

My eyes bulged, and he laughed quietly. "Yeah, he's home. So not a fucking sound or I'll stop. Got it?"

I nodded, my hips still trying to rock back into him. His eyes darted down, looking at where we were joined from behind. "Fuck, yes. Greedy little pussy."

Keeping his hand over my mouth, he started thrusting with fast, deep, and measured strokes. The slapping of our wet skin echoed off the tiles and set my head spinning. It didn't take long for my orgasm to come running.

"Open your eyes. I need to see them grow huge when you come," he grunted between thrusts.

I did, staring at him and moaning into his hand when he hit that exact spot over and over again.

I came hard, my hands slipping on the wall as my body shook. Felix grunted his release into me, holding me upright against his body before withdrawing and spinning me around to plant his mouth on mine.

He backed me into the wall, his hands framing my face

and his mouth devouring mine as if he was still starving. "Don't fucking lie to me again, Mags. In any shape or form. We're supposed to be a team." His voice was raspy, a whispered plea that made my heart clench.

"I won't." I dug my hands into his hair, sliding my tongue back inside his mouth.

A little while later, lying in bed and watching TV with his hand tangled in my damp hair, I could feel the remaining tension in his body.

I wrapped my arm tighter around his waist, my eyes about to close when he said quietly, "I'll quit working at the garage, get a better paying job. You're going back to college."

"You can't do that," I whispered into his t-shirt. "Darren needs you."

He cursed as if he'd forgotten that fact for a moment. "Yeah, but this shit isn't right. You need me more."

"I've got everything I need." I kissed his shirt. "Right here."

"You're going back. Next semester, you'll retake those classes."

I didn't answer him, partly because I knew I wouldn't go back, but mostly because I was settled in my decision. Even if he wasn't yet. He just needed time.

Life happened in unpredictable waves, and we just had to keep swimming above the surface.

As long as we had each other, we wouldn't sink.

CHAPTER EIGHT

Five Years Ago

Darren's death wasn't just hard on Felix. It changed him.

He got the call late one night while Jared was still sleeping. Darren had drunk too much, driven home from his friend's place, and hit a power pole. Felix went to identify his body, deciding not to tell Jared until he got home the next morning.

He refused to let me go with him and came home as the sun was rising, drunker than I'd ever seen him. But I wasn't mad; how could I be? He'd just seen the man who he thought of as a father in a way that no one wanted to remember seeing someone. Let alone someone they loved.

I supported him as best I could, picking up even more shifts at the diner when he stopped going to work. Jared was quiet, but he kept working at the garage, doing his best to make sense out of a business that was never really all that successful. I tried to help when I had the time.

"God, I don't think Darren filed anything." I closed the

drawer and leaned back against it, looking around the dingy office. Which was really more of a sectioned off corner in the shed created by miscellaneous car and bike parts and tool boxes.

It gave enough privacy away from the few other workers, though, to discuss how bad things were.

"Right." Jared sighed, running a hand through his hair. "Christ, I don't think he ever picked up a calculator in his life. Shit." He smirked sadly with a huff, looking over at the tax statements on the desk. "I'm surprised he even paid his damn taxes on time."

They weren't on time, but he did pay them. "What do we do?" I asked.

Jared frowned, his eyes softening as he stared at me. "It's not your problem, Mags. We'll figure it out."

I shook my head with a humorless laugh. "We? Felix isn't—"

"Isn't what?" said the man himself.

Jared and I looked over at him. He was here, and that felt huge after a week spent wondering what I could do to get him to talk to me.

"Hey. You're here," I breathed, feeling kind of dumb afterward.

He shrugged, straightening from the makeshift wall. "Well, I'm not fucking anywhere else, am I?"

"Dude." Jared scowled. "Why bother if you're just gonna be an ass?"

Felix gave him a hard look, and my insides started to knot. "Fuck off. And because the funeral's over, it's time to get this shithole sorted."

Neither Jared nor I argued with him. I think we were both just relieved he'd shown up.

We spent that afternoon sorting through boxes of receipts, client information, and trying to work out payroll before Felix decided he'd had enough.

"Going out. I'll be home later." He then left without a backward glance or before we could even say a thing.

I looked at Jared with my heart sitting in my throat.

He worried his lip between his teeth. "He'll keep coming around. Just give him some more time."

I didn't know if I believed him, but I wanted to.

Over the following week, he kept going into the garage during the day, and I thought things would get better.

But he still went out every night. Still was distant and would barely say two words to me.

Two weeks after the funeral, I woke up one night to the sound of giggling coming from somewhere. Felix wasn't in bed, he hadn't come home yet, but I tried not to let that worry me. It was sadly kind of normal behavior for him at the time.

I slipped my robe on and padded out of the room to get a glass of water. But what I saw in the kitchen stopped me in my tracks.

"Come on, just have a little. Ryan said it was really good shit."

Sam was sitting on the kitchen counter, swinging her legs back and forth as she used a credit card to scoop some powder into a tiny pile next to her bare thighs. Her denim skirt had ridden up, exposing some of the green of her panties. I didn't think she was in any state to care.

My pulse was stampeding in my ears. Felix was standing between her and some other guy I didn't know, sipping on a bottle of beer.

I didn't know what to do, so I simply walked my numb body over to the sink and got a glass of water, feeling their eyes on me the whole time I chugged it down.

"Mags," Felix slurred. "What're you doing up?"

Spinning around, I stared at his bloodshot eyes and the small smirk on his lips. Figures, he could give me some semblance of a smile while he was drunk.

"I heard laughter and woke up. I think the better question is, what are you doing?"

Felix's jaw clenched, his features hardening with annoyance.

Sam cleared her throat. "Sorry, Maggie. He said it was cool to come back here after the party at Ryan's."

I looked at her then, the way she swayed on the counter, a tiny smile on her pretty face and her blue eyes hooded with intoxication. "Ryan's?"

Her smile grew bigger. "Yeah, his birthday bash was tonight." She frowned then, looking back and forth between Felix and me. "Wait, you didn't know?"

I glanced down at the scuffed floor, shaking my head.

"Oh, sorry. I mean, Felix said you couldn't come, so I just thought—"

"Shut up, Sam. She's not my fucking keeper."

Ouch. Okay, well, I'd had enough.

Tears stung my eyes, so I kept my head down and walked out of the kitchen, waving goodbye over my shoulder. "Have a good night. I'm going back to bed."

Jared found me sitting on the bed a few minutes later. I guess he'd woken up, too. I couldn't hear anymore laughter from the kitchen, but I knew they were all still out there from the hushed murmurs and the occasional clinking of glass.

He plonked down on the bed beside me on an elbow. "You okay?"

I looked down at his sleepy green eyes, willing myself not

to cry, and shook my head.

"Who's Ryan?" I asked after I thought I had my emotions in check.

Jared cursed. "He *has* been hanging out with him again, then."

I picked at my nails in my lap. "Apparently. Scored some coke from him. It's on the kitchen counter if you want some." My sad attempt at sarcasm didn't go unnoticed.

"Hey." Jared sat up. "Look at me."

I did, still trying not to cry as Felix's harsh words bashed into each other in my head, trying to make a home for themselves among all the softly spoken declarations of love. He could be short, easy to piss off, and quiet at times, but he'd never treated me like that before.

It hurt. It hurt so badly that I didn't know what I would do to fix it, or if I could handle it if it happened again.

"He hung out with him when we were younger, doing some dumb shit. It wasn't long before he met you, actually, that it all got straightened out." I frowned, and he continued, "Ryan's bad news. Drug dealing, theft, you name it, he's either done it or is doing it."

Oh, God. "What happened? Felix did that, too?" I couldn't imagine that, but then again, thinking back to the boy I'd met all those years ago at a party, maybe I could.

Jared nodded. "Yeah, they got caught stealing cars. Felix almost went to juvie."

At my wide-eyed expression, he told me what happened, how Felix ended up getting roped into stealing cars and how Darren got him out of trouble.

"Holy shit." I stared at the blue sheets on the bed in a daze. Angry he'd never told me and scared out of my mind about what might happen if he was hanging out with that guy again.

"You got that right." Jared sighed. "So this? Well, it isn't good. I know he's in a bad place, but fuck, this is really stupid of him."

"What can we do?" I looked up at him, desperation strangling my vocal cords.

He chewed his lip, staring at me for a beat. "It needs to be you. You've gotta do something. I know he's hurting, I fucking am too, and hell, I'm sure you are as well. But he needs to wake up." He gave my shoulder a light punch. "And there's no one left who can really do that besides you."

He was right. Only, I didn't know if I was enough.

My stomach curdled, knowing he was out there with Sam. I didn't know what it was that made me believe it, but I just didn't think he'd ever cheat on me. I also didn't want to take the risk that things could get any worse, though.

Jared left a minute later, and I could hear him saying hello to Sam and that guy before telling them it was time to go. The voices faded. The front door closed. And I wondered if Felix was even still home.

He was. And lying next to him later in bed while he snored and stunk of beer and weed, I tried to think of what I could do to bring him back to me.

The next day, I worked until nine. By the time I got home, I found Jared half passed out on the couch and Felix was nowhere to be seen.

Jared was usually out on the weekend, so to find him home on a Saturday night surprised me. But I think a part of me had realized he was waiting for me to get home, seeing as that was something his brother would usually do.

"Hey." I slumped down on the couch next to him.

He blinked a few times, sitting up and stretching his arms over his head with a yawn. "Work okay?"

I nodded, tossing my purse on the coffee table. "Yeah, it dragged as it usually does with the late shift."

He stood. "Well, I'm gonna hit the sack then. I'll catch y—"

The front door opened and slammed closed. We both turned as Felix stumbled into the room, and I mean stumbled. The only thing holding him upright was Sam and some guy with blond hair and a sharp face. He wasn't the same guy who was here last night.

"Let go of me. I'm fine. Shit." Felix shoved away from them and almost fell into the wall.

Jared was there then, holding his arm and giving his brother a tremulous smile. "Big night, eh? It's not even ten; you're getting soft in your old age."

Felix chuckled. "Shut the fuck up."

The blond guy smiled at me. "Maggie, I take it? I'm Ryan."

I didn't trust his smile, not with everything I'd heard about him. But I stood and walked over to them, giving him a small hello in return.

"Well, we'd better get going." Ryan tucked his hands into his jean pockets. For someone who was supposedly on the wrong side of the law a lot, he seemed awfully sober. "This guy here tried to drive his drunk ass home. So I thought I'd better bring him home instead." He winked at me, grabbed Sam's hand, and turned for the door.

"Thank you." I forced a smile.

Sam waved, Ryan nodded, then they were gone.

"Fucking hell, you seriously tried to drive home like this?" Jared hissed.

Felix ignored him and pushed away from the wall and his brother, walking unsteadily out of the room.

"Felix!" Jared hollered, startling me. I'd never heard him angry like that before. "After everything that's fucking happened, you'd seriously do something that fucking stupid?" He followed him out of the room, and I started to do the same.

"Fuck off, Jared. I'm fine, aren't I?" Felix grumble-slurred. "Go babysit my girlfriend. You seem to like doing that."

I stopped in the hall, flinching at his venom-coated words.

"You fucking for real? Do you even hear yourself right now?" Jared groaned. "I'm trying to look out for her because you obviously don't give a shit anymore."

He looked over at me when I walked into the kitchen, wincing apologetically. I shook my head, trying to let him know it was okay.

He was right, after all. No matter how much the truth stung.

"Yeah, well, maybe Maggie should fuck off back home to Mommy and Daddy, save us both the trouble of having to give a shit about her."

What? He didn't just … *he did.* My heart met the pit of my stomach.

Tears leaked out of my eyes of their own accord, and Felix spun around from his perch against the kitchen sink, fear blanketing his handsome features. "Shit, no. I didn't …"

My feet carried me out of the room before he could form any more of a response, my heart splintering with every move I made as I grabbed my old duffel bag from the wardrobe in our room and threw it on the bed.

"Mags, Little Doe …" Felix came barreling into the room, grabbing the bag and holding it behind him. "I didn't mean it. I'm just … It's all messed up."

I sniffed. "What? *Us?*"

He shook his head, eyes pleading. "No, no. My head." He groaned, closing his eyes briefly. "Fuck me. I'm too drunk for this shit."

Snorting, I yanked the bag back from him. "When aren't you drunk lately, Felix?"

He cursed. "That's not fair. Come on."

"No." I threw the bag to the floor, anger and frustration granting me the courage to say what I needed to. "What's not fair is having to sit here, night after night, wondering when the hell you're going to come home." He went to interrupt me, but I kept going. "What's not fair is wondering what you're doing all hours of the night while I stare at the god damned ceiling with my stomach in knots. What's not fair is you hurting, and spiraling out of control, and not letting me help you." I pulled in a trembling breath, tears streaming down my face. "What's not fair is you breaking my fucking heart, Felix."

His face paled as he stared at me for a long moment before sitting on the bed, hanging his head between his knees and running his shaky hands through his hair. "You can't leave me. I'm not gonna let you do that."

Sighing, I sat down beside him. "I don't want to. Ever. But I don't know what else I can do, Felix." I stared at the carpet, trying to get the tears to stop.

His warm hand took mine, and I let it. It'd been too long since I'd had him willingly touch me like this.

He tugged it to his lips. "I'm sorry, so fucking sorry. It just hurts, Mags. It hurts so much, and I don't know how to make it go away."

His broken voice had my tears coming faster, and when I looked at him, his wet eyes had me climbing in his lap to hold him to me. "You need to let it out, big guy," I whispered in his ear, placing a kiss on his neck.

A choked sound left him, and I held him tighter.

"Let it go. It needs to come out."

And with his arms holding me so tightly I could hardly breathe, he finally did.

CHAPTER NINE

Five Years Ago

"**W**hat are you doing?" I laughed as Felix tugged my hand. He'd blindfolded me as soon as I got home from work and stepped out of my car.

"Shhh, you'll see in a minute. Step, step, step." He directed me up the stairs and into the house.

As soon as the door shut behind us, I heard it.

A meow.

"Oh, my God!" I tore off the blindfold, and Felix cursed. Frantically glancing around the floor, I saw nothing. With my heart pounding, I walked down the hall, dropping my purse and squealing when my gaze found a little ball of orange fluff trotting toward me.

I bent down low and picked it up. "Hey, cutie! You're so soft." Turning to Felix, I asked, "Where did you get him ... or her?"

He was smiling at me, and the little ball of kitten I held tightly to my chest.

"Found him in a box outside the garage."

My eyes almost popped out of my head. "What?" I glanced down at the kitten. It was tiny. Only a baby. Maybe seven or eight weeks old. "Were there any more?" I looked around, not seeing or hearing anything. "Oh, God. We have to go get them!"

"Mags." Felix cursed again. "Wait."

I stopped my journey back down the hall at the rough tone of his voice and spun around.

"What?" I asked.

He scratched his head for a second. "There were two more."

"Were?" My heart sunk.

He nodded. "Yeah, the other two ... they were dead." I swallowed thickly, my eyes closing. They reopened when he continued, "I found them a few days ago. This guy"—he pointed at the orange kitten—"has been at the vet for the past forty-eight hours so they could monitor him, hydrate him, give him some shots, and the all clear."

I smoothed my hand over the kitten nuzzling his wet nose into my neck. "Who would do that?" I whispered, not expecting an answer.

Felix gave me one anyway. "You know some lowlifes live around here, Mags. Besides ..." His lips pulled to the side. "I thought you'd like him."

"Like him?" I guffawed. "I *love* him, but Felix, we're going to need so much stuff, litter, food..."

He waved a hand. "Got it all taken care of."

Felix never seemed like the cat loving type, but I knew he'd done this for me. What with my cat obsession and all. "You're okay with this?" I raised a brow at him.

It had been a few weeks since he finally broke down after almost tearing my heart to shreds. But he was no longer going out drinking, and we lay awake late into the nights, sometimes talking and sometimes not. He told me about what happened with Ryan years ago and how Darren's death had left him feeling like he was missing something and could never find it or figure out what it was. Even though it was obvious.

How he loved me so much he was sometimes afraid I'd disappear too.

He was quieter than he used to be. But I handled it, knowing he was on the right track and things were getting back to normal. Well, as normal as they could be. He continued to work with Jared at the garage, and they had even changed the name of the business to Surface Rust. It was Jared's idea. He came home drunk the other week and declared he had a brilliant brain.

Felix didn't hate it and said it was better than Darren's garage, so it was done.

Felix shrugged, stepping closer and running a hand over the kitten's back. "Seeing you happy makes me happy." He smirked when the kitten lifted its head from my neck to try to catch Felix's big palm with its tiny paw. "And I guess he's kind of cute."

"What should we call him?" I asked a while later as the kitten ran across the bed between Felix and me while we were watching a movie.

Felix scratched at the sheets, and the kitten pounced, trying to eat his fingers. "You decide. I'll probably call him something tough, and this guy is too cute for that."

Smiling at them, I decided on, "Toulouse."

He frowned. "Where've I heard that name before?"

"*The Aristocats.*"

He laughed, and I rejoiced at hearing the deep, melodious timbre of it. "You're serious?"

"Uh-huh. Very much so."

He moved Toulouse out of the way and tugged me over to lay on his chest. "Then Toulouse it is, Little Doe." He tucked some of my hair behind my ear, then traced the outside of my lips.

Smiling, I said, "Thank you, for Toulouse."

He leaned in, whispering against my lips, "Thank me properly."

I kissed him, sweeping my tongue into his mouth to do just that, and moaned when his hands ran over my hips to grip my ass.

The bedroom door flew open. "Hey, you show her the cat— Oh, come on, guys. I've been waiting for this all day, and you decide you wanna bump uglies now?" Jared huffed. "Whatever. Where's the little guy? He doesn't need to see this shit."

I laughed, and Felix smirked against my lips. Turning my head, I watched as Jared scooped a meowing Toulouse up and headed back out of the room.

"His name is Toulouse!" I called after him.

He stuck his head back in, his brows scrunched. "His name is a what?"

"Toulouse. Like the Aristocats," Felix informed him smugly.

Jared chuckled. "Real fucking funny. As if you'd actually know that."

Felix shrugged. "Fuck off now, yeah?"

Jared bowed with Toulouse held tightly to his shoulder. "Gladly."

We waited until we heard the TV volume turn up in the living room, then I locked the door and jumped back on top of Felix, only for him to roll me underneath him.

He undid my pants and stripped me of my shirt in record time. "Ugh, I probably smell like beef patties and coffee. Let me shower first."

He grunted, undoing my bra, then pulled my panties and pants down my legs. "Good thing I love both those things, then."

Nipping the inside of my thigh, he roughly spread my legs wide then shoved his pajama pants down over his ass.

"Come here." I grabbed the sides of his face.

He kissed my nose, and I tugged his t-shirt off, throwing it to the floor and running my hands over the flexing muscles in his arms.

"I love you," he said, aligning himself and sliding inside me.

My head tilted back as every single one of my nerve endings started to sing.

His tongue traveled lazily up my neck. He bit my chin, then drove his hands into my hair and brought my mouth to his.

Tearing my mouth away, I breathed out, "I thought I was supposed to be thanking you."

His chuckle was low and heated as he rolled, and then I was on top of him. I moaned at the new, delicious depth of the position. "Then by all means, Little Doe. Go ahead and thank me."

His hands gripped my breasts, and I rolled my hips tauntingly before I did exactly what I was told.

CHAPTER TEN

"Say, woman, when's that fine ass man you got finally going to put a ring on that finger of yours?" Tabitha asked as I finished wiping down the empty tables.

She refilled the salt and pepper while I straightened the chairs, blowing a piece of hair out of my face.

It wasn't an unreasonable question. Felix and I had been together for almost eight years. I often used to wonder the same thing myself until I gave that up. There was no point.

Felix and I were forever—I felt it within the marrow of my bones—but we just didn't have the financial means to pay for a wedding, let alone an engagement ring. It'd be a dream come true to marry him. But sometimes dreams had to stay just that, a dream.

Surface Rust barely covered the basics to keep the business alive. What profit they made was paid to the employees and Jared.

Jared didn't seem to know, but I'd quickly figured it out.

His brother took his cut each week and put most of it straight back into the business to keep it going another week, another month. For however long it would take for them to finish paying off the debts Darren had left behind.

He had only owned half the business. So Felix paid the mortgage on that while I paid for both our share of the mortgage on the house. Darren had been behind on his payments for that before he died, and despite doing all we could, they still owed well over a hundred grand. It turned out Darren liked to refinance.

"I don't know," I settled on saying. "I'm not too concerned about it, to be honest."

Tabitha chortled loudly. I say the word chortled because that was often what she did.

"Girl, no. Don't tell me you're one of those new-age, fang-dangle types who"—she used air quotes—"doesn't need marriage to cement their eternal bond."

I started laughing, making my way back to the kitchen with her following. "No, I'd love to marry him." Sighing, I dumped my cloth into the hamper and moved to the sink to wash my hands. "It's just never the right time, I guess."

"Totally get that, but still." She eyed me from the counter she was leaning against. "Keep an eye on that handsome piece of man. You'd hate to waste all that time on someone only to be left broke and lonely one day, ya hear?" She clocked out and grabbed her purse.

"Night, Maggie."

"Night," I said quietly, scrunching the paper towel in my hands and taking a deep breath. Letting it out, I slumped back against the counter, wondering if her words held some merit.

I shook my head, determined not to let them get to me when I knew Felix, and so I knew better.

After clocking out, I walked outside to find the man himself standing beside my old Honda.

"What are you doing here?" I glanced around the parking lot. "Where's your bike? Or truck?"

He straightened, pulling me to his chest and pressing his lips to my forehead. "At home. Got Jared to drop me off."

Smiling, I asked, "Why?"

Amusement filled his eyes as he tucked a piece of hair behind my ear and rested his forehead against mine. "Because I wanted to drive you home. Been a while since we've done that."

"It has," I agreed, my eyes fluttering closed when his lips brushed softly over mine.

Tabitha's words became nothing but dust in the windy night, floating away thanks to my heart standing in front of me. My heart was never wrong, so I refused to second-guess a thing.

"Let's grab a bite to eat." He walked me back inside, ordering some fries and burgers from Will, the young guy who'd just started working here a few weeks ago.

We took a seat in the back corner, and I'd complain that eating dinner together at my place of employment was hardly anything special, but it was. We rarely ever went out together for dinner anymore. Not just because money was always tight, but because we were also both tired. Mentally and physically. If we ever had a day off together, we spent it getting groceries or lying in bed and watching movies.

So I'd take whatever I could get, and at that moment, what I was getting felt pretty damn awesome.

We laughed, we fed each other fries, and we felt like us.

"So you finished with that bike yet?"

Felix swallowed and took a sip from his water. "Nah, not yet. Maybe tomorrow." He sighed. "It'd wanna be; the guy's on our asses about it."

"Seriously?"

"Yeah, it's fine, happens sometimes. I actually kind of get it. They miss their rides, and it's hard, putting something you care so much about into the hands of other people."

I'd have laughed at how silly that sounded—the way some people got so caught up in their bikes and cars was kind of funny and ridiculous—but I'd heard variations of similar things from Felix and Jared over the years.

So it was oddly normal.

"What time you working tomorrow?" He grabbed one of my fries and popped it in his mouth.

I watched his square jaw move as he chewed. "Ten."

He nodded. "Means I can keep you up a bit later tonight."

I laughed, raising a brow. "Is that so?"

"You can bet your perfect fucking ass it is." Taking my hand, he brought my fingers to his mouth to run the pads of them over his bottom lip.

My blood started to heat, my breath quickening while I stared into his hooded eyes.

No matter how long we'd been together, he'd probably always have this effect on me.

"Well." I cleared my throat a little and grinned. "We'd better get going then."

Stretching my arms above my head, I blinked my eyes open when I felt the absence of Felix in bed beside me. The glow from the moon creeping inside the dark room had me glancing at my phone on the nightstand. It was just after two in the morning.

I should have gone back to sleep, my limbs were deliciously sore after the two rounds of sex we'd had earlier, but I didn't. I sat up, picked my robe up from the floor, and slipped it on, walking quietly out of the bedroom.

I found Felix sitting at the counter in the kitchen and paused in the doorway to watch him shuffle some papers around. He seemed to be mumbling under his breath, but I couldn't catch what he was saying. Highlighter in hand, he started scribbling on pieces of paper or discarding others to the side with a low curse.

Toulouse gave my presence away, walking over to me from where he was sitting on the floor at Felix's feet. I picked him up, cuddling him to my chest as he purred, and walked over to Felix.

"What are you doing up?" he asked with a severe furrow to his brow.

I reached out to smooth it away with my finger. "I was just about to ask you the same thing…" My eyes fell to the paper, and my stomach sunk like a stone in the sea.

They were bills. Overdue bills, to be exact, and quite a few of them.

"Holy shit," I breathed. "Darren had credit cards, too?"

I tried to pick the statement up, but his hand grabbed mine. "Don't. It's fine."

Frowning at him, I found that very hard to believe. What, with the worry and exhaustion marring his beautiful face. "Hey." I motioned to his lap, and he scooted the stool back for me to sit down on it. "Why didn't you tell me about this?"

His arms wound around my waist, his head falling to my boobs as he groaned out a pained sound. "Because I didn't know until a few months ago. He'd been dodging some of these creditors for years." He laughed. "Sneaky bastard."

It was said with affection, but I knew it still stung that the fallout was coming back to lay at his feet.

"But he's gone ... they can't just write it off?"

He nuzzled his face into my cleavage. "Nope," he mumbled, then lifted his head. "Not when he mainly used them for the business. A business that's still running."

Shit. One step forward, three steps back. A never-ending game that might never be won.

But I wouldn't let him shoulder this alone.

Felix stared down at the papers, chewing on his lip.

"Big guy, look at me."

He did, and I yearned to absorb all his worries, all his pain, and anything that troubled him. Even after everything I'd already done for him, I'd do more. Whatever he needed.

"We'll sort it out. We always do."

He stared at me, his eyes unreadable for a minute. "You shouldn't have to keep putting up with this shit, Mags. God, it's so fucked up." He moved his hands to my cheeks, fingers sinking into my hair. "You've had to deal with so much. This isn't anything like the life we imagined for us."

"Stop." I grabbed his face, resting my head on his. "We'll get everything we imagined. Someday. But first, we have tests we can't fail. We won't fail. We'll figure this out, and we'll look back on it one day and wonder what the hell we were even so worried about."

A choked laugh erupted from his mouth, then he was silent for a long moment.

"I love you, Little Doe."

I closed my eyes, rubbing my nose along the side of his. "Right back atcha, big guy."

CHAPTER ELEVEN

Twenty-Two Months Ago

Two tiny pink lines on two little white sticks.

I didn't have the money to buy more than one pack of two, but I didn't need to.

I was late. I was never late.

"Fuck." I exhaled shakily and sat down on the floor of the bathroom, wondering what the hell we were going to do now.

We couldn't afford a baby. We could barely afford to live ourselves. But despite all that, I let my hand drift down to my stomach.

A baby. An actual human being was growing inside me. One that Felix and I had unknowingly created but made from love all the same.

After sitting a while longer, I got up, packed the tests away into the box, and washed my hands. Felix would be home soon, so I went to the kitchen to start making some spaghetti Bolognese.

I'd worked the morning shift, which was torture. I didn't

think I had that full-blown morning sickness thing going on, but I'd definitely felt queasy in the morning for the past week. Another thing that gave me a not-so-subtle hint.

I finished prepping dinner just as Jared walked in the door with Felix, laughing and punching him in the arm as they walked into the kitchen.

"Get fucked. It looked like a turd's ass."

Jared chuckled. "Pretty sure turds don't have asses, but whatever. The guy wanted it. What the fuck else could we do?"

"Um, maybe not talk about turds when we're about to sit down and eat." I winked at them and slid their plates across the counter.

Jared grinned and sat down, digging right in. "You make the best spaghetti ever, Mags," he mumbled around a fork full of pasta.

Felix hugged me from behind, his hands smoothing over my stomach. I had to fight the urge not to flinch. He wouldn't be able to tell the difference yet, but this was definitely a conversation I was scared out of my brain to have. But one we had to have, no matter what happened after.

He kissed my cheek and then moved to sit next to his brother. I ate in silence next to Felix as he and Jared continued their discussion of the ugly paint job a client had requested for his bike.

Felix was waiting for me when I walked into the bedroom after my shower. I ran the towel over the wet ends of my hair before hanging it up on the hook on the back of the closed door.

"You're quiet." He looked me up and down, eyes narrowing. "What's up?"

Well, no point in putting it off. He'd either be furious,

ecstatic, or somewhere in-between. Somewhere in-between was the best I could hope for, really.

I sat down beside him on the bed. "I need to tell you something."

Humming, he eyed me thoughtfully. "Sounds ominous." He pulled me on his lap so I straddled him. His fingers started twirling around the wet ends of my hair before he tugged the strands to his lips, sucking the water from the ends and making me giggle. "Stop, ew."

"Make me." He grinned wolfishly, and oh, how I wished this could've waited.

But it couldn't, so in an effort not to stammer or have a panic attack, I squeezed my eyes closed and just blurted, "I'm pregnant. Please don't hate me."

I wanted to smack myself in the head because it came out as one weird word. *I'mpregnantpleasedon'thateme.*

Felix started coughing, and I hesitantly peeked one eye open to see his own eyes bulging, his lips slightly parted. "You just say you're pregnant?"

I nodded, closing my eye again.

It took a minute for him to say something after that. A minute that felt like hours with my heart roaring and my stomach clenched tight. "Mags."

"Mmmmm?"

He chuckled, but the sound broke off into a curse and another cough. "Look at me."

I opened my eyes to find that his had softened. "I'm not mad. Shocked as fuck but not mad." He laughed then. "How could I be? I put my dick inside you almost every night. You're not to blame."

I nodded vigorously, my head feeling like one of those bobble-head dogs you see in the back windows of some cars.

He chuckled again, grabbing the sides of my face to keep my head still. "But how did it happen? You've been on the pill for years."

Breath escaped me then, because this part was totally my fault. Still, I had to be honest. "I missed my pill. A few days in a row," I whispered brokenly.

He frowned. "What, like, you forgot or something?"

I felt a tear leak out of my eye. "I ... yes." Sucking in a few gulps of air, I tried again. "My reminder on my phone ... I must've accidentally switched it off, and so I forgot. It's happened once before, so I thought it'd be okay. It was only two, maybe three days." I sniffed, feeling stupid. "I was wrong."

"Jesus, Mags." His thumbs wiped up the few tears that had fallen. "Why didn't you say something?"

I shrugged. "Didn't think I'd need to. I'm sorry."

The silence that followed made me feel even more horrible, so I went to climb off his lap.

He stopped me with his hands on my hips, and I looked down at him, finding his eyes on my stomach. Lifting my t-shirt, his hand slowly moved in to gently splay over it. "A baby." A small smile edged his lips. "Fucking crazy. I mean, I always knew that you'd one day have my kids. Guess life got sick of us putting some things on hold."

"You did?" I asked.

"Of course. You're my girl, and that's never gonna change. You and me, Little Doe. Always."

I ducked my head, smiling and watching his fingers gently rub my tummy. He could still take me back—right back to where we first began. With just a look, a smile, or a touch, he could pull all my heartstrings as if he was responsible for its every beat.

And I guess he was. Every single one.

Two weeks later, I'd been to the doctor. We were lying in bed, Felix running gentle fingers over the skin of my stomach. I was only about seven weeks along, but he didn't care. He seemed to think I needed to be kept in bubble wrap. Even went so far as to tell me that I should stop working; that he'd find a way to take care of everything.

I'd laughed and told him I was pregnant, not sick. He'd grumbled and given me a sour look before slapping my ass.

"Hey." I looked up to find him almost asleep. He'd been at the garage late tonight.

"Hmmm?" He lifted one sleepy eyelid.

"What are we going to call him?"

He chuffed quietly. "Him?"

"Yeah, him."

"How do you know it's a him?"

I didn't. Just had a hunch. I could've been way wrong, but I went with it anyway. "Humor me. What will we call him?"

He opened both eyes then, blinking slowly. I lifted my hand to run it over his cheek. He kissed it when my fingers reached his mouth to trace his lips. "Archer."

"Archer?"

He nodded, closing his eyes again. "Archer. Darren for the middle name."

While I didn't exactly love the name, I pondered it as I stared at the ceiling, silently testing variations of it on my lips.

"Mags?"

"Yeah?"

"You're cute."

Crinkling my nose, I threw a scowl at him. He laughed huskily into the pillow. "Keep scrunching that tiny nose at me, Little Doe, and I'll have to do something about it."

I raised a brow at him, and he groaned, pulling me over him and lifting my sleepshirt from my body, leaving me naked. "Pull down my pants and put my dick in you."

Pulling them down, I placed him at my entrance, sighing at the friction as he slid inside.

Sex felt different while pregnant, though I couldn't put my finger on why or how. All I knew was that I wanted more of it, which he didn't seem to mind one little bit.

"Fuck." He shifted, sitting up and wrapping my legs behind his back. "Grind down on me, Little Doe. Yeah, just like that," he whispered to my neck, sucking and biting my skin as I rolled my hips and worked myself over him.

His hand snaked down my back, moving to my ass where he shoved his hand down under it, lifting it in sync with my bouncing hips and making my job easier.

We both came mere minutes later, and Felix laid back down, taking me with him.

After a few silent minutes of him rubbing my back, still inside me, he murmured quietly to my hair, "Summer."

"What?" I mumbled to his chest.

"If it's a girl, we're naming her Summer."

I laughed at the fact he didn't think I'd want a say in this. But strangely, I liked the name. "Why Summer?" I asked.

Placing a kiss on my head, he said, "Because I met you right before summer. Summertime always reminds me of you."

Sometimes, he surprised me with random bouts of sweetness. You never knew when it was coming, which only made it all the more sweeter.

I wrapped my arms around him tighter, thinking that I didn't just like that name.

I loved it.

CHAPTER TWELVE

Nineteeen Months Ago

February arrived, and I'd finally hit the three-month milestone.

Desperate to tell someone, I'd called my sister on my way out of work that night.

"*What?*" she practically screamed into my ear.

Genevieve was often dramatic, but I didn't think she was being so this time.

"Uh." I chewed my lip, suddenly feeling like calling her was a bad idea. "You heard me, Gen."

She blew out a loud breath into my ear. "Fucking hell, Maggie. What are you going to do?"

"What do you mean?" I asked, opening my car door and folding myself into the seat.

"Okay, okay, look." She sounded like she was walking fast somewhere for a few seconds. "I've got a number here for a place that can take care of …"

It was my turn to say, "*What?*"

"Oh, don't even start. I've never personally had one; I'm smarter than that. But I know a few friends back home who have. You'll be fine; I'll text it through to you."

"Gen, no, um, thanks. We're keeping it. We're happy, excited even."

She breathed out a stunned laugh, and I pulled the phone away from my ear momentarily. "Are you fucking serious right now? You? Having a baby with some joker who rides a motorcycle and lives in the slums?" She laughed again. "God, Maggie. Wake up. You were never meant to have that kind of life. Don't you want more?"

Anger sprouted in my heart, growing thorns and piercing the delicate flesh until all I could see, taste, and feel was red. "You know what? Fuck you, Gen. You're being a total bitch, and I don't need your crap. Bye."

I hung up, chucking my phone on the passenger seat and sighing heavily as I tilted my head back against the headrest. I was a twenty-six-year-old woman. I'd be twenty-seven before the baby arrived. I had a partner who loved me and made me happy despite all the stress in our lives. We could do it, and I wouldn't let anyone convince me otherwise.

Resolved to ignore Genevieve's nasty words, I turned the car on and started the drive home. She was another reminder of why it had felt so good to walk away from my family all those years ago. Though, sometimes, I did miss my mom. She rarely called anymore, but then again, I didn't make much effort either. But I didn't miss my old life.

Did I sometimes wonder what my life would be like had I never met Felix? Sure. Only, if I'd never met Felix, I just knew I'd never have found someone capable of owning every inch of my heart. Not in the way he did. So there wasn't much point in dwelling on what-ifs. Life could be hard and stressful.

Whose life wasn't at some point? But I'd pick happiness over an easy life without it.

And no kind of happiness was quite like the kind that love provided.

Parking in the driveway, I noticed the truck and none of the bikes were there.

I got out and went inside to a quiet house, kicking off my shoes and heading straight for the shower. I needed two after the day I'd had, but one would have to suffice. After scarfing down some macaroni, five pieces of milk chocolate, and an apple, I passed out on the couch.

Loud voices woke me up who knows how long later. I dragged my eyelids open, staring at the muted TV and wondering if I had the energy to move my growing butt to bed.

"No fucking way. You do something like this again and get caught, your stupid ass is going to jail, Felix," Jared bellowed from where I guessed was the kitchen. "And you fucking know it."

My eyes sprung wide, and I sat up.

"It'll be fine. Fuck, just let it go. You weren't supposed to know anyway."

Jared laughed, short and gruff. "Well, too fucking bad, huh? You should know better than to trust that asshole with anything. Sam's worried; can't fucking blame her, can you?"

Felix cursed. "What the hell has she got to do with it anyway?"

"She told me because she gives a damn. Unlike you. What the fuck are you going to do when your ass is sitting pretty in jail and Maggie is left high and dry with your kid?"

"It's not gonna happen. Besides, you got an extra twenty or thirty odd grand lying around to clear out some of this shit so I can actually have my girl at home to take care of my kid? Huh?"

Jared didn't answer, and I got up off the couch, my head spinning for a moment.

"Didn't think so," Felix snapped then asked, "Where's Mags?"

He came down the hall, then stopped when he saw me leaving the living room. "Shit, what are you doing up?"

I didn't answer him, and when he tried to grab my waist, I glared at him "Don't touch me."

"Mags, what the fuck …?"

"What's Jared talking about?"

He shook his head. "Nothing, nothing you need to worry about."

I scoffed. "Nothing I need to worry about? So talk of you doing something dodgy again isn't something for me to worry about?"

He looked at the ground, and I left the room, heading to our bedroom and barely looking at Jared who was frozen in the doorway to the kitchen.

"Mags! Maggie, stop." Felix followed and closed the door behind him. "Just hear me out, yeah?"

"Why? It's not going to be anything worth hearing, judging from what I've already heard."

He raked a shaky hand through his hair, and I sat down on the bed. "It's just one job. I just need to grab a couple of cars for Ryan … We could breathe a bit easier with the money I'd make from it."

"We don't need his dirty money, Felix. Forget it." My eyes begged, but he ignored them.

"I can't." He tugged at his hair.

My gut rolled. "Why?"

"Because … I've gotta do it next week. Besides," he hurried to add, "it's just one time. His guys do it heaps and hardly ever get caught."

Eyes widening, I whisper-hissed, "Do you realize what you're saying?"

"I know." He sat down beside me, taking my hand with his. "I know it sounds bad, but it's easy. I swear it'll just be the one time." I blinked, stunned that he was seriously going to go through with this. "One time. You can't keep working like this, especially not when you're further along in the pregnancy, Mags. And I can't leave the garage for another job, or it might go belly up."

I knew that. I knew it all. Yet I wasn't just going to let him do it. Not to me, not to himself, and definitely not to our baby.

Tears brimmed my eyes as I started to beg, "Please, no. We'll figure it out on our own. Hell"—I sniffed—"I could even ask my mom if maybe—"

His eyes hardened. "No. Fuck that, Maggie. You're mine, and it's my job to take care of you."

My head shook furiously, and he pulled me into his arms. "Stop, please. Let me go." He didn't, and I cried into his Henley. "It's not going to work. What if things go wrong, and then I'm …"

He shushed me, grabbing both sides of my face firmly and looking me hard in the eyes. "You'll never be alone. I'll never let that happen. But Mags …" His eyes squeezed closed and when they reopened, they were glazed, full of his own tears. "I've gotta do *something*. Please, you'll see. It'll be okay."

Except I knew it wouldn't be, yet I let him lay me down, strip me of my clothes, and sink inside my body.

Unsure of when the next time might be.

My heart had my feet frozen in the doorway as I watched Felix's chest rise and fall evenly, his face untroubled while he slept. But I knew when he woke up, that trouble would mar his features once again. Only this time, I wouldn't see it.

Because I'd be gone.

I glanced at the small note I'd left him on the nightstand, grabbed my bag, then moved down the hall as quietly as I could. Tabitha said I could stay with her for a few days, and I had hope that it'd be all he'd need. A scare, something to shock him enough to stop this insanity causing him to make desperate decisions.

He would. I had hope that he'd see reason, and he'd find me when he did.

And that hope helped my feet carry me away from him.

But despite the missed calls he left me over the coming days and the promises in the form of voicemail messages that I didn't respond to.

He never came for me.

If I had known that night would've been the last time I'd see him, I would've done so many things differently.

But that was the thing about perspective.

It was nothing but a cruel taunt.

One that had no qualms about reminding you it was too late.

CHAPTER THIRTEEN

Present
Maggie

"Sometimes, I still feel like I'm falling."

Dr. Hayes puts her pen down, her keen green eyes perusing my face. It takes way too much effort to keep still and not fidget under her inspection.

"How often?"

Giving in, I start picking at a thread on the hem of my skirt. "Not as much as I used to, just every now and then."

"Can you describe it this time?" she asks.

How do you describe the feeling of your heart plummeting to the ground as though it's trying to drag you with it?

Yet I try. "It's kind of like being on a roller coaster. That violent dipping sensation. Then it straightens out, I feel fine, and carry on like it didn't happen."

She doesn't respond, just stares at me before quickly scratching something down onto her notepad.

My gaze travels from her fast-moving hand over to the books that line the shelves in her stark office. Staring out the window, I watch as the white fluffy clouds float among the vast blue sky.

It's sunny today, warm. A beautiful day. So I have no idea why this weird feeling of trepidation insists on making its way into my body, trying to disrupt all the progress I've made.

"Well." Dr. Hayes puts her pen down again as I look back at her, clasping her hands together over her crossed legs. "Today is your last session, but if you feel as though you're not—"

She stops talking when I smile and shake my head. "I think I'm going to be okay. It's time … time to move on." I draw in a deep breath, letting it out slowly. Some of the tension in my chest eases. "And it's exciting, you know? I don't want to feel like I'm going backward in any way. I want to keep going forward. I *need* to."

She nods as if she understands. And maybe she does. She's seen many a patient like me before, probably many much worse than me, too. "You have my number. Call me if you need to." She stands, righting her pantsuit jacket and walking over to me.

Rising from the leather armchair, I grab my purse. Dr. Hayes takes my hand at the door, giving it a gentle squeeze. "I mean that, too. If you feel like you're slipping too much, make sure you do." She eyes me pointedly, raising a blond brow.

I give her my word, visit the front desk, and make my way back home.

"Mommy!" Warren mock squeals when I walk in the door of the two-story home by the bay. "She's back!" He starts jiggling Archie up and down in his arms with a big goofy smile, making Archie let out my favorite sound. His deep belly laugh.

"Come here, little guy." I drop my purse onto the hall table and walk to the doorway of the kitchen to snatch my boy from Warren.

"So does it feel awesome? Knowing you're not crazy enough to warrant seeing the good doctor anymore?" Warren waggles his brows while I plant smooches over Archie's chubby cheeks.

"Shut up." I laugh. "It does, though," I concede.

He nods, and I follow him into the kitchen. Pulling out some mugs, he prepares some coffee. "Thanks for watching him. Was he good?"

Warren gives me the eyeball over his shoulder, turning back to put the milk in. "Duh."

"Bub-bub-bub-bubba," Archie mumbles. One of the seven words he says at the moment. Which is apparently okay for an almost thirteen-month-old. I should know; I've obsessed over everything to do with him and his development.

"That's right. You're the bubba." I poke him in the chest, and I'm rewarded with hearing that musical sound again.

"Mik." His bottom lip wobbles when he catches sight of the milk carton.

Warren's eyes bug out, and he freezes by the fridge. "Busted, little dude."

Smiling, I put Archie down and move into the kitchen to grab his sippy cup, filling it up with some milk as Warren says, "Jake's going to be home for dinner tonight. I'm making his favorite, vegetarian lasagna."

He puts my mug down on the counter while I give Archie his milk, who takes it and plonks himself on the wood floor. "Ta, ta."

"You're welcome." I sit on the floor with him, drinking my coffee while he drinks his milk and moves one of his many toy cars around with his free hand. Glancing up at Warren, I smirk. "So, in other words, don't come a-knocking if the big house starts rocking?"

He almost chokes on his coffee, pointing a finger at me. "You're *so* not funny. But yeah, I wouldn't come knocking." He pauses. "Yeah, no. *I* totally would. *You*, on the other hand ..." He raises a thick blond brow, and I shake my head, flushing a little.

Warren and Jake are more than good looking, but I got used to their antics quickly. They're married. Jake's a doctor at Rayleigh hospital, and Warren runs his own sports gear website from home.

"Anyway, honey bunches, I'm going to finalize some orders. I'll be in the office if you need me."

I take the sippy cup once Archie's done, rinsing it and my mug out and putting them in the dishwasher. "I'm going to put him down for his nap, then I might run the feather duster through here."

Warren marches back into the kitchen, groaning. "Maggie, you don't need to do that shit. We have a cleaner who comes in every two weeks."

Shrugging, I pick Archie up, bending to pick up his car when he drops it and starts kicking his legs. "I know, but it needs it."

He scoffs. "What are you going to do once you start using that degree you just got? Be our maid, clean up your own mess, look after Archie, and work too?" He points a finger at me. "I don't fucking think so, sweetheart. Relax. God, watch a movie or read one of those smut-tastic books you like and masturbate or something." With that, he's gone, and I try not to cough in embarrassment.

I don't do that. Okay, so I totally read smutty books sometimes. But masturbating?

Yeah, I do that, too. But not very often. Sheesh.

"Come on, little guy." I hoist him higher on my hip. He's starting to get pretty heavy. We make our way out the back door and into the backyard until we reach the little two-bedroom guesthouse where Warren and Jake put us. It's cute and is the same pale blue color as their house, covered in vines and surrounded by flower pots. It sits right on the water, but thankfully, a fence stops Archie from wandering off down to the sand if we're playing in the yard.

Although picturesque, it's never really felt like home.

Still, it's the best one I've got, and for that, I love it all the more.

After changing Archie and putting him down for his nap, I stare at him for a moment, smoothing my hand over his head full of dark brown hair as I lean over his crib. He sleeps soundly, always does, this little ball of energy of mine. But some nights as I lay awake in bed thinking about all the ways things should've been different for him, for me, for *us*, I selfishly wish he wouldn't. Yes, I realize that makes me sound as though I need to march myself back to Dr. Hayes. But despite all the generosity, and the two men living practically next door, I feel most alone when it's quiet. When I have nothing to listen to except for the turning and twining of my own thoughts.

Sighing, I straighten from the crib. With one last glance at Archie, I soak in the way his long lashes rest on top of his chubby cheeks before quietly closing the door halfway when I leave the room.

Walking into our little open plan living area, I follow Warren's advice by perusing my mini bookshelf, when I realize I left my purse inside the house.

Snatching the baby monitor, I hop over the

stepping-stones to the back door, heading inside to grab it when there's a knock on the front door of their house.

My spine tingles strangely. That feeling that tries to choke the air from my lungs returns with a vengeance as I place the monitor down on the hall table.

My hands shake, but Warren doesn't leave his office, so I move to answer it just as they knock again, louder this time.

I should use the peephole. I always do. But there's no need.

My heart could feel him through any obstacle.

He's here.

I struggle to hold the tears back as all the words and all the feelings I'd planned on spilling to him seem to run away. My body reacts on impulse, though, opening the door to get what it wants.

"Mags," Felix breathes. One word. The same word I've been dying to hear for almost nineteen months now.

He looks so different. So much bigger, yet still the same.

I don't even think. I throw myself at him, tears escaping my squeezed shut eyes when I wrap my arms around his neck.

His scent, the feel of him, even with all the physical changes, have remained the same.

I'm so caught up in my relief that I don't register how long it takes for him to hug me back, for him to touch me with the same desperation emanating from me.

Then finally, he does. Thick arms hold me to him so tightly that I wonder if I'll be able to breathe soon enough.

He can take my oxygen, though. He can take it all.

He's back.

"Fucking hell, Mags," he says throatily into my hair. My rejoicing heart stops its celebrating when he says, "Where've you been?"

My body locks up, and he must feel it because he steps back, steadying me with his hand when that feeling of falling resurfaces.

"I've been here. We've been here." I smile shakily at him then reach up to touch his cheeks. He lets me, his brows furrowing while his eyes flick over my face.

My hands move to his hair, well, what's left of it. It's now gone, shaved into a crew cut. "Your hair," I whisper before I can think better of it.

He grabs my hands then, lowering them before slowly releasing them. "Jail, Mags. You know where I've been. Now answer the question."

No, I need more time. But I know, no matter how much time I give myself to prepare, the only reason I can give him isn't going to be good enough.

Felix stiffens, then moves me aside before marching inside the house. "Who the fuck are you?" His voice is low and unforgiving in its harshness. "Why the hell are you here with this guy?" He turns to me, eyes full of shock and incredulity.

Warren raises his hands. "Hey, whoa." He glances at me, and I try to give him an apologetic look. Felix looks back at him, steps forward, and with his hands clenching at his sides, stops right in front of Warren.

Warren's a fit guy who loves all things sports, and it suddenly occurs to me that unless you know him, you probably wouldn't even know he was gay.

Oh, hell. "Felix, stop. Back up."

Warren smirks at Felix. "Felix, hey? I'm Warren. Nice to finally meet you, man. And she's right." He nods at me without taking his gaze from Felix's hard face. "You should back up. I'm spoken for, and despite what you may think, she's not my other half."

Felix's confused eyes snap back to me, and my heart races faster.

"Although my husband and I wouldn't say no to a little playtime with our girl over there, she's not interested. And I'm way more interested in you than in her, if you get what I mean." He raises a brow, and Felix stumbles back so fast that he almost barrels me over.

Warren just laughs.

"You're …"

"Gay?" Warren supplies. "Why, yes. I guess you could say that I am." He looks at the picture of him and Jake on the wall above the hall table. One from their wedding on the beach. "Married three years a month ago." He sighs, turning his attention back to us. "Handsome pair, aren't we?"

A snort escapes me at that, and Felix turns around, relief stamped all over his face. "You scared the ever-loving shit out of me." He frowns then. "But how the hell did you end up here with these guys?"

The smile on my face slowly wilts, but Warren notices and thankfully steps in, diverting Felix's attention back to him. "She needed a place to stay, and we've got a guesthouse out back that we advertise for lease sometimes. So her and your boy have been living there."

That seems to make Felix's shoulders drop even more. I don't know why; maybe even with their sexual preferences, he's glad I'm still not sleeping under the same roof as them.

I used to, though. It took me a few months to work up the courage to move into the guesthouse. Not that I'm about to say that.

"Look, I'll just give you guys some privacy. Congrats on the jail break, dude." He slaps Felix on the back, who stiffens again, before grabbing the baby monitor and giving me a wink to say he's got it covered.

"Where is he?" Felix stares at the baby monitor in Warren's hand until Warren disappears at the end of the hall.

"He's taking a nap."

He turns back to me, his brown eyes closing for a brief second.

"I could maybe go and—"

"No." He cuts me off. "Don't do that. I'll come back tomorrow and see him. When's he awake?"

There's so much to discuss. What's been happening, how he's doing, what's going to happen now. Yet no way to know for sure if or when we'll get to cover it all. The thought makes my head spin a little, and my chest tighten. "Um, he's only sleeping before and maybe after lunch at the moment. He sleeps all night. So whenever you want, I guess."

He nods, stepping closer to me and grabbing my hand. "Christ, I've missed you. You're okay? He's okay?" He shakes his head as questions start to roll through his eyes. I can tell he has so many, but I already know I can't answer them all. "What's his name?"

"Archie," I supply quietly, absorbing the heat from his large, rough hand while I can. "Archer Darren Williams."

His eyes move from my hand to my face, glinting as a slow smile spreads across his face. "Archie."

I nod, and he lifts my hand to his lips. My eyes close to stop the barrage of tears gathering when he kisses each of my fingertips and then my hand.

"I need to know, Mags." He drops my hand. "Why you didn't come? I know there's gotta be a reason. I know I fucked up, but he's my ..." He swallows, not finishing. He doesn't need to.

Cold replaces any warmth that had enveloped me. I'm

suddenly freezing, and it's barely even the start of fall.

I'm completely stuck, unable to answer him.

He repeats the question, harsher this time. His voice like gravel that drags over the bruised tissue of my heart. "Maggie, *why?*"

I've been over this moment a million times in my head. Probably more. But every time, every single time, I could never form a coherent response. Not even for the Felix I silently pleaded and begged forgiveness from in my head.

Because if he knows why I didn't come—what happened—it could ruin everything for him all over again.

I can't do that; I can't risk that. He's made mistakes, ones we're all still paying for, but so have I. I can't risk making anymore, and neither can he.

So I take a steady breath and set my lies free. "I'm sorry, but you know why, and I regret it. I really do. I was just so … mad."

He steps back, shock moving over the now even harsher planes of his face. His arms, so thick now, bulge under his white shirt as he digs his palms roughly into his eyes. Dropping them, he snarls faintly, "Am I seriously hearing this right? I can understand you'd be mad, but not bringing my own kid to meet me, Maggie …" He shakes his head. "That's bullshit."

He stares at me for a heartbeat, and my blood freezes along with the rest of my body. "You didn't listen to me. What was I supposed to do? Just forgive you?" I clench my teeth and use some pent-up anger of my own to force my next words out. "And I didn't keep him from you. You ended up in jail, Felix. *Jail.* Did you really want me to bring our son to prison to visit you?"

The look he gives me is full of incredulous outrage. "What the fuck? Yes!" He studies me again, laughing humorlessly under his breath. "This is so messed up. You thought you were too fucking precious to bring our kid to see his dad in jail, is that it?"

"That's not it at all, but he's only a baby, Felix."

He spreads his arms out wide. "So what? Other inmates got to see their babies, toddlers, kids. But no, not me, apparently."

My hands start to shake, and I bunch them together in front of me to try to hide it. "I think you should go," I whisper, though everything I am screams at me for suggesting such a thing. "You can come and meet Archie tomorrow if you want."

Averting my gaze to the ground, I keep it there even though I feel the sear from his own burning into my profile. "So that's it, then? That's all you've got to say?"

I shrug, mumbling, "I don't know what else I can tell you, Felix, besides the truth. I'm sorry; it was wrong of me. But I just couldn't ..." I slam my mouth closed to stop from saying anything more.

I watch his black boots as he moves toward the door, pausing on the threshold. "I'll come over tomorrow after work, but you and me?" I glance over at him then, hope slowly melting away some of the ice until I see the look in his eyes. "We're fucking through, Mags."

CHAPTER FOURTEEN

Maggie

"**S**o he just showed up here? How the hell did he know where you were?" Jake asks the next afternoon when he gets home from work. He didn't end up getting his vegetarian lasagna because he had to work a double, and it looks as though he's about to fall over, the poor guy.

"I have no idea, and yes." I give Archie the truck, and he starts pushing it through the dirt in the flower bed.

Jake curses, and I give him a smile. He sees through it, though. "Don't." He points a finger at me. "Don't try to act like you're doing okay. Shit." Jake looks over at Warren, who's watering the plants nearby.

I try not to laugh because I should be more than used to it by now. But he's the epitome of an all-American jock, baseball cap on and all, with a purple watering can in hand as he hums under his breath.

Warren pauses, probably feeling our eyes on him. "What?"

He gives me a wink, and a little laugh escapes me. Like he knew I needed it and doesn't care that it's at his expense.

"Put the damn watering can down and get your ass over here."

Warren guffaws, still looking at me all wide-eyed with feigned indignation. "Honey bunches, the way he speaks to me is just appalling!"

"You love the way I speak to you. Don't pretend otherwise."

Warren chuckles, dropping the can and dusting his hands off on his cargo shorts. Which was pointless, seeing as he walks over to join Archie in the dirt. "What's up?"

"This Felix guy could have her back in therapy, that's what's up." Jake runs a hand through his jet black hair, making the wavy locks fall across his forehead. His brown eyes soften when Archie toddles over to hand him a flower. These two men like their gardens, but they love Archie, so they don't seem to care that he likes to play in them. Still, I try to smooth the dirt back over and make sure Archie doesn't pluck anymore flowers.

"What can ya do? The guy's done his time, and we've just gotta wait it out. See what happens." Warren shrugs. "Maggie insists she can't tell him, and if what I saw yesterday is any indication, she's damn right about that. The guy will lose his ever-loving mind."

"I'm okay," I tell mainly Jake, who's watching me. I'm not, but what did I expect? To be welcomed back into Felix's heart after keeping his son away from him? Maybe. But I'm not that stupid. I know him. His temper and stubbornness don't leave a lot of room for forgiveness.

And if I can't tell him, well, all I can hope is that he lets me back in and forgives me eventually. We've got too much past for him to just throw it away so easily.

Even if I'm terrified he'll do that anyway.

"Look at her." Warren bends down to sit beside me, squeezing my cheeks. "She's too beautiful for him to stay mad at. It'll all be fine."

Jake seems doubtful, but his lips curve into a small smile as he watches Warren fuss over me. Warren pulls my hair back off my face when Archie climbs onto my lap and tries to use it as leverage to stand.

"Car!" He shoves the car at my chest, and I grab it before it falls down my top. "Uh-huh, vroom, vroom." I make the noise for him, and he gifts me with a mostly gummy smile before snatching it back and walking over to Jake.

Jake picks him up, hoisting him high in the air and grinning at him.

"Remember that time you did that, and he drooled right into your mouth?" Warren laughs as he tidies up the flower bed.

Jake lowers Archie to his hip. "He did no such thing."

I laugh too, standing and dusting some dirt off my jeans, because he did. He's done it to me, too. Only it landed on my cheek and not in my mouth.

"Puts a whole new spin on spit or—"

Jake glares at Warren. "Don't speak like that in front of the baby, filthy bastard."

He then walks off with Archie still attached to his hip while Warren continues to laugh.

"Jake!" I call just as he's going inside. He turns around when I reach him. "Here, I'll take him. You need to sleep. Look at you."

He scoffs. "I'm used to it, and I want to hang out with him. It's been a few days since I've even been home."

I lift a brow and give him my best stern look. He huffs,

handing my baby over. "Fine. I'm seeing him before he goes to bed, though." With that, he kisses Archie on the head, smooths his hand over mine, and wanders off into the house.

Warren runs in after him, winking again as he closes the door and I step back outside.

Shaking my head, I make a beeline for our little house and put a movie on for Archie. He falls asleep in my lap, but I can't bring myself to move. So I stare mindlessly at the small flat-screen TV, thoughts of Felix turning my brain and heart to mush as I wonder if he's still going to come over and see Archie this afternoon.

An hour later, Archie's awake, and I'm changing him in his room when Warren knocks on the glass sliding door out in the living room and walks in. "Bunches? You've got a visitor."

I don't need to ask who it is. Again, I just know. The air in our little home seems to change, affecting my breathing and turning my heart inside out with anticipation.

"Thanks. Let him in if he wants. I'll be out in a minute." I toss the diaper in the small trash can under the table. After pulling up Archie's shorts, I kiss his head before putting him down in the bathroom next to me so I can quickly wash my hands.

I hear the murmur of voices from outside, but they stop when Archie runs out of the bathroom and turns left, heading down the small hall into the living room.

"Car!" he shouts while I quickly dry my hands then run after him with my heart in my throat. This isn't exactly the introduction I had planned. Then again, not much in this life of mine has ever gone to plan. I should've learned to roll with it by now.

Maybe Felix is outside still, maybe he's waiting … my thoughts halt as do my feet when I find him staring down at

Archie, who's picking up a handful of Hot Wheels cars and taking them to Felix. Unafraid of this strange man who he has no idea is his dad, he's just happy to be awake and playing.

Felix lifts his gaze to me. I stop myself from apologizing, knowing that even if I do it until I'm blue in the face, it'll never make up for it. He stares at me for a soul-twisting minute, his eyes glassy with unshed tears before blowing out a loud, shaky breath and returning his attention to Archie, who keeps dropping cars at his feet. He bends down, picking some of the cars up, and I don't know what I should do. Unsure if I should leave and give them some time to themselves or if I should stay in case Felix decides it becomes too much.

I clear my throat. "I'll just, um, clean up a bit."

He doesn't say anything, doesn't even look at me, just stays where he's now seated on the floor, moving the cars over the rug with Archie.

I busy myself with cutting up some apple for Archie, then I decide to clean up his already clean room. With nothing else to do, I move to my own room and sit down on the queen-size bed, staring at the wall while I listen to them play.

I feel like an intruder as I listen to Felix talk quietly to our son. Like I don't deserve to bear witness to any part of such a prominent moment in both of their lives.

After a little while, I wipe the tears from my face, check it in the bathroom, and make my way back out to give Archie his snack. He eats while he plays, dropping bits of apple on the rug and running over them with his car. Felix laughs, and I try not to do the same, for fear of ruining anything. Instead, I grab a wipe and clean up the car and the rug after he's moved on to his toy motorcycle.

"Beek!" He passes it to Felix, who finally looks over at where I'm sitting on the couch.

"He likes bikes?"

I nod. "He likes anything with wheels, really."

He looks over at Archie, and a fond smile relaxes some of his features. It hasn't escaped my notice that Felix hasn't tried to pick him up or touch him much. Not while I've been in the room anyway.

Archie runs over to the door, knocking on it, which is his way of saying he wants to play outside.

"He wants to go out?" Felix asks.

"Yeah." I stand, moving to the door. "He loves to be outside."

Felix stands too, following us as we head out to the grass.

Sitting on the grass, I watch them dig in the dirt of the flower bed together, wishing so many things were different about this moment but appreciating it all the same.

Felix walks over a while later, and I stand on unsteady legs.

"He's … incredible, Mags." He clears his throat. "I can't believe it, that we made him."

"I know," I whisper, watching Archie throw some grass into the air above his head. We're silent. A heavy moment that grows thick, pressing and pulsing until I decide to blurt, "Hey, how'd you even find me?" I tuck some hair behind my ear, feeling flustered. "Not that I'm not glad you did, but well—"

He puts me out of my misery. "Jared hired some PI."

My breath hitches. I'd never even thought of that. "Oh."

"Yeah. I just …" He seems to struggle with what to say. Our gazes meet, and my heart starts thudding at his nearness, at the hurt and questions brewing in his stormy eyes. "Why? Why'd you hide from everyone?"

Not everyone. "I didn't." It's all I can think to say. It's a lie, but it's only half of one.

"Yeah?" He steps closer, lowering his voice. "Well, why the

hell didn't your sister tell Jared where you were then, huh?"

My eyes widen, and his scowl deepens. "What? He asked Genevieve?"

He scoffs. "Oh, come on. You know he would've."

But I didn't. He realizes I'm not lying after a beat of time passes and curses quietly. "What a fucking bitch. I knew she didn't like me, but what the hell, Mags?"

I just shake my head because I don't know. I had no idea. She's never mentioned anything about that. "I promise. I'll talk to her and try to find out why." Even if it's too late to bother.

I glance over at Archie, finding him back in the dirt with his truck. Felix does the same then grabs my chin, turning my face to him. My eyes close, my head relaxing into his firm hold. "I've missed you," I whisper. "So much."

His voice is low when he says, "I don't fucking understand it, Little Doe." My eyes fly open at that name, warmth filling my veins and flowing through me. "For someone who destroyed me by leaving me alone to rot and not even bringing my own son to see me because of what I did, you sure seem to have changed your tune now."

Stunned, my heart thrashes with the injustice of it all. Its thud so powerful that it feels like it wants to tear my chest open to get to him. To make him take it and never let it go. To find its way home.

When I don't respond, he closes the remaining gap between our bodies, his scent filling my nose and almost overwhelming me with how close he is. So close, yet nowhere near close enough. "So what's it going to be, Mags? You want me again now? Now that I'm free? Is that it?"

My eyes close once more, only to reopen when his warm breath ghosts over my lips. They tingle in response as if they're trying to get to him too. Every part of me is desperate, and I'm the one stopping it all from getting what it needs.

I don't want to stop it. I want him. I'll always want him. "Y-yes," I breathe out.

His voice is a hissed whisper. "Yes, what?"

"I want you. Always." I close the distance and seal my lips to his. My heart sings, my arms wrap around his neck, and my shoulders deflate with bittersweet relief.

My lips press themselves gently to his, lifting, dropping, gliding, over and over. He groans but remains unmoving against their soft assault.

He grabs my forearms, and my stomach hollows out as he shoves me back. I try not to scream, to gasp or panic, knowing that no matter how much I've hurt him, he'd never physically hurt me. But no, for the first time in a long while, it's not the physical I'm afraid of.

He turns, barely looking at Archie who's banging his toys together in the garden before walking toward the side gate.

My feet send me running to him. "Felix …"

"No." He spins around when I reach him; his eyes darker than I've ever seen them. "Fuck you, Maggie. Don't fucking touch me again."

CHAPTER FIFTEEN

Felix

Almost three weeks have passed since I stepped out of the cesspit some might call a prison.

Two and a half weeks since I last saw my son.

Since I saw her.

I don't know what it is about this whole situation that's got my heart fucking raging at me, but my brain seems to be steamrolling the show here. And I'm in complete agreement with its leadership.

She didn't visit me. Didn't bring my baby to meet me. All because she was pissed that I fucked up?

I did fuck up and in a huge god damned way. I'll be the first to admit that. But she's taken my punishment too far. Not only is it not fucking fair to me, but it's not fair to Archie that he never got to meet me until two and a half weeks ago.

Archie. Archer Williams. I can't help the stupid smile that tries to take over my face when I think of him. Kid's cute as hell. All chubby legs, arms, and face. Big brown eyes and a head full of the same colored hair as his daddy's.

Daddy.

Well, shit.

Guilt slams me in the gut, so hard I almost choke on my next sip of Coke. Man, I need a drink. Fucking parole. I know I shouldn't be acting like a selfish prick—not seeing him just because I can't bear to look at his mom—but fuck, it's hard.

I'm just glad the little guy won't remember any of this shit.

"Felix." Badger walks out the back door of our small three-bedroom house. The same one I grew up in, well, for the years that mattered anyway. And the very same one I spent years sleeping with my heart right next to me.

Only to have her bail on me when I needed her the most.

Forcing my thoughts away, I stand from the folding chair to shake his hand. He pulls me in for a one-armed hug instead. "Good to see you. Now, don't go doing anything that'll send you back." He gives me a stern look; his blue eyes twinkle, though, betraying anything harsh he says. As usual.

"You've got nothing to worry about. How's that heart of yours doing?" I gesture to his chest with my can of Coke. "Don't think I didn't hear about that."

He shrugs, tucking his hands into his trouser pockets and smiling warmly at Vera when she comes over. "I've never felt more rested in my life." He leans in to whisper, "In fact, I think if anything, I'll die from boredom soon, if she's not careful."

Vera scowls. "I heard that. Speaking of careful." She points at me. "Give him your chair."

My brows rise, but I don't argue. "All yours, old man." I wink, patting him on the shoulder before heading to the kitchen to grab another drink.

Jared thought it'd be a good idea to have some kind of

118 | ELLA FIELDS

welcome home party for me. I told him not to bother; it's not like I can drink right now anyway. Then Vera got wind of it, and she's all about parties and giving that kid what he wants.

He thinks he's whipped. He doesn't realize how much he's got her wrapped around his fucking finger too, though.

"Oh, my God. Hi!" some girl with red hair in sky high stilettos says, walking into my kitchen. I glance around, wondering if she's lost. She's dressed up as if she's stepped off a runway or something. Then another one joins her, brown hair and huffing and puffing as if she's chasing after a delinquent child. "Jesus, Cleo, you couldn't wait two freaking minutes for me to get off the phone?"

The redhead is Cleo, I'm guessing. I remain frozen, partly because I'm still wondering if they're lost and partly because they're also blocking the way out of the kitchen.

"Uh, can I help you ladies?"

The one called Cleo moves closer, and I back up against the sink. "What was it like, you know, being in jail?" she whisper-hisses, as if it's some big conspiracy no one is allowed to talk about.

"You totally don't have to answer her," the brown-haired one says. "I'm Isla, by the way. We're Vera's besties."

"Besties?" I mumble to no one in particular. Figures, though.

She smiles. "Yep."

"So ..." Cleo moves in next to me, nudging me with her elbow. "Is it true what they say?"

God damn, this chick has smothered herself in the harshest perfume known to mankind. I try not to wrinkle my nose, or breathe, and simply raise a brow at her.

She lowers her voice. "You know, about dropping the soap?" Then she goes and makes it worse by trying to wink or some weird shit, her eye twitching a little.

I bite my tongue to suppress my laugh.

"Cleo!" Isla scurries over, grabbing her arm.

"What?" Cleo shrugs. "I'm just asking what everyone's probably wondering. Yeeesh."

I humor her because damn, it feels good to smile. I'm thankful for that much, at least, even if she's asked a random as fuck question. "Sometimes true. But didn't happen to me." I lean in, not breathing in case I choke on her perfume. "Iron grip, you know?"

She nods slowly as if it's useful information she's storing away.

"Step away from the convict, Cleo." Vera marches into the kitchen, swinging open the fridge door and placing a bottle of fancy champagne on the counter. Isla and Cleo clap, moving to open it and grabbing glasses from the cabinet.

Guess they've been here before.

I look up to find Jared standing outside the doorway, smirking at me.

With the girls distracted, I head back outside, catching up with Troy and Butch, who work at the garage with us. Troy's missus is pregnant again and watching him fuss over her damn near makes me want to hit something. I make my excuses and head back inside, needing solitude for a while.

Closing the door to my bedroom behind me, I take a seat on the bed and hang my head in my hands for a good minute. Toulouse appears from under the bed. He must've been hiding from all the commotion outside.

"Hey, little fella."

I don't touch him ... can barely stand to look at him, to be honest.

Him, and everything about this damn room—hell, this

house—reminds me of her. All the years we spent together, the late nights, the early mornings. All in these walls, this bed. A bed I don't even want to sleep in now. In fact, I spend most nights on the couch.

A familiar, crumpled piece of paper catches my eye. Snatching it from the nightstand, I read the same words I've memorized by heart. It's the note she left me before everything went to hell.

I'm sorry, but I can't watch you do something like this. You're risking so much for something that might end in disaster.

I'm staying at Tabitha's. If you start to see reason, come find me.

I love you.

"Hey."

I look up, finding Jared in the doorway. Kid's always been sneaky.

I crumple the note again, tossing it back on the nightstand. When I don't say anything, he closes the door, taking a seat beside me on the bed.

"Maybe this wasn't such a great idea." He sighs. "I just thought it might help, since you're always looking so down, so pissed off."

"Not much is going to change that right now, kid. Doesn't mean I don't appreciate you giving a damn, though." I clap him on the back, and he pretends to wince, making me chuckle.

"Shut the fuck up."

He's been giving me shit about bulking up ever since I got home, and it's starting to piss me off.

When he just continues to sit there, drinking his beer, I ask, "Did you come in here to check on me or escape from your woman's crazy ass friends?"

He pauses mid pull, his green eyes shifting to the side. Busted.

He swallows, whispering, "They're awesome chicks and all, but damn ..." He chuckles.

"Bit fucking much, eh?" I offer.

He nods. "Don't ever let Frost hear you say that shit, though," he says. "She's liable to try to kill you with her eyes."

"Jared?"

"Speak of the devil," I murmur, and Jared punches me in the arm.

"One minute!" he calls out to her, then glares at me. "Don't speak shitty about her, or I'll put Toulouse's litter tray under your bed, motherfucker."

He goes to leave at that, and I'm left smiling once again.

Until he stops near the door. "When are you going back to see her?"

He doesn't even need to say her name, and my body tenses.

I shrug, and he curses. "Felix, fucking hell. I'm going to drag my own ass out there to meet my nephew if you don't do something about this mess. You're out now. I don't understand why you aren't trying to fix it."

Glowering at him, I growl, "You can't fix something that broken, kid. Leave it alone. I'll figure something out with Archie. You'll meet him soon."

"Knock, knock," a familiar woman's voice sounds from behind the door.

"Really? So to make matters even worse, you invited Sam?"

My jaw clenches. "I didn't invite her, if you must know."

"Rash," Jared hisses. "God damned rash." He flings open the door. "Wassup, Sam? Party's that way; Felix'll be out soon."

She pops her head around the door, blue eyes wary when they land on me. "Sure, okay."

I flick her a halfhearted wave, wondering how she heard about this little party of mine.

Jared closes the door with a quiet groan. "Tell me you're not going to go there."

His attitude is starting to grate on my already split nerves. "No, and even if I did, it'd be none of your damn business."

He doesn't respond right away, and I keep my eyes trained on a stray pair of socks on the floor. I should really clean up this room before Vera comes in here messing with my shit and does it herself again.

"You know, if you really wanted to screw up your life some more, I'm sure we could arrange for some coke, maybe some weed. Let's see how your next piss test comes back then, yeah?" He guffaws. "Or hey, I know. How about you start fucking Sam, all the while you're ignoring the fact you've got a kid and a woman who probably still gives a damn about you."

"Back off, Jared." I run my hands through my hair, the tiny thread I'm keeping on my anger starting to fray. "If she gave a damn about me, she would've fucking came to see me."

His laugh is low and full of disbelief. "Yeah, that's pretty fucked up on her part. But you know what? Sitting around here and showing up at work like someone keeps pissing in your Cheerios isn't going to change what's happened. Making it worse will only do just that, make it worse. Think about that with your brain before you start thinking with your unused dick."

Like he can fucking talk. I'm on my feet in an instant—
to do what, I don't know—but he doesn't back down; he just
gives me a hard look. "Stop being a stubborn idiot. Now, get
out there and at least spend an hour with some people who,
shock horror, *do* care about you."

He leaves and I just stand here, anger making my arms and
hands shake. My heart pounds furiously throughout my head,
causing it to ache as my gaze falls to the picture frame on the
dresser.

"Fuck." I grab the photo of Maggie and me, throwing it at
the wall and watching the pieces rain down onto the carpet.

The photo lands face up; our smiling faces, covered in
shards of glass, mocking me.

Taunting and tormenting me.

How is it possible to love someone so much while fucking
hating them in equal measure?

CHAPTER SIXTEEN

Maggie

Felix stormed out of Warren and Jake's backyard over two weeks ago, and I've been in a tailspin ever since. This constant feeling nagging and gnawing at my insides won't let up. It kicks and screams for me to tell him the truth. To tell him what happened.

But as much as I want to be selfish, I just can't.

So much more than my own heart is at stake here.

My sister's voicemail greets me again, and I almost growl, hitting end call and dumping my phone on the counter before shoving my hands roughly through my hair.

I should be doing so many things, but instead, I'm letting Felix's reappearance and now disappearing act turn my shaky little world upside down.

I finished my degree in early childhood education a month ago, and I've yet to even try to find a job. Fear isn't holding me back because I know I can do it. Join the real world again.

It's the uncertainty of *everything* that's holding me back.

Once again, I'm letting my feelings for Felix control the way I'm living. Yet I can't seem to snap out of it or make heads or tails of what's going to happen next, and I hate that. It makes it even harder to sleep at night and control the racing of my heart when I try to work out the jumbled mess inside my head.

I look over at Archie when he babbles quietly in his sleep. He passed out on his little fold-out couch after eating lunch. He doesn't know, he's untroubled by all this, yet the anxiety rolling off me in steady ripples has somehow exhausted him.

My phone rings behind me on the counter. I quickly spin around to answer it before it wakes Archie and step outside to talk to my sister.

"Thanks for finally getting back to me," I say dryly.

"God, what crawled up your butt and died?" She tells someone in the background that she wants a skinny flat white before saying, "I've been busy. You know how it is. Robert's got all these charity events coming up for the surgery at the end of the year. I'm on committees. It's not exactly easy."

I roll my eyes because screw it, she can't see me. "Right. Anyway, why didn't you ever tell me about Jared trying to get in touch with me?"

She's silent for a few seconds. "Who's Jared?"

"Jesus, Gen. Felix's brother."

"Oh," she says. "Dark hair, green eyes? Good looking, for sure. I can see the appeal, sis. Too bad he runs on the wrong side of the law and is probably broke as hell. Just like his brother. I'm surprised he even has access to social media, let alone the balls to repetitively contact me over it."

My teeth grit, and I inhale deeply through my nose. "Yes, that's Jared. So again, why didn't you tell me?"

She sighs audibly. "Because those kind of men are garbage, Mags. You finally got to break away from the shit life you'd fallen into by being with Felix."

"But at what cost? And who are you to say we had a shit life? We didn't. It was hard, but that's just life in general. Not everyone needs to marry a doctor or a fucking rocket scientist."

"Calm down," she hisses. "I'm not going to apologize, okay? I did the right thing. You're so much better off without those lowlifes in your life. Now you and Marty can move on and find a better man to be his dad."

"Archie, Gen. It's Archie." She'd know if she ever visited, but she stays in New York. Though she did FaceTime me a few months after he was born. If that even counts for something.

"Whatever. Gotta go. And hey, have you heard from Mom?"

"No, not in a while. Why?" I watch the dark clouds gathering in the sky.

"Just thought I'd ask. I haven't gotten her monthly phone call yet is all. Talk soon."

She hangs up, and I stare at my phone disbelievingly.

Felix is right. She's a serious bitch.

I've always known that, but I at least thought she cared about me to some extent.

And as for my mom … Gen gets a monthly phone call? That stings. When I called her a few months after Archie was born to give her my new number, she checked in when she could—usually to ask about Archie—but it's been a few months now. Last time we spoke, I finally told her where I was staying in hopes that maybe she'd like to visit us, but I've heard nothing from her since.

I head back inside, but the anger intensifies as each minute passes until I feel like I'm going to throw up or start crying.

I'm so sick of this. I know what I want, what will fix this, and it's him. If he can't be with me the way I want him to, then maybe we can at least be civil. Friends. Maybe then he'll remember what it's like to be us again.

I've got big hopes when it comes to that one, but I need to cling to something right now.

I grab my keys and bag, stuffing a fresh diaper into it before taking Archie out front to the car.

"Where are you going?" Warren walks out his front door just as I finish buckling Archie up.

"To see Felix." I climb in and shut the door, starting the engine.

He opens the door. "Hey, hold up a minute." He looks warily at Archie in the back and then at my face. "You sure that's a good idea?"

He thinks I'm not ready for such a long drive, especially when it has to do with Felix. I don't drive much anymore, and when I do, it's usually just to somewhere local.

I'll show him. I'll show myself too while I'm at it.

"I'll be fine. I'll call you if I have any trouble, okay?"

He chews his lip. "I'm coming with you."

"Warren, no …" He shuts the door, pointing at me with a stern look that says I'd better not leave before running to lock the house.

We sit in silence the whole way to Rayleigh. I can practically hear the questions being yelled at me from Warren's head, but I don't speak. I need to do this, take some control back.

Glancing at the time, I realize Felix is probably still at work as I make my way through the city to the old familiar shed on the south side of Rayleigh. Surface Rust.

After parking, I turn the car off and try to breathe as a thousand memories threaten to suffocate me all at once.

"You okay?" Warren asks.

I nod, swallowing and closing my eyes over the tears.

Taking a deep breath, I undo my seat belt and climb out of the car, pushing the door closed behind me when I see Sam walking out of the rolled-up door.

She looks over at me as she stops at her car, a blue Kia, then smiles at Felix, who follows her out.

My heart jumps into my throat, and my feet stop moving on the cracked asphalt halfway across the small lot, when she moves her hands to his chest.

His eyes flick over to where I'm standing. It's so brief that I don't know if Sam even notices.

Those hands, hands that aren't mine, keep traveling up his chest and around his neck. He seems a little shocked, staring back down at her. Then his features morph into something else entirely.

His top lip curls, and Sam must take that as a sign, because she moves his head down at the same time she rises on her toes to whisper in his ear.

Then her lips are on his, and his are on hers.

Something cracks. Nobody else seems to hear it, though. Nobody except me. Which would make sense.

Seeing as it's the sound of my heart splitting in two.

I can take his anger, the hurt, the words he slings at me that hit a bull's-eye every time. But this? I don't think I can take this. Especially when he doesn't pull away from her. No, his head lowers more while hers tilts. His arms have moved around her waist, and he looks straight at me while their kiss goes deeper. It's as if he wants me to see I mean nothing, that he meant every word he said to me the last time I saw him.

"Bunches," Warren calls out from the car. "Come on, let's go."

He's right; I should. And the message has been received anyway. I don't think Felix could've made it any clearer if he tried. Turning away, I will the tears to wait just five more minutes until I'm away from here.

Before I can get in the car, the sound of another starting fills my ears, and Felix grabs my arm. I spin around, yanking it back as I watch Sam drive out of the lot.

"What are you doing here?"

I keep looking at her car until it disappears, and I'm left with little option but to bring my attention back to Felix.

"I just ..." I shake my head. "Nothing, don't worry about it."

"Don't. Just spit it out already."

Anger rattles my heart, telling it to shut its whiny trap so I can muster up some damn courage. "You haven't been back to see Archie. I don't have the same number, and I don't know if you do either, so I couldn't call ... and I was thinking that we should at least try to be friends..."

His laughter puts a stop to my rambling. "Friends. Right." He rubs his hand over the thick scruff on his jaw. "Tell me, Magdaline, how's that supposed to work when I don't even want to see you? When I can't even stand to look at you?"

"Oh." My chest burns as if he's punched a hole through it. "Okay, well, um, we might have to try to get past that."

He scoffs. "Oh, yeah? Why?"

I look him square in the eye then, raising a brow and trying not to let his proximity affect me. "Our son."

"Oh, so he's *our* son now, yeah?" He laughs dryly. "Now that I'm out, I'm actually allowed to see him, now am I?"

"Felix, don't do this," I plead. "I know you're mad, and you've got every right to be. But don't take it out on him."

His brows lower, his jaw clenching tightly as he seethes,

"Fuck you, Maggie. You don't get to make me feel guilty."

My nose scrunches along with my heart. "Why would you feel guilty, Felix?" I lower my voice, my next words slipping past my lips before I can stop them. "Because you're with Sam now?"

Stepping back, he runs a hand through his hair. "Unbelievable." He shakes his head, his top lip curling. "That really doesn't concern you."

Breath whooshes right out of me.

How is it that he's able to move on so easily? I don't think I've even looked at another man in the past decade.

"Okay." With nothing else to do, I throw my hands out. "Well, you know where Archie is."

I climb back into my car and start it without another word. He doesn't stop me, but I feel his eyes on me the whole time I'm backing out of the lot.

Once I'm a few streets away, I pull over and step out of the car.

Leaning over the trunk, my head spins wildly as I try to breathe normally. Warren joins me, rubbing my back and counting them with me. Thunder booms overhead. The sky darkens, and with it, those last flickers of hope I'd been holding on to.

"That's it. Good," Warren says quietly, brushing my hair off my tear-stained face.

"It'll be all right, bunches. Promise."

"It won't." I heave out a breath, straightening from the car. "I can't keep living like this."

"Like what?"

"Like …" I shove my hands into my hair, and they slap back down to my sides as I admit, "Like I'm not moving again. Like I can't move at all. While everyone else just moves on around me."

His eyes turn soft. "Like Felix has?"

He doesn't need me to answer that, but I nod anyway, my stomach folding over itself.

"For what it's worth, Maggie, I think you're better off, as far as I can see anyway."

I know he's probably right. But he doesn't know the same Felix I do.

Though maybe I don't really know him anymore either. And maybe that's all my fault.

Because he may have made us fall apart, but without meaning to, I scattered our broken pieces.

Now they're nothing but waning memories, drifting away with time.

CHAPTER SEVENTEEN

Felix

I watch her car drive away, the same Honda Accord she's had since we first got together.

Would've made it pretty fucking easy for that PI to find her then, so I hope they didn't pay him too much money.

Sighing, I scrub my palms over my eyes and down my face, wiping my lips. As if I can erase the feeling of having Sam's there just minutes ago.

If I wanted Maggie to know how much she's hurt me, how much I hate her right now, then why do I feel like such a dick and kind of nauseated?

I've never been very good at controlling impulsive urges.

And the second I saw Maggie, I used Sam's whispered offer like the asshole I am to try to hurt her the same way she's hurt me.

Only, I don't know if I actually want to succeed at that, now that she's gone.

When Sam came in here, claiming she wanted to see if I could look at her car, I told her we were busy, because we really are, but maybe another time and walked her out.

A low groan escapes me. Shit. Wouldn't be surprised if she comes back tomorrow now.

I can't completely shut her down, though; she's done so much for me over the past year or more. Being her friend is the least I can do after she was there for me.

"Come on, asshole. Get back to work," Jared hollers.

Turning, I find him leaning against the tin siding of the door, his eyes narrowed and his arms folded over his chest.

"Don't give me any shit." I walk past him and return to the old Buick, grabbing my wrench and sliding back underneath it.

Staring at the undercarriage while lying on the cool concrete floor, I take a deep breath and close my eyes for a second. Just a second, in an effort to tame all these fucking conflicted feelings.

Maggie's right. I shouldn't let how I feel about her get in the way of my seeing Archie. Too bad I can't help it.

She's all I see, all I've ever wanted. Just being around her makes this hold I'm desperately trying to keep on my anger loosen.

And I need to keep it. The anger.

Because I honestly don't know if I can ever forgive her.

I'm lying on my bed later that night when Jared walks in and dumps something on the nightstand.

"What's that?" I don't take my eyes off the TV.

"All your missed wages."

That makes me sit up. "What do you mean?" I swing my legs over the side of the bed and grab the large envelope, my eyes widening at the sight of all the cash inside.

"There's a check in there, too," he says, before making his way out of the room.

"Wait." I toss the envelope back on the nightstand. "I can't take that. I didn't work for any of it."

He shrugs. "Your business, too. Don't think I didn't figure out that you were taking scraps for years before you went to jail and giving us the rest. Besides, I didn't realize how damn hard it'd be to find Maggie, and I'd planned to give it to her when I did."

Damn. How the hell he turned out to have such a kind heart after all the shit we'd been through was beyond me.

"I'm not taking it, kid." I flop back onto the bed, giving my attention back to the old Western movie that's playing.

Jared sighs. "Figured you'd say that. Well," he says. "Guess I'll just take it to Maggie on your behalf then."

I stiffen. "I'll do it."

He doesn't respond for a beat, but I can feel the smug smile he's directing my way. "Right. I'm going to meet Vera at the bookstore. Later."

"Hang on a sec." I sit up again. "That PI you used, did he get Maggie's number?"

Jared nods, leaving the room and coming back a moment later with a long, thin envelope full of Maggie's details. Bank details, car, driver's license, phone records, even some of her medical history. I skim over most of it, grabbing what I need and entering her number into the cheap cell I got last week.

Jared's bike starts up outside, and I toss the envelope onto the nightstand. It falls to the floor, probably under the bed, but I'm too busy staring at these numbers to give a shit.

I could call her. Hear her voice anytime I want.

It feels surreal after having no way to see or hear from her for so damn long. After calling her old number from the shitty prison phone and hearing that monotone voice repeating the same thing every time. That the number had been disconnected.

After spending night after night locked away in a six-by-eight-foot cell, with nothing but a weird cellmate and my bone shaking regret for company.

Gritting my teeth against the urge, I shut my phone off and head out to the garage after locking up the house.

Starting my bike, I do my best to ignore the memories of a certain auburn-haired woman who used to love riding with me on it, almost as much as I did.

I need solitude, but being on my own isn't enough.

I need the steady rumble vibrating beneath me and filling my ears until it drowns out my thoughts. The wind on my face and the feeling of freedom only the open road can provide.

I need to remember that I'm out. I'm in control.

Pulling out of the driveway, I head south toward the warehouse district. My muscles relax, and my mind quiets. And for the first time in fuck knows how long, my heart almost feels free.

CHAPTER EIGHTEEN

Maggie

Loving someone really shouldn't hurt this much.

Loving someone should feel good, and I know first-hand just how good it can feel.

Maybe that's why, despite everything that's happened these past few weeks, I'm still clinging to that love.

But I think it's time to try to let it go.

I guess things can only fall apart for so long before you need to stop trying to hold them together.

Archie's cries fill the baby monitor sitting on Warren and Jake's counter.

"Bunches, I'm going into the city to deposit some money and send some shit. Wanna come?" Warren leans against the wall, scowling at the towel in my hand.

I put the last dish away and fold the towel over their oven door. "Sure. Archie's been a grump today. I think he's getting some big teeth." I sigh tiredly, picking up the monitor. "Maybe the ride will help him settle a bit."

Warren nods. "I'll meet you out front."

I head back to the guesthouse, changing Archie and grabbing him some milk before heading out the front to put him in my car. It's the only one with a baby seat other than Jake's, so Warren doesn't argue and hops in the passenger side.

"Feeling okay?" Warren asks once we're on the highway.

I nod, staring at the sunlit road ahead. "I'm okay."

"You will tell us if you feel like you're not, right?"

Nodding again, I bite the inside of my cheek. "You know I will."

Seemingly appeased, he turns around and starts babbling to Archie until we're pulling up outside the bank. He holds Archie while I move to the trunk to grab his stroller.

Except when I open it, I remember I'd left it at home after walking him down to the bay yesterday. Well, crap.

"I forgot the stroller, but it's okay." I close the trunk and hold my arms out for Archie. "He can do a bit of walking, or I'll hold him. I'm going to grab a few groceries from that old grocery store around the corner."

"All right. I'll try not to be too long. Got your phone?" Warren asks, walking backward into the flow of pedestrians. I smile and nod then put Archie down, holding his hand while he waddles down the sidewalk.

At this rate, it'll take us twenty minutes to get to the grocery store, but I let him walk a few more minutes before picking him up.

He's not happy about it, but I try to distract him with a banana once we get inside.

He shoves it into his mouth, smearing it between his fingers in the process. I grab a few things we need while he's content for now. He's usually a happy baby, but some of those teeth have given him a hard time, so I'm betting these new ones are giving him hell, too.

My phone buzzes in my pocket, so I drop the basket to the ground and dig it out.

"Hey, Jake's finishing up soon. Will you be all right if I head back with him?"

Archie looks at me, pulling at his bottom lip. I think I would be okay, usually. But Archie's unpredictable mood swings these past few days make me a little nervous to be out right now.

Still, I can't keep relying on other people. I'm strong enough to do this on my own. If he wants to spend time with his husband, I'm not going to let my stupid little fears stop him.

The car is around the corner and across the street.

I'll be fine.

Perfectly fine.

I repeat those same words to Warren, reassuring him when he asks again, and hang up.

"Right." I hoist Archie higher on my hip as he fidgets. "Just you and me, little guy."

We head to the checkout, and that's when Archie decides he's about had enough.

"Ma, ma, ma," he bellows and tugs on my hair.

I give the guy working the register a twenty and tell him to keep the change, before grabbing the two bags and walking out of there as quickly as I can.

As soon as we're out on the street, his whining turns to a full-blown meltdown, and it takes every bit of strength I have not to drop him.

"Shhh. We're almost at the car, little guy."

But he doesn't care. He flings himself backward with an ear-splitting cry, and I drop the bags in my effort to keep from dropping him.

"Shit," I whisper underneath the sound of his wailing. My heart starts racing, my blood pumping too fast and roaring in my ears. The world starts to spin, but I grit my teeth against it and try to concentrate.

It's hard to decide what to do first. Try to console him or save our groceries.

Naturally, I try to do both when my peripheral vision snags on a familiar pair of boots farther down the sidewalk. Felix. Felix is walking straight toward us with Sam. I don't think he can see me, so I try to squash my growing panic and put Archie down.

I wrap an arm around him and use the other to stuff the milk, some probably now smashed bananas, and chips into the bag. The rest I can do without and are being skirted around by impatient city goers anyway. I take a few deep breaths in through my nose and slowly exhale out my mouth, feeling ridiculous yet unable to control the panic that's taken hold.

Just as I'm about to get up, something whacks me in the side of the face, sending me to my ass. That's all I remember before everything turns dark once again.

CHAPTER NINETEEN

Felix

"Sorry," I mumble. "I'm not exactly used to this. Company." My shoulders lift, and I tuck my hands into my pockets as we step out of the coffee shop and onto the street.

"I totally get that, but I'm just glad to be spending time with you again." Sam playfully nudges me in the arm. "So try to cheer up a little."

I grunt in response, wishing she'd found something else to do besides come see me at work again. I knew what I did the other day would have consequences.

Just didn't think I'd be paying for them with coffee. As it is, I turned her down yesterday and the day before that. But feeling like an ass after how I used her, I told her I'd shout her this once.

Besides that, I've been wondering why the hell Ryan hasn't shown up to see me since I got out. And I was hoping Sam might have the answers about what he's up to, yet she's been oddly evasive.

The sound of the seagulls flying above pierces the air, the noise from the traffic flowing in either direction drowning out my repetitive thoughts. Then the sound of wailing hits me like a punch in the nuts, making me think of Archie. Christ, I need to get my shit together.

The wailing doesn't stop, and pretty soon, I'm not even nodding at whatever it is Sam is saying, because there's no way I can pretend to be listening over the volume of it.

It quiets suddenly, turning to low whimpers as we stop by a bunch of people huddled together on the sidewalk.

"What on earth is she doing?" someone asks loudly.

"Maybe we should call 911."

Someone gasps at the same time Sam does.

"Holy shit," Sam breathes. "Is that …?"

My stomach lurches when I catch sight of the auburn hair. "Felix, what the hell is she doing?" Sam asks.

Maggie appears to be rocking, holding Archie tightly to her chest. Which would be sweet and all if she wasn't sitting in the middle of the fucking sidewalk on a busy city street.

I don't even give myself time to question it. I tell Sam I'll see her later and shove my way through the onlookers, who're just standing there like stunned idiots.

"Felix!" Sam cries, but I shoo her away with the flick of my hand and bend down.

"Back up," I growl at the people hovering around my kid.

Maggie lifts her head then, her doe eyes looking vacant as they try to focus on me.

"Mags." I grab her face. "What happened?"

She blinks, and it's as if whatever spell she was under breaks. "Shit," she hisses.

Maggie looks around, her cheeks turning pink when she realizes all these people are watching her sit on the ground.

"I-I don't know." She swallows and tries to stand. I grab her arm and help her, then without even thinking, I take a whimpering Archie from her and hold him to my chest, his head flopping to my shoulder. "He was screaming, and I dropped my stuff. I was picking it up and hurt my head or something."

I can tell she's lying without even looking at her, but I let it go. For now. "Your car?"

"Yeah, ah, parked just around the corner."

We head back toward the coffee shop and around the corner to where her car is parked across the street. She removes her arm from my hold and digs a shaky hand into her pocket to grab her keys.

I take them from her, and she doesn't argue, just hops in the car while I try to work out how the hell you buckle a baby into this weird contraption.

I figure it out after a minute, then end up just staring at Archie. "Car!" He grins, kicking his legs and blowing a snot bubble out of his nose. Which is probably thanks to all his crying.

Well, he seems happy enough now. I bend down and grab one of the toy cars from the floor and pass it to him. He shoves his thumb into his mouth and holds the car to his chest.

Resting his head against the side of his seat, he looks as though he didn't just almost cause a riot of curiosity in the street.

It makes me chuckle as I move out of the back seat and open the driver's door. "Out."

Maggie looks up from where she was staring at her hands, that small nose scrunching. "What?"

I jerk my head to the passenger side. "I said get out. I'm

driving you home."

She shakes her head. "You really don't have to do that."

Sighing, I pinch the bridge of my nose as I mutter, "I kind of do. I don't know all of what happened back there, but I'm not letting you drive home with our son after whatever that was." I raise my brows at her, then pull out my phone to text Jared. "Don't make me say it again."

She obeys, silently getting in the other side and staying that way most of the drive back to Bonnets Bay.

When the silence only increases in volume, I finally ask, "Gonna tell me why you were sitting on the sidewalk?"

She shakes her head in my peripheral vision, a nervous laugh bubbling out of her. "Like I said, all I remember is dropping my stuff, trying to pick it up, and then getting hit in the head with a heavy bag maybe as someone walked by."

Teeth gritting together, I tell myself not to ask.

Don't ask.

Don't ... "Are you okay?"

Idiot.

"Yeah." She reaches up to touch the side of her head. "I'm fine. Just ... I think it shocked me more than anything."

She's quiet again after that, and I try to figure out how much truth sits behind her words.

"He sick or something?" I ask when we hit the turnoff and I see in the rearview mirror that Archie has fallen asleep.

"No, just teething."

That's all she says, keeping her gaze directed out the side window, where it's been the past twenty minutes.

Her despondence puts me on edge. The quietness a glaring contrast to the woman who's been trying to reason with me for weeks now. And the same woman I used to know so well.

Sensing she needs it, I let her have her quiet and try not

to inhale that familiar scent of strawberries that I know comes from all that thick, beautiful hair. My dick hardens, as memories of what I used to enjoy doing with that hair try to invade, and I almost growl.

Dicks are fucking traitorous things.

I soon pull into the driveway of the large, two-story light blue home that sits in front of the bay, and not knowing what else to do, I turn the car off and just sit here for a moment.

Maggie's phone rings, and she steps out of the car, digging it out from the back pocket of her jeans and answering it only after she closes the door.

"Well, little man," I murmur, looking away from her ass and lifting my eyes to the rearview mirror to look at my sleeping kid instead. "Hell if I know what to do now."

When she hangs up, I watch her for a minute, wondering if she thinks I can't see her standing near the rear of her car. She rubs her hands over her cheeks, then shoves them into her hair, roughly pulling at the thick strands and closing her eyes.

I wish I wasn't such a stubborn asshole because right now, I know she really needs a hug.

Blowing out a breath, I undo my seat belt and hop out, opening the back door to unbuckle Archie and carefully carry him to the house.

Maggie walks over to the side gate, holding it open for me to walk through.

Right. She lives in some tiny little shack out the back. I walk through, my heart swelling when Archie mumbles and blows hot little bursts of breath onto my neck in his sleep.

My arms hold him tighter to me in response, and I wonder how the hell I was so afraid to touch him like this.

It's one of the best damn things in the world.

So much so, that I continue walking to the rear of the yard, sitting down on the grass in the shade, and keeping him held to my chest.

Maggie disappears inside her little house, and I try not to wonder what she's doing.

We're out here for what has to be at least twenty minutes when I hear her footsteps crunch on the grass as she approaches.

"Want me to take him?" she asks.

I shake my head, and Archie stirs, his chubby hand whacking me in the chest and making me smile.

His eyes spring open, his head snapping up. "Ma," he blurts hoarsely.

"Hi, little guy."

Little guy. Like she used to call me big guy. Something lodges in my throat.

He then looks at me, blinking before he asks, "Mik?"

The fuck? I'm starting to get real sick of all these new men popping up in their lives. "Who's Mik?"

Maggie laughs softly, and the sound tries to tunnel through my ears to my damn heart. "He wants milk."

Oh. "Ah." I grin at Archie in relief. "Milk, eh?"

"Mik," he affirms with a smile, then tries to shuffle off my lap. I let him go, watching him walk over to Maggie, who lifts him up and kisses his cheek.

Fuck me. *Time for me to go,* I think.

I get up, grabbing my phone to call Jared as Maggie walks back inside.

"Hey, can you pick me up?" I ask when he answers.

"I guess, where the fuck are you? You said you were taking lunch, not a damn vacation."

I look over at the water beyond the fence. "Yeah, I kinda ran into Maggie. I'm in Bonnets Bay."

He whistles. "Text me the address."

I'm tucking my phone away when Archie comes running back over the grass, stumbling and falling on his ass and dropping his sippy cup in the process. He looks from it to me, his bottom lip wobbling like he's about to lose some serious shit.

I rush into action, grabbing his milk first 'cause I know that's what's important to him. Then I sit down beside him while he drinks it and try not to feel all cocky about my crisis averting skills. But shit, watching him smile at me around his cup like I've saved the day makes me feel like I'm the king of the world.

He drops his milk a minute later, on purpose this time, and waddles off back to their little house. I notice Maggie sitting on the porch steps at the back of the main house, watching us.

"He'll be back," she says, then returns her attention to her hands.

She's right. He's back not even a minute later, dumping trucks, cars, and motorcycles into my lap and pointing at them all while he babbles.

We play in the grass for a little while until my phone beeps, letting me know that Jared's probably out the front.

I'm hit with a wave of unease as I look at my boy. Maybe now that it's all sunk in, it's so much harder to say goodbye. "Hey." I pick Archie up and poke him in the tummy. "I'll see you soon, little man." I kiss his head, inhaling his scent and walk him back over to where Maggie's still seated. He climbs into her lap and rests his head on her boobs.

Shit. Shit, fuck, shit. I clear my throat, inwardly cursing out my hardening dick and trying not to get choked up from all these damn feelings and the way she looks. Which is more beautiful, if that's even possible, than she's ever been before. Motherhood looks good on my Little Doe.

Leaving them stings differently this time, but I head for

the side gate and make my heavy legs move.

"Thank you," Maggie says so quietly, I almost don't hear her. My feet stop for a second. But I don't turn around, and instead, I force myself to keep walking, closing the gate behind me.

"How the hell did she end up here?" Jared asks as soon as I get in the truck.

Letting out a sigh, I put my seat belt on as he reverses out onto the street. "Good fucking question."

CHAPTER TWENTY

Maggie

My eyes blink open, once, twice ... and on the third, I can keep them open long enough to remember where I am. Beeping. The smell of antiseptic.

Hospital.

And as if the realization holds the trigger, my ribs scream out in pain. My nose and jaw throb and my casted arm pangs. But my head ... my head hurts the most. As if someone stomped on it repetitively.

And I'm thinking maybe they did.

I'm not a religious person, much to my parents' dismay growing up, but I thank God or whoever is out there for the pitiful mercy of sending my world dark after the first or maybe second blow to the head.

My free hand reaches down to my stomach, panic gripping hold of my throat and causing tears to spring to my eyes. I remember them saying I was lucky to be alive. That the bleeding on my brain had now stopped, but I'd need to be monitored. Yet right now, all I can think about is this gripping fear. This overwhelming sense of doom that maybe they'll be back to finish what they started.

Voices drift in through the crack of the almost closed door to my room. Voices I haven't heard in a really long time. Which somehow only makes me feel worse.

"She got beat half to death by some gang of thugs! No, this shit has been wrong from the start. She's not bringing that kind of trouble to our house."

"Martin ..."

"You think they'll stop here? No. Those kind of delinquents won't stop until they get what they think is rightfully theirs. It's not happening. She's not dragging them to our door. No fucking way. She wouldn't even talk to the detective who came by."

"But the baby ..."

"No, Elodie, don't even try to test me on this. The answer is no."

They fade away after that, and my hand stays pressed against my stomach. I'm both shocked and so damn relieved that this little life has somehow managed to survive the beating my body took.

My nose burns, which makes the pain flare, and I close my eyes against the onslaught of tears.

They reopen sometime later when someone clears their throat from beside my bed.

I startle, wincing as the pain wracks my body from the tiny movement.

"Hey, sleeping beauty," a man with blue eyes, blond hair, and a mischievous smile says from the chair by the wall.

"Who ..." My dry throat makes it hard to get the words out. I clear it and try again. "Who are you?"

He continues to smile, his elbow leaning on the armrest of the chair and his square chin resting on his fist. "Let's just call me your fairy godmother."

My brows rise, and he chuckles quietly. "Well, one of them anyway."

I shoot up in bed, covered in sweat with my heart's violent pounding beat reverberating through every limb of my body. Pushing my hair back from my face, I try to take deep, measured lungfuls of air while counting backward from ten. When that doesn't work, I try counting back from thirty.

Phantom pain takes hold of my arm, my ribs, my nose, my head, and my heart.

I check the time, realizing it's only five thirty, and get up to check on Archie.

He's sound asleep, his thumb resting on his bottom lip and his chubby limbs sprawled out in his crib. I move the blankets over his little body and go take a shower, hoping the hot water will help bring me further into the present.

It's been a while since I've had nightmares. They stopped becoming so frequent after I started seeing Dr. Hayes before Archie was born.

I don't know if that's what I'd call a nightmare. Perhaps it's only my conscience screaming at me.

It felt like a bit of both.

After getting dressed, I make some coffee, peeking out the sliding glass door while I drink it and watch the sun's final ascent into the sky.

Archie and I spend the morning watching cartoons and lazing around on the couch. Well, he plays; I just stare at the TV like it's got all the answers I'm seeking while feeling strangely hollow. That dream is not only an ugly reminder of what Ryan's awesome friends did to me, but it's a glaring reminder that I haven't seen my parents since.

Picking up my phone, I hesitate for a good five minutes before deciding to just do it.

"Hello? Ma chérie?" My mom sounds surprised and a little panicked.

"Hi." I tuck my legs under my butt. "Um, how are you?"

She exhales loudly in my ear, and it sounds like she's crying when she replies, "Good now. Much better when I get to hear your voice."

A small smile curves my lips at her slightly broken English. "And how are you? How is the baby?"

"Archie is good." I watch him roll over on the rug, throwing Duplo pieces into the air and laughing as they fall on top of him.

"Archie." Her smile is evident in her voice. "Goodness, it's been so long. I actually meant to call you soon. I have news."

"Elodie, who're you speaking to?" my father asks in the background.

Her breath hitches, and my eyes close.

"I need to go, but I will call you soon. I promise. Take care, my darling."

My eyes reopen when she hangs up. Blowing out a breath, I drop my phone, frowning as I wonder what kind of news she could have and if my father will always stop her from trying to have any kind of relationship outside their own.

"Good morning, handsome devil," Warren says, walking inside and dropping down onto the rug beside Archie.

Archie gives him a block. "Da!"

He doesn't know what he's saying. He calls lots of things *da*.

"Why, thank you," Warren says, stacking it on top of

another one. "So you were okay driving home the other day?" He had called me when Felix pulled into the driveway, making sure I was okay. But it's a lot easier to lie over the phone. He and Jake stayed in the city for the afternoon and had an early dinner. Warren's been locked in his office catching up on work ever since.

I try to quickly prepare a lie, only to be stopped with a knowing look. "Shit, bunches." He shakes his head. "Christ, what happened?"

I tell him everything, and he curses again quietly under his breath before staring at me with sorrow filled eyes. "I'm so sorry. We thought …" His head shakes again. "You've been doing so well for so long now. You should've told me; I would've—"

"No." I stop him there. "I thought the same thing. I think …" I fiddle with the couch cushion on my lap, staring down at it before returning my gaze to Warren and shrugging. "Maybe recent events are just shaking me up a little."

He crosses his legs and puts Archie in his lap. "Do you think maybe you should give Dr. Hayes a call? Might be a good idea to resume sessions for a while longer." He holds up a hand when I go to protest. "Just until you get used to Felix being back and everything that entails. None of us really knew what would happen, but it's clear the situation could take some time to settle down. Your feelings included."

He's right. But I've come so far, and I know I'm not in danger of going back to where I was, not entirely, but the fear is still there. The problem is, I think it's never really going to leave. I just need to continue living regardless.

"We'll see what happens, I guess. He was … different after he drove us home."

Warren's brows shoot up as Archie climbs off his lap and goes to his basket of cars. "How so?"

"I don't know, just quieter. Not so—"

"Rah, rah, I'm angry with the world?" Warren suggests.

Laughing, I nod. "Well, yeah. Not as much of that."

Warren hums. "Did you guys talk at all?"

"Uh, not exactly. He just spent some time with Archie then left."

My phone rings next to me, and Warren says he needs to get some work done and will check in with me later before leaving.

The unknown number has me wary, but I answer it with a hesitant hello anyway.

"Hey."

His voice. Even after so long, it still has the same effect on me. "Hi," I say again, and immediately want to slap myself in the forehead.

"I've gotta leave work early this afternoon. Got a meeting with my parole officer. But I thought I'd come out there to see Archie maybe."

He seems different all right. Like he's not sure if I'll let him, which is ridiculous.

"Of course, we'll be here."

His exhale is loud, and I can just picture his big shoulders dropping with it. "Okay. I'll probably be there around four."

"Okay." It's all I can come up with. I chew my lip, trying to find something else to say, but even with all the questions and thoughts rolling around in my head, I can't settle on one.

"Do, ah, do you guys need anything? Diapers, milk? Um, maybe …"

A small laugh escapes me before I can stop it. "We're okay."

"Mags." He sighs. "Please, let me do something."

My eyes shut at hearing that nickname, but I refuse to let my heart cling to it. "We could always use more diapers. He's in size three."

"Okay, sure. Any specific brand?"

It sounds like he's getting up to write it down, which makes me want to laugh again. "No, any will do."

"Got it. I'll see you later then."

"Yeah." I open my eyes. "Bye."

I hang up and wonder what it is that has him letting go of some of that anger. If it's got to do with what happened a few days ago ... well, I just hope he doesn't start asking questions.

Because even if I could tell him, it's too late now anyway.

There's a fresh wound in my chest every time I think about what's happened since he got out.

Even if I can understand, it doesn't mean he hasn't caused damage to something that was already fighting to heal itself.

Felix knocks on the door at exactly four that afternoon. Archie's just woken up from his nap, so he's a ball of excited energy that races to the sliding door.

Felix opens it when I walk over, smiling and dropping low to pick Archie up.

"Da!" he blurts, and I cringe when Felix freezes.

He looks at me. "He say that a lot?"

"Sometimes, yeah."

He seems to understand what I'm not saying, and the two of them head outside to play. I watch for a little while, trying to ignore the way Felix's jeans hang low, revealing his gray boxer briefs when he squats on the grass with Archie. Or the way the sun seems to reflect off the sharp lines of his face, his teeth, and that growing scruff that's fast turning into a beard.

Damn it. My thighs squeeze together when old memories resurface. I head back inside and give them some privacy. The last thing I need to be doing right now is ogling him, especially when a switch has flicked for Felix and he seems to be handling this all a bit better.

An hour later, Archie starts crying, and I jump up from the couch. I try to slow my pace once I get outside, not wanting to seem like I don't trust Felix, but I'm worried all the same.

"He's okay, just whacked himself in the head with his truck." Felix rubs Archie's head and sets him back on the ground. Archie runs off as if nothing happened.

I offer a weak smile, turning to go back inside when he stops me. "Hey, if you want to watch him for a sec, I'll go grab those diapers."

He jogs out the side gate and returns a moment later with two huge boxes full of diapers.

"Want them in his room?"

"Yeah, thanks." I grab Archie and show Felix inside.

He dumps them by the changing table and glances around, his lips parting when his gaze falls on the photos on Archie's dresser.

He picks up one that Jake took not long after he was born, running his finger over the glass. "Shit," he breathes the word out raggedly, as though it hurts. And it must. My own chest twinges when I think of all the things he's missed.

"There's more, if you want to see," I offer quietly.

He shakes his head, sniffing and placing the photo frame back. His white shirt pulls tight over his chest and arms as he lets out a shaky exhale. "Thanks, but maybe next time."

I nod, even though he's not looking at me, understanding that it might be too much right now.

"Ma! Car!" Archie barrels into the room on wobbly legs,

falling over on the carpet then getting right back up.

Felix laughs under his breath. "When did he learn how to walk?"

I take the car from Archie, spinning its wheels and bending down to give it back to him.

"He started almost two months ago." I smile as Archie waddles off. "He's determined, but I think it'll still be a little while longer before he stops falling over so much."

Felix lets out a small grunt, and I straighten, looking at him and finding a soft smile pulling at his lips as he stares out the door. He notices me watching and shifts. "I'd better go."

"Right, sure." I move out of the way for him to walk past.

He kisses Archie and hugs him tightly to his chest before heading for the door. "Can I come back on Saturday?"

Wringing my hands together, I watch as he digs his keys out from his pocket. "Of course."

He hesitates at the door, then curses. "Forgot to give you this." He retrieves a folded over envelope out of his back pocket and places it on the counter.

By the time I open it up to find all the money stashed inside and run outside to give it back to him, he's already gone.

CHAPTER TWENTY-ONE

Maggie

Pulling up outside the familiar yellow house, I turn the ignition off and let my eyes soak it all in for a moment.

I didn't even think; I just grabbed the envelope, put Archie in the car, and drove.

Now that I'm here, though, I'm not so sure it was a good idea. Good intentions or not.

That house is like a treasury, one that holds so many moments in time that lay trapped in my head and heart. It feels like I'm stuck in some warped sense of déjà vu as I see it again while sitting in the same car I drove while living here. Except this time, I'm not parked in the driveway.

The house has been repainted, the roof replaced. Two motorcycles are parked in the half-open garage, a Volkswagen in front of the garage, and a familiar white truck behind the Volkswagen.

Chewing on my thumbnail for a second, I decide that

maybe I should just go. Then the door flies open and out comes a man I haven't seen in almost two years.

Jared stops on the porch when he notices my car. I start to freak out, thinking that he's going to be mad at me or something, when a huge grin takes over his face. I can practically see his eyes twinkle even with the distance between us.

He jumps over the railing of the porch and jogs across the lawn. Before I know what's happening, he's opening the back door of my car and looking at Archie.

"Car!" Archie says to him.

"Holy motherfucking shit." It all comes out in one whispered word as Jared stares at his nephew. He doesn't look at me, doesn't say a word to me, just unclips Archie from his car seat and removes him from the car.

Crap. Well, cover blown, I grab the envelope and get out, locking the car behind me and slowly moving over to where Jared is standing on the lawn.

"He's so awesome, Mags." He smiles at Archie, letting him pat his cheeks with his chubby hands.

"He is." I fidget with the envelope, feeling kind of awkward.

He finally looks at me then, and I don't know what it is, but something about his smile seems different. Lighter. As though nothing weighs it down anymore.

"Don't get all nervous and shit. I'm not mad. Did I wish I knew where you were so I could help you, and you could put me and Felix out of our misery?" He shrugs, hoisting Archie higher on his chest. "Yes. But it's none of my business. I'm just glad you're both okay."

Smiling at him, I say, "Thank you. I'm sorry … I never knew you asked my sister where I was, not until Felix told me. I wasn't trying to hide from you, I just—"

"Jared, can you grab some of those chocolate drops while

you're …" A stunning woman with jet black hair walks out onto the porch. "Well, shit. Leave you alone for two minutes and you go and find yourself a baby."

Jared's eyes narrow on me for a split second before he clears his curious expression and spins around. "You said you wouldn't give me one. This lovely lady here has agreed to let me keep hers." The beautiful woman scowls at him, her hands going to her hips. He chuckles, walking over to the porch. "Vera, meet Maggie, Maggie, Vera. And this is Archie."

Vera's brows rise when those words seem to penetrate her ears. She looks from Archie to me, and I make my way over to the porch.

"Hi." I wave, still feeling awkward as hell.

She grins, and I don't know whether to think she's the most beautiful woman I've ever seen in my life or the scariest. Possibly both. "Maggie. Heard a lot about you."

That's all she says before turning back to Jared. "Does it stink?"

Jared guffaws, moving a hand up to cover Archie's ear. "Don't let him hear your child hate. Excuse us, we've got important business to attend to."

He walks inside with Archie, leaving me here with Vera. Okay, I'm totally willing to admit I'm a little scared. But then her features soften as she watches Jared babble back to Archie while they walk down the hall. She wipes that softness away when her gaze returns to me.

"Where've you been?"

"Uh." I twist the envelope in my hands. "Bonnets Bay?"

She shakes her head. "No. I mean, *why.*"

Swallowing, I look away, unable to explain. And if I can't tell the truth to Felix, I most definitely can't tell her.

A car backfires down the street, and that, combined with

the mounting tension in my bones makes me jump a little. I look back at Vera, finding her ice blue eyes assessing.

"What happened to you?"

I blink and try to stop my eyes from giving anything away. *What the hell?*

She points a finger at me, grinning. "Gotcha."

Panic sets my heart thumping faster, and I start backing up toward the stairs. Where I'm going, I have no idea. "Hey, shit. Stop."

"Sorry," I mumble, waving the envelope around. "I'm fine. I just wanted to return this to Felix."

Vera doesn't even look at it. "I won't say anything. But just so you know, these guys spent a lot of time worrying about you."

Jesus. This woman doesn't miss a beat. I nod slowly. "Yeah, I know."

"I'm getting married in almost a month's time. We'll both be expecting you there."

Wait, *huh?* "You're ... what?"

"Getting married," she says slowly. "To the guy with tattoos who likes to test me ten times a day." She rolls her eyes. "I know, crazy, right?"

She heads inside, and I follow, trying to shake off the whiplash from all that just happened.

I close the door behind me as she says, "Oh, and if the kid poops while he's here, I'm not going near that."

Then she disappears down the hall while I struggle to wrap my brain around Jared marrying anybody, let alone someone who appears to be an ice queen.

Crazy is right.

I follow the noise of Archie and Jared down the hall until I find them in Felix's room, looking at a picture on the dresser.

"That's Daddy, but you'll take after me, don't worry, kiddo."

I lean against the doorframe, my chest caving as all the feelings, memories, and snapshots from years gone by stare back at me from this room.

"Maggie?" Turning around at the sound of his voice, I find Felix behind me, running a towel over his short, wet hair.

My tongue sticks to the roof of my mouth when my eyes fall to his bare chest.

He's only wearing a towel. A towel that hangs so deliciously low on those even more defined hips that I almost think I'm going to start salivating.

What do they do in prison? Train for body building contests?

His body is all bulky, sinewy muscle. His abs so defined now, you could run water through the dips and ridges between them. The urge to drag my finger over them, to feel the bumps for myself, is extreme. I snap out of it when he clears his throat, my eyes widening and my cheeks flushing.

Awesome. I've been caught blatantly ogling him.

His lips twitch, like he wants to smile at me but is stopping himself.

"Hey." I swallow hard, trying not to look at his arms when they bulge like giant boulders as he lifts the towel to wipe it over the side of his neck. Wow. Shit. I'm doing it again.

Shaking my head a bit, I lift the envelope. "You left before I could catch you." I lean into his room, putting it on the nightstand. "I'm not taking your money, Felix."

Jared clears his throat. "Yeah, ah. We're just going to go …"

He and Archie leave, and Felix looks at Archie when he squeals over Jared's shoulder, "Ba, ba!"

"So you came here to … drop it off?"

It does seem kind of stupid when he says it like that. My

cheeks start to flame again, and I feel like that naïve eighteen-year-old girl under his curious gaze once more. So I duck my head. "I guess. Sorry, I should go."

"Wait, give me a second." He walks into his room and without pause, drops both towels to the floor and opens a drawer, pulling out a pair of gray sweatpants and tugging them on.

Holy smokes. Is he serious right now? I bite my lip, my face on fire, and look away as soon as I see those perfect ass cheeks staring back at me. Of course, he's serious. He doesn't give a damn.

He never did.

Turning around, he runs a hand over his short hair and sighs. "Should've known this might happen. Look." He steps closer to me, picking up the envelope and holding it out. "It's yours. If you don't take it, it's just going to sit here until you need it." He shrugs. "May as well take it, yeah? I didn't get to be there; I made a stupid decision that changed everything. But you can at least let me do this."

I look away from his brown eyes and take a shaky breath through my nose. It escapes my lips on a gasp when I see the dent in the wall, and what probably caused it.

Without thinking, I move past Felix and walk over to it, bending down to brush the glass away from our smiling nineteen-year-old faces. He probably threw it at the wall, but the picture seems to be in okay shape.

He's silent, but I feel him watching me the whole time I stare at the picture. Tears sting the backs of my eyes. These faces, these two people … they had no idea that life wouldn't allow them to follow any of their heart's plans. But they clung to each other regardless.

Until it all became too much and they fell apart. No matter how much they tried to hold on.

Something brushes up against my butt, and I know who it is the moment I hear that telltale meow. Straightening, I don't look at Toulouse and move back out the door, ignoring Felix and his money, too.

I need to get out of here.

"Maggie." He follows me, grabbing my hand in the hall. The touch sends a painful spark right to my heart, and I tug my hand away at the sting.

"I really should go. I'll see you on Saturday."

He looks like he wants to say something, but what else is there to say?

Nothing.

So I grab my baby and let Jared help me put him in the car while Felix watches from the porch, then make the half hour drive home as the tears slowly slide down my face.

CHAPTER TWENTY-TWO

Maggie

I t's strange. The way some days hold more significance, more weight in your heart than others. First dates and first kisses. First love and first heartbreak. My firsts are all tied in with the same man. And as my mind untangles the past, playing those days in a torturous loop, I'm afraid that everything I do, everything I feel, and everything I think will always lead back to him.

Felix came over on Saturday morning and spent a few hours with Archie down in the sand by the bay. Something stirred in my gut when I watched them walk off toward the water together. Anger, maybe. Or irritation at the way my heart still longs for me to spend so many moments absorbed in him in any way I can. Fighting against what it wants takes strength I didn't know I still had. But I'm somehow doing it.

I spent the time he was here polishing my resume. I sent it out to a few local preschools via email on Monday morning, in hopes I can get some part-time work, and maybe even more of my independence back.

It's now Wednesday, and I haven't heard from or seen Felix since Saturday. So when the phone rings, I try not to let my heart jump. It needs to cooperate with my brain in thinking that it's past time to move on.

It lurches anyway. But for a whole different reason.

"You what?" Warren almost yells when I race inside to tell him. "That's brilliant, bunches! When do you start?"

I laugh at that. "It's just an interview. But they want me to come in tomorrow."

His eyes roll. "Doesn't matter. It's so going to be yours." Clapping his hands, he practically squeals, "I'm making dinner reservations!"

I groan, grabbing his arm. "Don't. You might jinx me."

He guffaws. "Nonsense. But you're right, priorities. Let's go find you an outfit. I'm thinking smart, a little sexy, but not too much. Don't want those old timers or other mammas giving you the stink eye."

We spend the afternoon trying to choose the perfect outfit. But my options are limited, on account of never needing to own anything very fancy before. I settle on a cute floral skirt and a white blouse and grab some black ballet flats from my wardrobe to pair with the matching black knitted cardigan.

"There." Warren eyes the ensemble on my bed with a jerk of his head. "Cute, sassy, but sophisticated enough for any ninnies."

"Ninnies?" I raise a brow.

"Yep. There'll be at least one, trust me."

Before I can ask him what he means by ninnies, he's walking out of the room and calling out goodbye for the night.

Archie yanks my skirt off the bed, and I dart over to him,

grabbing it just in time to stop it from going into his mouth. His bottom lip wobbles, and I hurry to distract him. "Mac and cheese?"

He kicks his legs out when I pick him up and take him out to the living room, getting him situated with some toys while I make us some macaroni.

The remainder of the night is spent staring at my book, when really, I'm just trying to ignore the fact I'm waiting for my phone to ring.

It doesn't.

He never calls, and I go to bed thinking that stupid saying about things happening for a reason might be correct in a lot of ways.

Especially regarding Felix and me.

Setting Archie on the ground after I've changed him, I fix my gaze on the photos on the dresser.

After washing my hands, I open the bottom drawer in my wardrobe and pull out some photo albums. Archie squawks at the door, dancing and bobbing up and down to a silent beat.

Smiling, I look back down at the first album, willing myself not to go there. Not to open it and look inside.

It's one I've had since I was fifteen and tried my hand at photography. I spent the next few years taking photos whenever I remembered, and I sucked. But I'm thankful I did it all the same. This album doesn't just hold pictures of Felix and me. Before him, I had a life. I had friends. Not many, but a few I enjoyed spending time with.

Giving in, I flip it open to the second sleeve of photos, my finger trailing idly over Lucy's sixteen-year-old smile. I wonder how she's doing. She used to send me the odd email here and there, but we grew apart when she left for college. She's married to a dentist now with two kids of her own. Last I heard, she was living in New Jersey.

Life rolls on, taking everyone in its path with it. I sometimes wonder if it's forgotten me, or maybe the decisions I've made over the years have forced me to stay behind.

Closing the album with a sigh, I put it back in the drawer.

Underneath it sits a little blue box. My eyes stay glued to it for a minute before I close the drawer and take the other album out to the kitchen, the one I was originally looking for, and place it on the end of the counter so that I remember to give it to Felix the next time he's here.

That way he can look at them in private.

I finish getting ready, trying to ignore the nerves that are slowly setting in with every passing minute.

"Come on, little guy." I grab Archie's hand and my bag, locking the door once we're outside. "Wish Mama luck."

"Ma, ma, ma." He shakes his other hand in the air and tries to stop to play with his toys in the yard.

"No time for that right now; you've got a date with Uncle Warren."

I pick him up and take him into the house, getting him settled with Warren before making the five-minute drive through Bonnets Bay to the preschool. I did work experience there when I was studying online. It was hard. I had a panic attack right in the little parking lot I'm now pulling into. Warren had dropped me off, though, and was there to help me through it. And eventually, I made it inside.

The fact I've worked here before helps a lot, even if I'm still apprehensive.

Looking at the clock on the dash, I let out a heavy breath. I'm right on time, which I'd planned. I don't want to sit around and give myself any illogical reasons to start panicking or over-thinking this.

Shutting the car off, I head inside through the brightly painted, noisy rooms until I find the director, knowing that even if I don't get the job, I've still accomplished something huge today.

Today's the day I started moving again.

CHAPTER TWENTY-THREE

Felix

A pair of doe eyes have been stalking my every move, no matter how much I try to ignore them. Maggie hardly looked at me on Saturday. But she sure as fuck looked at me when she came by to give me that money back last week.

I'm kind of ashamed to admit I've lost count of how many times I've jacked off since, remembering the way she stared at me, all flushed and overwhelmed.

Kind of.

Throwing the lid of my toolbox closed, I lean back against the workbench, trying to wipe some of the grease off my fingers with a rag while ignoring the stirring of my cock.

Jared left work a little while ago, some crap about having to help Vera settle a dispute with the venue she'd picked for their wedding. I can only imagine how the spitfire is going to handle a "dispute." It makes me laugh under my breath. No wonder he wanted to bail and be there. Vera doesn't get mad;

no, she gets scary evil. The likes of which even I don't wanna mess with.

And Jared's marrying her. Christ.

I still can't believe my shithead brother is getting married. It sets off a weird pang in my chest, and I don't know why. Could be that I wish I'd been around to see Vera knock him on his ass. But I know it's more than that.

I always thought I'd be first. Maggie and me. We were as solid and unyielding as a block of fucking concrete. But I guess even the strongest of things can start to wear over time. Pity I didn't realize that each chip, that every crumbling piece that tried to break us, would one day lead us here.

Not so indestructible now.

"Yo, Fel. You heading out soon?" Butch hollers then winces with a chuckle. "Should probably stop calling you that, now huh?"

Shaking my head, I toss the rag into the plastic bin and head to the wash bay to scrub the shit out of my hands. "True either way, isn't it? And yeah."

"True indeed." He shrugs. "Felix, felon."

I shake my hands dry and step out of the way for him to wash his own. "How's that Panhead coming along?" I ask him.

He grunts. "It's fucking coming, all right."

Laughing quietly, I head for the door. "You all right to lock up?"

"Sure thing, Fel."

I make my way out to my bike—a 1947 Knucklehead that I've pulled apart and put back together so many times I've lost count. I'm about to start it when a familiar voice startles me.

"Hey, stranger."

Sam. *Fuck.*

I spin around, not knowing how I didn't see her there

leaning against her car on the other side of the small lot. "Hey, Sam."

I go to start my bike anyway, wanting to get home and call Maggie if I can work up the courage. It's only been four days since I last saw her and Archie, but it feels fucked as hell that any amount of time should separate me from my son after all the time I've already missed.

It's obvious Sam came here for a reason, though.

My hands drop back to my sides as I curse repeatedly in my head. I might be a dick, but I need to draw the line somewhere.

"Been busy?" she asks, walking over and swinging her keys around her finger. "I called the other day, but you didn't answer." She adjusts the low-slung tank she's wearing, and I move my eyes away, not wanting to ogle her fucking tits.

"Flat out. Finally catching up now, though," I admit.

She nods. "Want to grab some dinner?"

I scowl, raising an eyebrow at her, and she rushes to say, "Just a quick bite."

Chewing the fuck out of the inside of my cheek, my eyes fall on her blue ones and she smiles. Maybe this time, she'll talk. And this time, I'm not going to let her evade the questions either. "Sure. I could do with a burger or something."

I tell her I'll meet her there, not wanting to be cramped in the interior of her small car with her. She's determined. For what reason, though, I don't know. Well, yeah, I guess I do. But she's also been a part of my life for even longer than Maggie, so I do care about the chick—as a friend—but even that says a lot, coming from me.

We grab some burgers and fries from a small diner in the middle of the city. Even though the food isn't great, I wanted to avoid showing up at Shake N' Burger with Sam. Just the thought of going to a place with her that I often frequented with Maggie makes my gut churn.

She talks to me about work while we wait. She's a hair-dresser and always has funny stories about some of her clients. Takes a lot to make me laugh these days, but she cracks one out of me.

"You seem to be doing a lot better," she remarks after we start eating, taking a sip from her shake. Shrugging, I take another bite from my burger. "You've been seeing Archie?"

Brows furrowing, I say, "Yeah, quite a few times now."

Sam looks down at her half-eaten burger. "How is she?"

"Maggie?" I watch as she gives a short jerk of her head in affirmation. "To be honest, I have no idea."

She lifts her head then, confusion wrinkling her brow. "But you've seen her?"

I don't want to get into this shit with her, but I guess I should tell her something, especially if I want some answers of my own. "Of course, I have. She's just … quieter, I suppose. Got no idea what's going on in that head of hers anymore." Which is fucking with my own head and heart in a way I never predicted. It almost seems like Maggie's only half there. The other half of the girl I used to know is hiding, or even worse, gone.

Guilt crawls over my skin when I watch Sam's face fall. "Sam, about the other week … the kiss—"

"Don't," she says. "I offered, knowing you'd only do it to get back at her. No need to explain."

"I know, but shit, I'm still sorry." She sits back in the booth, glancing away. I seize the opportunity. "You and Ryan, you never answered my question when we had coffee."

She quirks a blond brow at me, smirking. "Why do you want to know?"

I shake my head, taking a sip of water before saying, "Haven't seen him since I got out. Just think that's a bit weird."

Her eyes shutter momentarily. "He's probably busy, being his usual money-making self."

"Right." I take a few more bites of my burger, washing it down with more water. "You got his number? You know I got a new phone."

She starts fidgeting with the straw in her drink. "Why do you want to talk to him?"

"I don't. Not really," I admit. I don't admit that it's more of a *need to* at this point.

"Look, I think you should let it go. Being around him only causes you trouble." She laughs shallowly. "I know that better than anyone."

I wouldn't say her and Ryan were ever serious, but they've been together on and off since Maggie and I got together. A damn long time. So it's fair to say that she does know.

"I know what I'm doing." My voice lowers as my ire rises. "You don't think I've learned from my mistakes?"

She sucks her bottom lip into her mouth, and I start to grow more impatient. "But … don't you owe him money?"

"*What?*" I almost spit the word at her.

She looks a little sheepish now. "The advance he gave you. You know, that you got before you, well, attempted to do the job."

Is she for real? Is *he* for real? He never said anything about that five thousand. Most of it was sucked into paying for my legal team, anyway. Gone a long time ago.

"You're shitting me, right?"

She shakes her head, then shrugs. "It's just something he mentioned a while ago. Can't even remember really."

I wipe my mouth with a napkin, then fist it in my hand, trying to rein in the disbelief that's making me want to throw something. "That's bullshit. He's never said anything about it."

She doesn't say anything else either, just silently finishes more of her fries.

I decide I've had enough. I need to get home and talk to Jared about this latest revelation.

Tossing the napkin and some money onto the table, I stand.

"Wait," Sam says. "I'm sorry to be the bearer of bad news. Maybe it's not even true. I don't know."

I don't respond, just wait for her to get up, then walk her to her car.

My spine tingles when we reach it, my eyes scanning the small crowd on the street outside the string of restaurants until they find that auburn hair.

Maggie. What the hell is she doing here?

She's with those guys.

"Lix?" Sam says, touching my arm just as Maggie spots me standing here. "I'll see you soon?"

I nod absentmindedly at Sam, and she kisses my cheek before getting into her car.

Maggie stops, the two guys she's with not realizing until they reach me, then backing up to see what she's doing. Which is staring at me with sorrow filled brown eyes.

I've been through a lot of shit in my time on this earth, but I don't think anything's worse than having the woman you love look at you like you've torn her heart out one too many times, and she's had enough.

With my own heart in my throat, I look away, like a coward, and my eyes find Archie.

One of the guys is holding my boy. Without thinking, I walk over to them, moving to take him from the tall dude with black hair who I haven't met, but he scowls and steps back.

"Oh, uh, that's Felix, Jake."

Jake looks at Maggie, then back at me, muttering, "Wonderful."

"Yeah, hey," I mumble distractedly, my gaze still pinned on my sleepy son.

"He's pretty tired," Jake says, hard eyes never leaving me. "We should get him home, Maggie."

She agrees silently, and Jake moves around me with Archie, putting him in a fancy black Rover parked by the curb. It's similar to the one I stole. Well, attempted to. My fists clench.

"Bunches," the other guy says. Wayne maybe? Shit, I really wasn't paying much attention to his name the few times I've met him.

Maggie looks at me, and damn if I don't feel like she's taken a sledge hammer right to my chest, knocking the wind out of me with that one final look. She nods then skirts around me, too.

I grab her arm. "Mags, wait."

She pulls it free. "It's getting late. We really do need to get him home."

She doesn't look at me again before getting in the back of the car.

CHAPTER TWENTY-FOUR

Maggie

"You sure you're okay?" Jake asks the next morning when I stop by to clean up a bit for them.

"I'm fine." I'm not, but what choice do I have, really? "I just need to keep busy."

I give Archie a cracker from their pantry and watch as he plonks himself on the floor, shoving half of it in his mouth to suck on.

"You're not fine. And I hope you're not in here to clean." He glares at me, trying to adjust his tie. I step closer and do it for him, and he gives me a soft smile.

He has several meetings this morning with the board of directors at the hospital.

Dodging that last comment, I walk him to the garage door just as Warren runs down the stairs. "Fuck, I slept in way late." He runs over to Jake, grabbing both his cheeks and kissing the life from him while Archie starts pulling his cracker apart and smearing it onto their expensive wood floor.

"Crap," I mutter, grabbing a wipe from the kitchen and cleaning it up.

"I'll be home tonight. I told them to take me off call. You." Jake points at Archie, walking over and bending down to run his hand over his hair. "Be good for your mom." Archie grabs his large hand, squealing as he yanks it up and down. Bits of cracker are sticking to Archie's chin with the help of some drool. I wipe that up, too. Jake straightens, says goodbye, and makes his way to the garage.

Warren follows, coming back in after the sound of Jake's car has left the garage and driveway. "That asshole's got another thing coming if he thinks he can see some big breasted Barbie on the side while still pining for his baby mama." He leans against the stairwell, eyes fixed on me.

"You were looking at her breasts?" Yeah, that's what I choose to ask first.

He shrugs. "She's got some big knockers. And hey, I can appreciate a good set when I see them." His eyes dart to mine, and I scowl, which makes him laugh.

"And he's not pining," I grumble. "Far from it, actually."

Warren snickers. "Whatever you say, bunches."

"He's not. He's made it abundantly clear that he's moving on." I blow out a breath, trying to ignore how much that hurts. "So I'm trying to do the same."

"And you should be so damn proud, beautiful."

Flushing, I pick up Archie and make my way to the back door. Warren's not going to let me clean a damn thing for them anyway. "Thanks for last night. It was nice." I smile over my shoulder at him. "Most of it anyway."

Warren gives me a wink, straightening from the stair railing and moving into the kitchen. "Don't mention it. You deserved it."

I close the door behind me and step across the stones until we reach our little house, getting Archie set up with some toys before making myself a cup of tea.

Jake and Warren took me out to dinner to celebrate my job offer yesterday. I smile, stirring some sugar into my tea as I remember the way the director's eyes lit up when she saw me. Caroline told me she'd been waiting for me to inquire about working there and asked if I could start in two weeks before we'd even sat down in her office. I'll only be working part time, two days a week. But even so, it was a good day, one that I don't mind playing on repeat in my head. A first of many hopefully, where I gain even more of my old self back.

Except for what happened at the end of it. I could do with forgetting that part.

It seems he likes to force his way into every moment I try to take for myself. I should know it's futile to do anything without him affecting it in some way by now.

Sam. I shake my head, staring at Archie as he lies on the floor with his thumb in his mouth.

Out of all the people to move on with, he chooses someone else from his past? Someone he knew and had been with long before he met me.

It more than hurts, but I know that if I let myself acknowledge just how much it does, it might very well destroy me.

A tapping sound has my head snapping over to the sliding door.

My stomach flips when I see Felix staring back at me. It takes a few seconds, but I finally snap out of it and let him in.

"Hi." I step out of the way for him to walk in, closing the door behind him.

"Hey, sorry I didn't call first. I just …" He runs his hand

over his bearded jaw, letting out a loud exhale as he stares at me. "I wanted to see him."

I let my eyes quickly dance over his white shirt, noticing the way his coveralls are hastily wrapped around his waist. He must've left work to come here. "You don't need to work today?"

He looks away, brown eyes landing on Archie, who finally realizes we've got company and rolls over onto his tummy, grinning at Felix. "I did, do. Yeah."

That's all he says before kicking off his boots and walking over to Archie, who pushes himself up on wobbly legs and lays his head on Felix's shoulder when he picks him up.

Felix stands there for a moment, eyes shut and his lips resting on top of Archie's hair, and my stupid heart warms to dangerous levels at the sight.

"I might just … Yeah." I grab my tea and make my way to my room.

Felix doesn't stop me, which only adds more fuel to this ever-present burning in my chest. God, this co-parenting thing is hard, and I have a feeling that unless I can somehow magically eradicate him from my heart, it's only going to get harder.

I come out half an hour later, bored from sitting there staring at the pages of a book I'm not in the mood to read, and find Felix standing in the kitchen. Archie's asleep, his head still on Felix's shoulder with his dad's hand resting over his diapered bottom. His other hand is flicking through the album I'd left out to give to him.

I'd almost forgotten about that.

Felix hears me approach but doesn't remove his eyes from the photos. "I've missed so much."

Guilt assaults me, thick and crushing as it weighs heavily on my heart. "I'm sorry."

"It's not entirely your fault." He huffs. "If anything, it was always mine. It just ... it kills me." He caresses the picture of my huge thirty-eight-week pregnant stomach. "It went okay? The pregnancy?"

"Yeah, it was pretty uneventful," I admit. "Well, except for growing so huge I felt like I wouldn't be able to get up off the couch somedays."

We're silent for a heavy minute, and I lean against the counter after rinsing my mug out. Felix glances over at the sink, his lips twitching. "Still love cats."

"Hmmm?" It takes me a second to realize he's talking about my mug, which has cat faced patterns on it. "Oh." Heat crawls up my neck, and I dig my fingers into my hair, glancing away. "Yes, I still do. Though I've tried to tame it a bit."

When I look at him again, his gaze is on me, which only makes the heat rise until my cheeks flame, as well as my insides. Something about the way Felix looks at me has always felt so ... intense. As if he's not just seeing me; he's seeing everything about me with a single inspection. It's petrifying and absolutely thrilling at the same time.

Trying to remind myself that things are different now, I blurt out something I've wanted to ask for a while, even if it hurts. "How's Toulouse been?"

He snaps out of it then, returning his gaze to the pictures. "He seems fine."

The way he doesn't elaborate or say much makes me frown, but I let it slide. "I actually got that out for you, you know, to take with you."

"What, the photos?" He turns those brown eyes on me.

"Yeah, but you don't have to take them if you don't want to." I don't tell him that every single photo I took was for him. That they're all snapshots I captured and printed for him to see.

"Up to you."

I move away, thinking I can busy myself with sorting the dirty laundry. His voice stops me, though. "Want to go sit outside?"

He closes the album when I turn around, rubbing his hand over Archie's back. "It's a nice day." He shrugs as if he's the kind of guy who likes to sit outside on nice days.

He's not. Rain, hail, or shine, he's working on his bike, watching old movies, or reading magazines. He's never been one for pointless outings or simple things like sitting outside in the sun.

I don't remind him of any of that, though. I simply nod and follow him outside, uncertain but curious. We walk out the gate at the back of the yard that opens to the bay and take a seat on the sand. I kick off my flip-flops, digging my toes into the warm sand until they find the cool grains hiding beneath.

Archie remains asleep, his parted lips resting near Felix's neck while we gaze at the flat water rippling in the breeze.

"What was it like?" I finally dredge up the courage to ask.

He knows what I'm talking about. "Boring, depressing, and eye opening." I look over at him then, finding his jaw clenching. "Each day, same shit. Same sounds, same men, same guards, and same food. The routine was almost maddening."

"You worked out a lot there? Did that help in some way?" I bite my lip, glancing away. He knows I've more than just looked at him, but that question would confirm it.

He doesn't answer for a minute. "Yeah, they have a gym there. To be honest, I think it was the only thing that really helped keep my head straight."

"You didn't get into any fights?" I can't even count how many times I'd lain awake, worrying, stressing, thinking the worst.

"A few but only at first. Never anything too bad." He gives me a small smile when I chance another look at him before he averts his gaze back to the water. "I learned quick enough to keep my head down."

A portion of my rattling mind seems to calm at hearing that.

Time passes. I'm not sure how much, but the tension in my body slowly fades as I listen to the sound of the water lapping against the shore and watch a few kids run by, chasing a ball.

"I'm not with her, you know," Felix suddenly says.

When I don't respond, he continues, voice quiet to keep from waking Archie. "I know it looks bad. And I feel like a dick because at first, well, I wanted it to look that way … but I don't know. It's actually not like that at all."

I suck my lips between my teeth as an overwhelming sense of relief encases me, my pulse racing frantically. But I don't respond for a minute. When my heart rate slows, I exhale shakily. "Okay."

We don't talk again after that. But it feels nice, just being for once without all the baggage accompanying us. The wind rustles the hair off my shoulders, and I tilt my head back, eyes closing while the sun's rays warm my face.

The sound of something hitting the sand in front of my feet has my eyes opening and my head snapping back down.

"Charlie!" a blond man calls out from near the shore. "What was that?" He laughs, his white teeth glinting in the harsh light from the sun, before jogging closer.

Wow. I try not to let my eyes bug out as they absorb the sight of him before me. A woman sits farther down the sand with a big floppy hat covering her long, golden hair, which thankfully helps to keep my jaw from dropping. She smiles at us apologetically while the boy runs over, mumbles an apology, and grabs the ball before running back to his dad.

"All right, move it back down here now," the man says, shaking his head and grinning at us as if to say, "Kids."

The boy, Charlie, chases after him, grumbling loudly. "But it wasn't my fault. Greta got in the way!"

"Hey! Did not," a little girl yells as she runs after them both, struggling to keep up.

Felix and I watch the family for a while, and I wonder if he feels the same way I do. Regretful. But with that regret, there's a tiny thread of hope. A voice that says maybe. Maybe one day.

I know better, though. *One day* doesn't always arrive.

"I'm going back inside," I murmur, getting up and brushing sand off my jeans.

"Maggie."

I barely hear him, too engulfed by the sound of my hurt and regret screaming through my body and making my head ache.

Felix remains outside a while longer, returning around lunchtime with a very awake and grumpy Archie. "He had a play in the sand, but I think he's getting hungry?"

He would be. I get up off the couch and make him a sandwich, removing the crusts before cutting it into tiny little square pieces and putting it in a bowl for him.

"I think he needs his diaper changed." Felix walks over to the kitchen, Archie bouncing in his arms. I pass Archie a piece of sandwich before reaching for him, but Felix steps back.

"Think I can maybe do it?" he asks.

"Uh, sure. Let me show you."

I watch while he does it, but he doesn't need much direction. Taking the diaper when he's finished, I deposit it in the trash and wash my hands. Felix joins me, and I think he'll wait for me to move, but he doesn't. He stands right next to me, the hairs on his arm brushing the skin of my own. I suck in a breath, hoping he doesn't hear, and move away to dry my hands on a towel.

Shaking my head, I tell myself to snap out of it and chop some banana for Archie before filling his sippy cup with water. I place it all on the tray of his high chair then pick him up and strap him in.

"Ta, ta." Archie's chubby hands go for some bread and banana at the same time, and he shoves them both into his mouth.

"You're welcome, little guy." I smooth his hair back and walk over to the fridge to grab a drink of water, realizing then that Felix is standing in the doorway, eyes darting back and forth between Archie and me with his arms folded across his chest.

Clearing my throat, I ask him, "Do you want a drink or something?"

He tilts his head, looking at me for a heartbeat more than I think my heart can handle. "Nah." He straightens, walking over to Archie and kissing his cheek. "I need to get back to work."

I take a sip from my water bottle, nodding and almost choking when he says, "I'll be back tomorrow. 'Kay?" he asks, though it doesn't come out as much of a question.

A bit too shocked to reply, I watch him grab the photo album and slip his boots back on before walking outside and closing the door behind him.

CHAPTER TWENTY-FIVE

Maggie

"That's good, right?" Warren asks. "That he's coming over more."

Jake scowls at him. "For who? Archie, yes. But not Maggie."

I sigh from my perch on a stool at their kitchen counter. "Who knows what it is, really."

Jake turns that scowl on me, leaning against the sink with his hands wrapped around his coffee mug. "You're okay with this? With him just barging in whenever he pleases?"

Warren snickers, saying something under his breath that I don't hear.

"I wouldn't say he's barging in." I idly run my finger over the counter, the sun glinting off the granite and making some of the specks glitter. "He's his dad. I'm not about to keep them apart just because I don't know if I can handle seeing him all the time. Especially after everything that's happened."

Jake stares at me over the rim of his mug, taking a sip of coffee. "Are you going to tell him then?"

Warren straightens from the wall and walks into the kitchen, scoffing as he stops beside Jake with his arms crossed over his chest. "We've been over this. You've met the guy now." He looks up at Jake, who's a head taller than Warren; it's kind of cute.

"So?" Jake asks him.

Warren's brows pull in. "*So?* So you can't imagine him going all Incredible Hulk on some thug asses?" He chuckles as soon as he says that. "Man, that totally came out wrong."

Despite his annoyance, Jake grins. "Or did it?"

They both start chuckling, and I'd roll my eyes if they didn't feel so damn heavy. Sleep eluded me again last night. My thoughts too tangled, too messy to shut my brain off and let me sleep for longer than an hour at a time.

"Anyway." I stand and grab the baby monitor off the counter. "It'll be okay, hopefully. We need to work out a way to do this whole co-parenting thing at some point. Probably better that we're getting the show on the road now."

They both return their attention to me; Warren's eyes mischievous and Jake's worried. My heart warms with affection as I smile at them. "I'll see you guys later maybe."

"I'm off for the whole day. Do I need to be one of those overprotective father types? Sitting on the porch or peeking out one of the top floor windows when he arrives?"

Eyes bulging, I stop at the sliding back door. I spin around, and they both smirk at my expression. "You will do no such thing." Jake frowns, and I'm quick to add, "But I love you for caring enough to suggest such craziness." I wink at him, and his chest seems to puff out in response as he smiles.

Walking out the door, Warren calls out to me, "What about

me, bunches? I'm supposed to be your favorite!"

"You're both my favorites!" I laugh and close the door behind me while Warren mutters something about that being bullshit.

I spend the morning cleaning up before making Archie and myself some lunch and organizing some laundry to do over at the house.

The day drags, and my anxiety becomes a living, breathing monster that seems to fill the whole room. I lose count of how many times I need to calm myself down with stupid breathing techniques. Not stupid, I guess, seeing as most of the time, they do seem to work.

And that's exactly how Felix finds me when he walks inside, not bothering to knock this time. "What's wrong? You sick?" He kicks off his boots.

I'd laugh; I'd laugh so damn hard at the irony of that statement. But I can't.

Lifting my head, I offer a smile, hoping it looks more reassuring than it feels. "Just a headache. I didn't get enough sleep last night." Both are true, and he doesn't question me further, just keeps those brown eyes pinned on me for an excruciating minute before looking at Archie, who's sitting in his high chair next to me and eating some melon.

Felix lets out a low laugh, walking over to him and raining kisses all over his cantaloupe covered cheeks and forehead. I take the reprieve to smooth my hair back off my face and take a few deep breaths. Strangely enough, though, now that he's here, I don't feel so bad.

God, this is all so weird.

"How was work?" I ask, getting up from where I was sitting on the arm of the couch and grabbing some wipes.

Felix takes them from me, his fingers lightly grazing mine

and sending tingles zipping over my skin. He plucks some from the pack and cleans Archie's hands and face before unbuckling and lifting him out of the chair to his chest. "Good. Got a lot on, but we're managing."

"That's good." I wring my fingers together before asking, "How was the shop? While you were gone?"

He yanks another wipe from the pack, cleaning the melon residue from the high chair tray with his free hand while Archie tugs on his short beard. Felix doesn't seem to notice, or if he does, he doesn't care.

"While I was in jail, you mean?" His eyes find mine, hard and unflinching, and I jerk my head, nodding once. "It did okay. Jared stepped up and kept everything afloat."

I'm glad and relieved, knowing how much that business means to them. I don't say that, though, and instead, move around him to open the cabinet under the sink. He sees the trash can inside and tosses the wipes into it.

"He seems happy. Jared." I close the door and lean back against the counter.

Felix smirks, running his hand over Archie's back. He must've showered before coming here. He's in fresh jeans and a t-shirt. Grease stains his fingers permanently, but they're cleaner than they would be if he'd come straight from work. "He sure is." He shakes his head. "Never thought I'd see the day he used the word marriage in a sentence referring to himself."

"I don't know." Thinking about it, I smile. "He's never been the type for relationships, sure, but he's always been soft at heart, you know?"

Felix's eyes snap to mine and darken. I tuck some hair behind my ear, feeling like I may have said something wrong. Three heavy heartbeats later, he sighs. "Yeah, despite everything, you're right about that."

He puts Archie down when he wriggles and babbles loud-ly. "Ba bub, car, da bub."

Felix adjusts Archie's shirt, his shoulders shaking with qui-et laughter before glancing up at me. "Cute."

"That was all Warren. He likes to shop, especially online. He finds all sorts of weird and adorable outfits."

Archie's black shirt has a white picture of an old vintage classic car with a tadpole or sperm driving it, and underneath, it says, "I won the race."

Felix straightens, tucking his hands into his jean pock-ets while watching Archie waddle to the TV unit and use it as leverage to bop up and down to a children's song playing on the TV.

"They seem like good guys," Felix says gruffly as though it takes a fair bit of effort for him to admit that.

"They are. Some of the best I've ever known."

He swings his head around to look at me, and heat climbs into my skin.

"Want to take him outside to play?" I ask in an effort to stop it, while hoping Jake minds his own business.

Felix continues to pierce me with those dark eyes of his before finally saying, "Sure."

At my suggestion, we take some toys down to the bay, and I hope that if Jake is playing a peeping Tom, then he won't be able to see much when we're all the way down here.

Felix tries to show Archie how to shovel sand into the bucket but ends up having to do it for him. Once it's full, Archie takes it and tips it upside down, laughing as the sand all pours out into a pile between his chubby legs. Felix's responding smile is contagious and does funny things to my stomach. They repeat the process over and over until Archie gets distracted and starts running his cars through the sand mounds instead.

"It's nice here," Felix says, looking around. "But how do you pay for the guesthouse?"

Unprepared for the question, I struggle to find a way to answer it. Because I don't pay for it. They wouldn't let me if I tried, which makes me feel rotten at times. "I'm between jobs right now," I say with as much confidence as I can muster. "I actually start a new one in about a week and a half."

"Yeah?" He takes his gaze from Archie, giving it to me. Except I don't want it right now. It's too much. "Where at?" he asks when I don't respond, too caught up in looking at his lashes when he blinks.

"Oh, um, the local preschool. It's a few blocks away. I graduated with a degree in early childhood education."

His brows rise, a huge smile lighting up his face. *Oh, Jesus.*

I look away as he says, "So you're finally becoming a teacher after all."

My shoulders lift because it's not exactly the kind of teaching I envisioned. I never really thought too much about that, but primary school would probably be what I'd have picked. It's a start, though, and it works for now. "Yeah, I guess. The best thing is, I get to take Archie in with me. He'll be in the nursery while I work in the preschool room, but even so, it helps a lot."

"How many days are you going to be working?" His voice turns rougher.

My eyes move back to his with a will of their own. "Just two for now while Archie is so young. I'm job sharing."

"Good," he grunts then pauses. "How's that going to pay for everything, though?"

Shit. "I'll figure it out. I can always work another day if they need me. And the rent here is cheap." *So damn cheap*, I think sarcastically to myself.

"No." His jaw tightens. "I gave you that money, and I'll

bring it back. Use it to be at home with Archie more. Don't pick up any more days."

I shake my head, and he grumbles, "Still so god damn stubborn."

"Much like someone else I know," I blurt without thinking.

He tenses, and so do I, before he says coldly, "I'll be helping you, Mags, and you're going to take that help and not give me any shit."

Archie waddles off toward the water, and Felix jumps to his feet, jogging after him. I have to tear my eyes away from his ass when his jeans lower even more with the movement. He lifts Archie into the air, who lets out a loud belly laugh while Felix holds him above his head.

Walking back, he puts him down, and Archie wanders over to the trees next to us, his face going kind of red.

"Ah, what's he doing?" Felix tilts his head.

"Just pooping." I smirk when Felix's eyes widen. He rubs a hand over his mouth, obviously trying not to laugh as Archie squats a little, his face turning redder. He then barrels back toward us as if he isn't carrying around extra baggage in his diaper.

"Better go change him," I mutter, laughing lightly and standing. It's getting late anyway; he's going to need a bath and dinner soon.

"What, he just plays happily with a turd in his pants?" Felix stares at Archie, looking perplexed.

"Yep. He only gets upset if it's been in there for a while, and I haven't realized."

I grab the bucket, dumping the cars and spade inside it while Felix gets Archie.

"Though it doesn't usually get to that point. It's really hard not to—"

"Notice the stink?" Felix offers with a chuckle, cradling Archie in his arms instead of holding him with his hand or arm under his bottom as he'd usually do.

"Uh-huh." I grin and open the gate for him, closing it behind us and leaving the bucket with the rest of his toys outside before following the boys inside.

Felix is already laying him down on the changing table in Archie's room when I walk in.

"Ah, are you sure you want to—"

He cuts me off. "I got this."

Right.

Thirty seconds later, he cringes, looking at his hand like it's about to sprout another finger. "Shit. There's shit on my hand."

My teeth sink into my lip so hard I think they're going to puncture the skin while I hold back a laugh. "Want me to take over?"

He looks down at Archie, scowling. "You're lucky I love you so damn much, boy."

Archie tries to grab his chunky legs, and I rush over, holding them still while Felix fumbles with the dirty diaper and tosses it into one of the plastic bags I keep below the table.

"He needs a bath now anyway. Don't worry about a fresh one." I head into the bathroom, turning the water on and putting some baby wash in.

When I get back, Felix is still standing there, one hand on Archie's belly and the one with a tiny bit of poop on it held far away from his body. "You don't think he's gonna piss on me now for good measure?" He raises a wary brow at our son's exposed private parts.

The laugh escapes, and he scowls at me before his chest heaves and he starts to laugh too.

When our laughter subsides, our eyes meet and stay stuck

for a moment before I clear my throat. "I'll take him, so you can wash your hands."

"Thanks," he murmurs.

Putting Archie in the tub, I grab his washcloth and run it over his skin when I hear Felix finish up at the sink behind me. "Do you think I can help?"

I glance over my shoulder at him from where I'm squatting on the ground. "Oh, yeah. Sorry."

"Don't do that, Mags."

"Do what?" I give Archie his toy turtle before rising on shaky legs.

He's too close, and this room is too small. I swallow thickly under his gaze.

"Don't apologize for being his mom and doing what you're used to doing. Do I need to wash his hair?"

"Yeah." I point at the bottle, tell him to use a small amount of the baby wash, then leave them to it.

Grabbing Archie's pajamas and a fresh diaper, I set them on the changing table and lean over it, trying to get my emotions in check. He only needs to look at me, and they all scramble, wanting to surface. Jumping and climbing over each other while I try desperately to shove them back down.

Felix walks into the room a minute later, carrying a naked Archie wrapped in a towel against his chest, sucking on his thumb.

With my thoughts turning to mush, I step closer, running my hand over Archie's hair. He stops sucking, smiling around his tiny thumb at me. Felix rests his lips against his damp hair, then lifts his head, eyes dropping to mine. My lungs almost seize as the moment seems to swallow up all the air in the room. A moment where I'm standing much too close, feeling way too much, and mere millimeters separates our bodies.

Averting my gaze, I step back, sucking in air and walking out of the room to drain the tub and tidy up. But the bathroom is pretty clean, with only the bathmat needing to be hung up. Feeling antsy, I glance out the window at the orange and pink hues of dusk, deciding now's as good a time as any to get Archie some dinner.

Digging out a pouch of spinach and pumpkin risotto, I empty it into a bowl and chuck it in the microwave, cutting up some bread and putting it on his tray while I wait.

The microwave dings just as Felix walks out, blowing raspberries on Archie's exposed tummy. He giggles, and I start to think Felix is becoming as addicted to the sound as I am, for he keeps doing it until he realizes I'm standing there watching.

"Dinnertime, I'm guessing, little man." He deposits him in his chair, and I don't even ask, just hand the bowl and spoon over to Felix. "Just stir it a bit first."

He sits on the arm of the couch, dragging the high chair over to him.

Archie starts tucking pieces of bread into his mouth while Felix blows on his food and mixes it around with the tiny spoon. It looks so small in his large hand.

Archie's starving, and he loves to eat. He opens his mouth for more as soon as he's swallowed a mouthful.

"He always love his food this much?" Felix asks, looking at the green gunk in the bowl suspiciously.

Smiling, I wipe my hands on a towel. "Yeah. Though it does taste a lot better than it looks."

He raises a brow at me. "You'd know, would you?"

My shoulder tilts. "I may have tried it once or twice." I laugh at his expression. "Don't tease; I was curious after looking at it the same way you are right now. Besides, baby custard tastes awesome."

Felix stares at me like I've just started dancing and singing on the spot. "What?" I shift some hair behind my ear, finding it hard to keep eye contact again.

"Nothing." He returns his attention to Archie when he whacks his high chair. "Ma!" He opens his mouth wide, and Felix shakes his head with a chuckle. "So it tastes better than it smells, then?"

"It definitely does." I busy myself with getting Archie's milk ready; it's almost seven thirty, and I'm wondering if maybe Felix would like to settle him for the night before he goes.

"Uh, I don't usually do much for dinner on the nights I give him those." I point at the discarded pouch on the counter. "But I can make you a grilled cheese or something, if you want?"

Felix doesn't take his eyes off Archie, but his hand pauses on the way to his mouth. Impatient, Archie grabs his hand and shoves it toward his mouth, causing the green goop to splatter all over his cheek. I grab a wipe and quickly lean over to clean it up before it drips down onto his pajama top.

"I'm good. I'll just grab something on the way home," Felix says a tad croakily when I step away.

I heat Archie's milk and give it to him. He guzzles it, eyes slowly drifting closed while Felix tries to clean up some of his dinner and the leftover bread off the tray.

After tossing the wipes out and putting the bowl in the sink, he unbuckles and lifts him out. Archie gives up on his milk, almost dropping it as he nuzzles into Felix's neck. Felix catches it and passes it to me, then starts swaying side to side a little, walking to Archie's room.

I guess he doesn't want any help then. Not that he needs it since Archie's almost out anyway.

Yawning myself, I quickly move the high chair back by the

wall and then wash up. I'm drying my hands and staring out the window when I feel Felix approach. "Out almost instantly."

I hang the towel over the oven door handle. "Doesn't usually take him long, unless he's sick or teething."

"He's …" I turn around, finding him right there, leaning against the fridge. Not even a few feet away from me. "There's seriously no words to describe him."

His voice is raspy, almost broken, and it has my body swaying closer. His seems to as well; his hand lifts and my eyes close when those rough fingers gently tuck my hair behind my ear. "We made something pretty fucking amazing."

A tear drops down my cheek when my eyes open, and his follow its descent before his thumb scoops it up. He rubs the wetness between his thumb and pointer finger, his eyes turbulent when they return to mine.

I don't know who moved, but suddenly, our lips are an inhale of breath apart. But I don't breathe, and I don't close the distance, despite everything inside me raging at me to do so. Because it's then that all his anger, all the hurt that still lingers inside the both of us, decides to shove its way to the forefront of my mind.

I step back, my ass hitting the edge of the counter hard. But I don't really feel it. What I can feel is him looking at me, and his hesitation and presence seem to scatter all conscious thought from the room.

He doesn't come for me, though. And I tell myself to be glad when he turns away, grabbing his boots before walking out the door and quietly closing it behind him.

CHAPTER TWENTY-SIX

Felix

My finger drags over the plastic sleeve covering a picture of Archie as a newborn.

Born August 14th at 2:33 p.m.

Maggie's familiar perfect handwriting sits above it and all the rest, too. My finger moves over them all, landing on one that says he's seven months old and crawling.

Archie's on all fours, smiling at the camera with a string of drool hanging from his tiny bottom lip.

God, I love him.

Sure, he's my son and I expected to, but I had no idea it'd be like this. That I'd feel like a whole different person and start to see things so differently after knowing him for such a short span of time.

Turning the page over, Maggie's smile has my chest constricting. Her face lit up with love and affection as she holds our boy on her lap and looks down into his upturned face.

The caption reads eight months old.

I remember a time when it wasn't hard to get her to smile like that whenever I wanted her to. Her laughter ... Christ. I'd almost forgotten what it sounded like. It's one of my favorite things about her.

What happened to that girl?

Did I drag her through the muck of my life too much and for too long before it irrevocably changed her?

Tonight, I saw glimpses of her. The one who stood by me, forfeiting her plans because she fell in love with an asshole from the wrong side of the tracks.

So why did she betray me? And after everything she's done for me over the years, all we've been through, why is it so hard for me to forgive her?

Maybe I do. Maybe I fucking get it. If I'm being honest, I wouldn't want my kid visiting someone in jail. But I'm a selfish bastard, and my need to know him would've had me begging her to bring him back every chance she could, regardless.

Still, she went and did this. She created an album full of memories that I'll never hold within my own mind or heart.

And it's my fault. It all started with the desperate, stupid decision I made that led us here.

Placing the album on the bed, I grab my keys and head out of the house to the garage, starting up my bike and clipping on my helmet.

It's getting late, but I doubt Jared and Vera are asleep, so I don't really give a shit how loud I am as I peel out of the driveway.

I just need the wind on my face and my thoughts to quiet the fuck down.

I ride for what feels like hours, though, in reality, it's probably only an hour before I find myself turning onto the now familiar street and letting my bike idle into the driveway.

I wheel it down the side of the house, chucking my helmet on the seat and shoving my keys into my pocket before marching through the side gate.

Knocking on the door, I suddenly realize I have no idea what I'm fucking doing. Or how I ended up here. But I think if left to its own devices, the part of me that belongs to her will always lead me back to her.

"Felix?" Maggie slides open the door, her auburn hair mussed but her eyes wide and alert, like she hasn't slept yet even though it's probably close to eleven at night. It's dark in her little house. The glow from the TV behind her the only source of light.

I don't say a word. The blood rushes from my head in a wave that almost makes my knees buckle as it flows straight to my cock. Her loose tank top outlines the perfect swells of her tits, her nipples hardening under my gaze. My cock turns painfully hard, then she's in my arms, the door closing behind me before I lower my mouth to hers, absorbing her surprised squeak and walking us backward into her small living room.

She stumbles over a toy, but I keep her upright and lower us to the couch, groaning when she finally opens those soft lips for me to dip my tongue inside. She tastes exactly how I remember, sweet and perfect and all fucking mine.

"Felix." She pants, her hands grabbing the sides of my face and forcing my lips away from hers. I growl, hating it, and grind my rock-hard dick into her softness.

She moans, and I grin. "Miss me, Little Doe?" My brows lower as I study her flushed cheeks and the glazed look in her big brown eyes.

Nodding, she bites her lip. "But what are you …" She trails off, her lashes fluttering when those eyes drop to my mouth.

"Need you, so fucking bad." I take her lips with mine again, harder this time. She's delusional if she thinks either of us are going to be able to stop this.

She doesn't stop me, though, and instead, runs her hands over my back, trying to lift my t-shirt. I pull away to tear it over my head and damn near lose my mind when I hear her harsh intake of breath. Her hands smooth over the planes of my chest and travel down to my abs.

Fuck me, I think I'm about to come in my pants with the way she's looking at me. That and it's been so fucking long.

Moving back, I tug her sleep shorts and panties down her long legs, throwing them to the floor then unzip my jeans and shove my boots off.

Settling back between her creamy thighs, I don't waste another fucking minute. She whimpers when my finger tunnels inside her pussy. So wet and warm. My dick feels like it's on fire. I pull my finger out, watching those doe eyes glow as I suck her wetness from it.

She reaches down, aligning me at her entrance, and I thrust forward, sinking inside instantly.

"Holy fucking mother of ..." My eyes almost roll back. Tight, so deliciously tight.

I stay buried to the hilt, my head dropping down to her neck, teeth biting her soft skin while I try to control myself. Tingles shoot up and down my spine, and her ragged breaths fill my ear.

When I think I'm good, I rear back, grabbing her leg and putting it over the back of the couch for me to go even deeper.

Then I move; hard, deep, and almost crazed by the sensations tearing through my body.

She takes it, whimpering with each thrust when I start pounding into her with a desperation I've never felt before. Her nails score into my biceps, her breath hitching and brown eyes flaring when I rotate my hips on each pump, hitting that sweet spot I remember so fucking well.

Her pussy tightens, and she soon explodes, silent cries escaping her parted lips as her body shakes. I follow, grunting and pounding into her as I fill her pussy with my cum. That knowledge seems to make my orgasm go on and on as I think about filling it all night long.

Her nails run over the short hair at the nape of my neck a few minutes later, her beating heart slowing back to a normal rhythm beneath my cheek. "Felix." Her voice is quiet and tinged with uncertainty, even as she touches me as if there's nothing else she'd rather be doing.

"Don't." I lift my head from her breasts, staring down at her. "Tonight, you're mine again."

Seeing the protest forming in her eyes, I don't give her a chance to voice it. I kiss her softly, gentle pecks that soon have her sucking my tongue into her mouth. Her legs wrap around me when my lips journey over her neck, and I shove her tank up to suck on her tits and squeeze them. She grinds into my already hard again cock, and I reach down, kicking my jeans all the way off before positioning myself and slipping easily back inside her.

At the ass-crack of dawn, I stumble half asleep from her tiny house to the side gate, still doing up my jeans.

Maggie's still asleep on the couch, so I grabbed a blanket from her room and laid it over her, watching her mumble something in her sleep before turning over, soft snores leaving her perfect lips.

My heart and head feel like they've been at war for an eternity, but despite how much she's hurt me, I know with a certainty that makes every step away from her painful that I don't think I'll ever be able to let her go.

She didn't say she loved me, but she didn't need to. I could feel it with every touch of her hands and every look in her eyes. Which only makes it that much harder to leave. But I've got a business to help run, and a ton of shit to sort out before I go charging full force into her life again.

This time, we're not teens with no idea of what we're doing. This time, it needs to be fair. She needs to talk, and I need to listen, to try to understand why she never came to me. I need to somehow see where she's coming from even if I don't agree with it.

Because I know she's not telling me everything, and it's about time she did.

My tired eyes open wide when I close the gate quietly behind me and find a familiar tall guy leaning against the seat of my bike.

"Felix."

I nod, feeling like a teenager who's been busted doing the walk of shame. Something that's never actually happened to me.

"Jake," he supplies when I just stand there.

"Right." I fold my arms over my chest, jerking my head at my bike. "I know it's loud, but I really need to get going."

Jake tilts his head, eyes narrowing on me before he glances at the gate, in the direction of where I just came from. "I won't hold you up."

He straightens, grabbing a small, blue box from behind him off the seat of my bike. "She might hate me for this, but you should know. And she's too damn stubborn and worried about you to tell you anything herself." He sighs, shoving the box at my chest. Frowning, I grab it before it can tumble to the grass. "You don't need to read them now. Tomorrow. Or next week. But you will read them." His eyes demand almost as firmly as his words. "They won't tell you everything. But until she's ready, they'll tell you enough."

With that, he walks away, leaving me confused as fuck.

I don't have time to ponder it or open the damn thing, though. Slipping it into my saddle bag, I then do my best to wheel my bike away from the house before starting it. But the damn thing weighs a ton, so I give in, starting it and taking off quickly, in hopes that it will help in some way.

The sun finishes its journey into the sky by the time I pull into my driveway twenty-five minutes later. I jump off, forgetting all about the box in my haste to get inside, shower, and get over to the garage. After backing up and grabbing the box, I'm about to leap up the steps when a figure sitting on the top one suddenly says, "Long time, no see, buddy."

Fuck. Ryan? I step back, taking in the small smirk and the blond hair. He hasn't changed much since the last time I saw him, but something about him seems wary, and it puts me on edge. My rush to get to work on time vanishes.

"Heard you've been asking for me," he says when I just continue to stare at him. "I should've come to see you sooner, but the truth is …" He sighs, standing and walking down the steps. "I've been a bit of a pussy."

"What's this shit about me owing you money?" is the first thing that comes out of my mouth.

He chuckles. "Yeah, it all comes back to that, doesn't it?" Cursing, he blurts out in a rush, "It wasn't that big a deal, looking back. But that's the thing about perspective, huh? It always chooses the worst time to show up."

"Spit it out. What the fuck are you getting at?"

"Guess you really don't know shit then." He glances away, then gives me a look I've never seen on him before. Fear. Such a strange thing to find on this wise ass who'd do anything and everything to make a buck, not giving a damn who he tramples over or ruins in the process. "Sam's always loved you. You know that, right?" I don't say anything, and he goes on. "I thought she'd gotten over it. But women ... confusing fucking things, they are." He shakes his head. "Anyway, I told the guys I needed that five-grand back when I found out you'd be doing time. Hellsy and Smith, those feral fuckers can get money out of a stone; that's why they work for me. But I didn't know—"

"Didn't know *what?*" My voice lowers, trepidation fueling an inferno that's now blazing inside my chest.

"That they'd hurt her. Chicks, I mean, it's just common sense, isn't it?" He laughs. Laughs as if it's a joke. "You don't hurt them; fuck 'em, sure, but not hurt them. Besides, I told the guys to get the money from *you*. I didn't know until it was too late that Sam told them you probably didn't have it, and that if anyone did, it would be Maggie, with you going to jail and all."

My vision turns blurry, then turns red. The little box falls to the ground, and my hands are grabbing fistfuls of his shirt, pinning him to the railing of the porch. "What the fuck did they do to her?"

The front door bursts open a second later, Jared jumping down the steps and trying to tug me away from Ryan. I manage to shrug him off as Ryan says, "They beat her up, man. But as fucked up as I am, I'd never condone that shit. And I didn't know ... I didn't know until days later. I swear to you."

My fist flies, connecting with his jaw with a force that sends his head banging into the metal of the railing so loudly that even my ears ring. I swing again, hitting him in the mouth before Jared grabs me, shoving me hard until I almost stumble onto my ass.

"You fucking sent your dumbass henchmen after *my woman*?" My heart is screaming in my ears. "And she was fucking pregnant!"

"What the fuck?" Jared growls, still trying to hold me back.

Ryan rights himself, his jaw already swelling and blood dripping from his split lip. "I'll let those two slide, but you're not getting any more." He straightens the collar of his dress shirt. "I tried to make sure she was okay after I found out. Even went to pay her hospital bills, but they'd already been taken care of."

"Why the fuck wouldn't you just ask me?" My hands squeeze my head, grief and anger warring together. The pit of my stomach swirling and knotting.

"That's what I told them to do, talk to you or Jared. Like I said, I never would've sent them after her. Call me old school, sexist, whatever—women have no business in my business. Sam wasn't even an exception, but still, she knew too much."

"Sam?" Jared asks, bewildered. He lets go of my arm, but I don't go after Ryan. There's nothing more he can tell me anyway.

"For what it's worth," he says from the open door of his Corvette, "I really am sorry, and hey, you've got no debt with me anymore. Congrats on the kid, man."

His car speeds off at the same time I collapse onto the grass and throw the empty contents of my stomach up.

"Holy fucking shit," Jared breathes.

CHAPTER TWENTY-SEVEN

Felix

Felix,

    It's been three weeks since everything changed and the Thompson men took me in.

    I have no idea where they came from.

    Warren said he was my fairy godmother upon meeting me while I was in the hospital.

    I would've laughed if it didn't hurt so much. But I guess in a way they are. Saviors, almost.

    I don't know why you had to go and set off this rapid chain of events.

And even though I should blame you, I still don't.

Does that make me stupid?

Who knows. I'm not really sure of anything anymore.

Jake said I should go and see someone. He's made an appointment for me, actually.

I don't know if I can do it, though. What's the point?

Some of my ribs are still healing, and my arm is in a cast. So I guess I have a good excuse not to.

It's weird being here and not being at home with you. But I feel safe here. Not wholly safe but safer. I don't think they'd find me here, if they're even looking.

I wonder where you are sometimes when I lie awake in the early hours of the morning.

What jail you might've been sent to.

I wish I knew.

Then I might actually send this.

What I do know is that despite everything that's happened, I still love you.

Maggie

My fingers shuffle through the small pieces of torn out notepaper. My eyes leaking tears onto them, smudging the ink.

Felix,

I got in the car today, put my seat belt on, and even managed to reverse out of the driveway before my foot slammed on the brake so hard that my head almost smacked into the steering wheel.

It starts with shaky hands.

Or just a shortness of breath.

Then there's this tightness in my chest that grows progressively worse.

Soon, my limbs might start to tingle, and sometimes my head spins.

And I don't know why or what exactly sets it off. But I'm so sick and tired of it. Of being so worried and so scared.

I'm sick of checking every face in every crowd. Of feeling like I'm being watched.

All the time.

It's strange because I'm pretty good at not thinking about what happened. It's almost as if my brain has blocked it out.

The day I failed to leave the driveway was the same day I agreed to start seeing Dr. Hayes.

She said that I suppressed the memory, and that it was normal. It was my way of trying to cope.

Is it normal for a fear you block out to control your life? Your hopes, dreams, and the longing in your heart?

Anything is possible when something holds that much power over you, Dr. Hayes says.

And I guess it does hold that much power.

But at night, all bets are off.

At night, while I sleep, I can still feel the blows. To my ribs, breasts, back, and worst of all, my head. The blows to my head were both my saving grace and the scariest part. Everything went black after that.

But the worst part of it all?

The thing that haunts me the most?

Their laughter.

They laughed as they hurt me.

They laughed as I struggled to crawl away.

They laughed as I curled into a ball, my arms covering my stomach to protect our baby.

They laughed and laughed and laughed.

They've ruined my life, and the sad thing is, I've let them.

And I'm trying, Felix. I promise you that I'm trying.

But how can you get away from something that constantly chases you? That haunts your every sleeping moment until your nightmares insist on controlling your waking hours?

I don't know. But I'm trying.

And with every breath that leaves my body, I try harder.

I love you.
Maggie.

Felix,

Archer ~~Darren~~ Williams was born 9 pounds 7 ounces via emergency C-section on August 14th, exactly one week ago from the day I'm writing this to you.

I've been sore, but every day I feel better.

I was in labor for almost 15 hours with a breech baby who refused to turn.

Good thing Jake works at the hospital. He stopped in on his break to see how I was doing and started asking questions that led to me being wheeled out of the room to get prepped for surgery.

It was a whirlwind after that. But despite all my fears, it didn't hurt.

It's hard to describe how it felt, but it wasn't exactly pleasant.

It was almost like someone was rummaging around in a handbag, only it's your insides. So yeah ... Kind of really freaking weird.

Anyway, Warren got it all on video, which I still can't bring myself to watch.

But it's here, if you decide you ever want to watch Archie's entrance into the world.

Right now, it's hard to tell who he looks like. With his face being all smushed like newborns are. But he's got some hair already, and it's brown. Which for some reason, makes my heart ridiculously happy.

He sleeps and poops a lot.

It was love at first sight.

And for the first time since I left you behind, I feel like a tiny part of my old self has returned. She's a little different but back all the same.

I love you.
Maggie

I glance down into the box, digging through more letters, some ultrasound pictures, and discover a small USB sitting underneath. Grabbing more, I read on in no particular order, with a fist held to my mouth and my heart breaking with every word.

Felix,

Archie said his second word today.

Dad or "Da."

I know it's more of a sound than a word, being that he's only seven months old, but it's a sound that weighs heavily on my heart.

You should've been here to hear that sound.

I'm not mad.

If you've read these at all, then you know I stopped being mad at you a long time ago.

But I'm still sad. So horribly sad that some days the only thing that can tug me from within its miserable grasp is the sound of Archie's laughter. Or a toothless grin.

And as I sit here, watching him sleep beside me, I start to wonder who or what is there to pull you out of such misery? If you're even miserable at all.

I can't imagine being in jail is fun, but I can imagine you're being your usual self. Strong, self-assured, and stubborn as hell.

The thought puts a smile on my face.

And in an effort to keep it there, I'm going to put this pen down.

I love you,
Mags.

Felix,

Last week, I put Archie in the stroller and went for a walk. Warren followed me, but I think it still counts, right?

I made it to the water at the end of the street before I had to turn around and walk back. I felt kind of stupid, feeling proud of myself for doing something so insignificant to most everyone else. But Warren acted like I'd walked my way into the Olympics and had won a race.

We celebrated with brownies. It was a good day.

Today, I made it to the next street, and Warren and I made a cake.

I'm trying, but it's taking longer than I thought it would.

Archie's now eight months old.

Warren has offered a few times to take me to see you, if I'm ready.

I think I am. But are you?

Would you even want to see me now? After it's been so long?

That's something I can't answer, and something I don't think I could handle the answer to just yet.

So like the coward I've turned into ...

I'll still be here, waiting.

I'm sorry,
I love you,
Maggie.

CHAPTER TWENTY-EIGHT

Maggie

Mornings feel different when your heart feels lighter. I know I shouldn't let it, but I bask in as much of it as I can, deciding to overanalyze it later.

Loving someone and forgiving someone are two very different things.

I love him. I'll probably always love him.

But can I forgive him and just forget the damage he's inflicted since he walked back into my life? Forgive, maybe. Forget, never.

Some things are easy to forget, whereas some hurts are so huge, you simply choose not to see them again.

And some are a reminder you need to keep close to your heart in order to guard it from any more injury.

"Maggie, hey," a familiar voice says.

Glancing up from my shopping list, I find Sam standing before me. What she's doing at the plaza in Bonnets Bay is beyond me. "Hey, what are you doing here?"

For some stupid reason, I feel kind of bad, knowing how she feels about Felix, how she's probably always felt, standing in front of her and still tasting him on my tongue.

"Just passing through on my way out of town, stopped in to see a friend." She looks around. "Where's your baby?"

"At home." I don't really feel like explaining everything to her, nor do I feel the need to.

She nods. "Cool. Well, I know I'm probably not your favorite person. But—"

Seriously? "Don't bother, Sam. I know you would've visited him in jail. I've seen you place yourself in front of him at every opportunity available." I square my shoulders. "You're not a nice person. In fact, *you are* my least favorite person."

She just stares at me, jaw slack, then clears her throat. "Right. Well, at least I made the effort to go see him. I don't remember you ever doing the same."

"Oh, fuck you." Someone walking behind me coughs, obviously hearing our conversation, but I don't really care.

Sam's lips tilt down into a sad smile. "Anyway, it doesn't matter now, does it?"

She walks away, and my teeth grit together as I watch her go. She snatches some chips from an end display on her way to the register, and a memory assaults me at the sight of her hand.

The memory of those exact hands, *her* hands, touching me, her voice shaky and panicked, asking if I could hear her.

"It was you," I whisper to no one. She's the one who found me. *How did she find me?*

My heart pounds as I watch her walk out of the store. I feel terrible all of a sudden. She might be the very reason I'm alive, that Archie is okay. We might both be here today, thanks to her finding me in that back alleyway.

Shivering and trying not to let any more memories take hold, I grab the rest of the items on my list and make haste to the checkout, wanting to get home in case there's any chance of a repeat of the other week's panic attack.

Once home, I settle down and have coffee with Warren and Jake, a little put off by Jake's silence but too lost in my head to think about it much right now.

Later that night, I open the wardrobe to get my box. I keep spare paper and pens in there, so when I want to write to him again, it's all where I need it. It helps to get it all out on paper. And that's what I think I need to do right now.

Write him a letter.

When I started seeing Dr. Hayes, she told me it was good to write to Felix. And even though I didn't send them at the time due to not knowing where he'd been sent, she said that was probably even better. An outlet for me to write out my feelings and fears without being held back by the worry of anyone reading them.

Only, it's not here. I pull everything out, a container of old hair ties I thought I'd lost, scrunched up paper, Archie's keepsake capsule, my old photo album, and a couple of stray photographs. Everything, and still not here.

Tugging on my hair, I sit back on my haunches, my breathing turning shallow.

"Fuck." Getting up, I race through our little home, tearing open cabinets, drawers, and making a mess in my desperation. They're not here. I know that, yet I keep searching.

"Looking for this?" My head snaps up from where I'm sitting on the floor again in my room, surrounded by random items. Felix steps slowly into the room, dodging them, with my blue box tucked against his stomach.

My own hollows, lurching wildly when I think about

what he might've read. What he might know.

"Mags." He tosses it onto my bed then drops to his knees in front of me, his eyes watering and his jaw rigid as if he's trying not to cry. "Why the hell couldn't you tell me?"

"No, no." I back up, getting away from him. "You can't know. *How?* Did you go through my things?"

"Doesn't matter." His voice turns colder. "It's too late to worry about that."

My hands shoot to my eyes, as if shoving my palms into them can stop me from seeing this moment, can prevent any more trouble coming for us.

"Tell me, Maggie."

"You know why!" I cry out, dropping my hands. "You'll, you'll just …"

"Just *what?*" He growls. "Go after the deadbeats who did this to you? Who messed you up so badly you became a shell of a fucking woman?"

Closing my eyes, I reluctantly nod. That's exactly why.

He sighs loudly, pulling me onto his lap until my legs straddle his waist.

My eyes stay closed. "You can't leave again …" I plead, my head shaking. "You can't."

With his hands tunneling into my hair, he whispers, "Look at me, Little Doe."

Tears overflow when my eyes open, and he watches them, one by one, slide over my cheeks and sail toward my chin before lowering his hands and scooping them up with his thumbs.

"I won't leave you again. Ever."

When I just stare at him, he gently shakes my face. "Do you believe me?"

"I don't know what to believe anymore," I whisper

brokenly.

His face crumples. "Christ, Mags." He sniffs. "Did they …?"

"They ran tests and said there wasn't any sign of … that."

Felix's eyes close briefly, his relief palpable yet his arms start shaking. He drops them to my waist, resting his forehead on mine and squeezing my hips. "I've been such a dick." He laughs gruffly. "Scratch that. I've been a complete, selfish asshole."

"Stop."

"No, I should've seen it; hell, I think I did. I just got too caught up in my head, in my own self-righteous bullshit, when I should've been listening to my heart." Tears start to run down his face, and I feel that little slice of anger inside me eat itself and disappear at the sight. "I'm sorry, so fucking sorry. This, everything, it's all my fault."

"Shhh." I grab his head, tucking it in my neck. His body quakes with the force of his torment. His cries silent, yet his sorrow so loud I can't hear, see, or feel anything else.

I don't want to do this. I don't want to let him fall apart and tell him that everything is going to be okay.

Because it would be a lie.

But I also can't leave him alone in this. He needs me, but I've needed him more. So I wrap my arms around him, running my hands up and down his back while his tears dampen the skin of my shoulder.

After a while, he sniffs, lifting his head to look at me. "I love you."

Giving him a shaky smile, I simply nod and kiss his cheek. He frowns, brown eyes studying every inch of my face. I don't let him look too hard, whispering, "I don't want your pity, Felix." I've never needed or wanted that, only him.

A broken breath leaves him. "You don't have my pity. You have every fucking part of me."

My heart somersaults, my resolve crumbling. And as much as I want otherwise, it's probably time for him to go before we end up in one of the same positions we were in last night.

"I should get some sleep soon. Someone kept me up late last night." I try for a joke, rising from his lap.

He sees past it, trying to pull me back down, but I tug my hand free of his and step backward.

"Mags."

"No, Felix. I need …" I pause, laughing sadly. "I don't even know what I need."

"Me," he says resolutely. "You need me, and I need you. Like we always have."

"That's true, but I've also realized that I don't." I tilt my head, meeting his gaze when he stands. "Maybe we fell apart for a reason, Felix. I mean, think about it." I throw my hands out at my sides. "When has it ever been easy for us? Why has it always been so hard?"

His brows pull in. "That's the thing, Mags. It's easiest when it's just us. Sure, life complicates shit, but only if we let it."

"But we did, Felix. We let it. And it was effortless, the way we gave into it."

He steps closer, his voice lowering. "Don't say all this, please."

"You're not getting it, though." I draw in a slow breath then release it, not sure how to put it into words. "I love you. I'll probably always love you. But sometimes, it's just not enough. You left me, and I had to find out who I was without you, and the second I was discovering who that woman might be, you barged into my life again, which would've been okay, except for the fact that you tore any progress I'd made into irreparable pieces."

"I said I'm sorry. Look—"

"Stop!" I shout then freeze, afraid I've woken Archie. When I don't hear anything, I mumble, "Please, just go."

He doesn't move. "What about last night?"

"What about it?" I glance away.

He steps closer, crowding me against the wall. "What about it?" he rasps out. "What about the way I made you come three times on my cock and once on my tongue? What about *that?*"

My stomach quivers at the memory. "Felix—"

"What about the way you looked at me while I drove you crazy, huh? As if you'd finally found home again …"

"We can't—"

"Because that's what it felt like for me, Mags. It felt like I'd finally come home. Only now, you're saying you don't know if I'm welcome anymore, is that it?"

At a loss for words, I nod, my heart slamming against my ribcage as his breath fans over my cheek.

He nips the skin of my neck. "Wanna know what I think about that, Little Doe?"

I don't think I do, and I keep my mouth shut. His finger tilts my chin up, his lips resting over mine when he whispers harshly, "I think that's fucking bullshit."

He steps back, grabbing my blue box from the bed and leaving the room. With a sob trapped in my throat, I watch him go, listening to the sliding door close before sitting down on my bed and trying not to cry too loudly.

CHAPTER TWENTY-NINE

Felix

Running my palms down my face, I sit back, the old chair creaking loudly under my weight.

"Hey, you got that receipt for old Howey?"

Spying what Jared's after, I slide it over the desk. Snatching it up, he scans it before sticking those inquisitive green eyes on me. "How you doing?"

"Yeah, I've got no idea."

He nods. "And Maggie?"

I glance away because it's been a few days since I stormed out of her place with my heart in my throat. It's been lodged there ever since.

"The wedding's only weeks away, man. We kind of wanted the both of you there."

Dragging my eyes away from the boxes lining the side of the desk, I glare at him. "I know that, and you know I'll be there. It's just, she doesn't seem to know what she wants anymore." I snort then. "No, I fucking know what she wants. But I've …"

"Fucked it up royally?" he supplies.

I nod once, picking up a pen and squeezing it in my fist. "I want to be there for her, and it's wrecking me. But it's kind of hard to do that when she doesn't want me to."

Jared frowns, crossing his arms over his chest. "You don't have to be fucking her to be there for her, Felix." My jaw clenches in irritation and irrational anger. "That right there." He points at my face. "Cool it a little. Just keep being there for them. You guys are as permanent as the fucking grease stains on this floor. You've just gotta wear her down, reassure her you're in this for the right reasons and all that good shit."

"Right reasons?" I growl incredulously. "I fucking am!"

Raising his hands in the air, he chuckles. "All right, all right. You know that, and I know that, and deep down, she probably does, too." He shrugs. "Just gotta make her realize that."

He's right, which irritates the shit out of me. Chucking the pen to the table, I exhale loudly, trying to calm down. "If she'd just told me, though, things might've been different."

"Different, as in you landing your ass back in jail for breaking parole after beating those asshats half to death for what they did?" Jared asks. "And that's probably why she didn't tell you when you got out. So think about that for a hot minute before you prove her fears right."

"I know, fuck," I mutter. "But I was offered a fucking plea deal." Laughter escapes me, void of any humor. "And I told them to shove it up their ass."

"I know," Jared says. "But you're no rat, Felix."

"Then, no. Now? Well, now, I fucking wish I was." We're both quiet for a few beats, letting what might've been fill the tiny ass room we call an office. "She got hurt because of me, because of what I did. But what they did to her, Jared …" I trail off, my voice catching.

"Yeah." He sighs. "I'd wanna kill them, too. Hell, I *do* want to kill them. But what are the chances of finding them?" I look at him then, raising a brow in question. "You know they'd know you found out what happened by now."

"Yeah, figured as much."

"They're not the smartest pair, though." He snickers. "They'll still be lurking around somewhere. What're you going to do about Sam?"

My blood boils just hearing her name. "I don't think Maggie even knows about that. But what can I do?" I try to breathe through the anger. The guilt. *I fucking kissed that bitch.* Cursing again, I scrub my hands over my face. "I honestly never thought she'd do something that fucked up. What? Is it jealousy? Revenge?"

Jared studies me. "My guess is as good as yours, but you're right. There's not a lot you can do about it. And if you want answers, it's probably best to leave it until you cool off a little, yeah?"

He's got a point. I'd never hurt a woman, but fuck if I don't feel like I need to destroy something every time I think about what Sam's done.

"Anyway, let me know before you do anything reckless this time. You know how I like to be included." He winks and swaggers out into the garage.

Shaking my head, I look out the dirty window, wondering when my younger dipshit brother became the wise one out of us both.

Parking the truck in the driveway, I jump out and head to the door.

The front door this time.

Time to be more of a respectful asshole, it seems.

Warren answers it after I knock once, a curious smile on his face and his head tilted. "Well, well. Hey, dude. The side gate not working?"

Scratching at my head, I take a deep breath, letting my hand drop back to my side. "Actually, I came to see you and, um, Jake," I say with obvious uncertainty.

"Jake." Warren grins in affirmation. "He's at work, but it's your lucky day; you get me all to yourself." He steps back, opening the door wider.

Blinking at his statement, I shake my head and walk in, kicking off my boots and looking around the foyer again.

I don't know why I'm puzzled. The place resembles a bachelor pad, only with nicer shit and a few homely touches.

"Coffee, tea, beer?" Warren gestures for me to follow him to the kitchen. "I'm pegging you for a beer and spirits kind of guy. But"—he flicks on the coffeemaker—"being an ex-con and all, coffee it is."

"Coffee's fine." I lean against the wall in the doorway. "Thanks," I mumble.

He grins over his shoulder knowingly, then gets to work. "No sugar? Milk?"

"Milk, no sugar."

He sets them down on the counter a few minutes later, and I untuck a stool, taking a seat.

"So." He leans against the counter on the opposite side. "You know Maggie's home, right?" He smirks then. "She doesn't get out much."

"That have to do with what happened?" I ask.

He nods. "Yeah. She's getting more adventurous, though."

We drink our coffee in silence before I decide to get to the point of this visit. "About that, I want to know what happened. How she ended up here with you guys."

Warren frowns, putting down his mug. "I thought you knew what happened now?"

"I do."

"Right, you want the whole sordid tale, but you don't want to upset her by asking."

When I jerk my head in response, he scrubs a hand over the scruff on his jaw, staring sadly down at the counter. "I was watching the latest episode of *Game of Thrones* one night when Jake called me, saying I needed to get my ass to the hospital where he works. I was pissed; if you watch that show, you'd know why. Everything's a fucking cliffhanger. People are always dying."

Looking at me, he takes note of my furrowed brow and chuckles. "Don't guess you do, then. We'll have to do something about that. So I get to the hospital and meet Jake. He tells me about this woman who'd been brought in a few nights before." He swallows, glancing out the window. "It was bad."

"How bad?" My voice is a husk.

He looks back at me, his eyes watery, but I nod, indicating I can handle it. "She was …" He inhales deeply, waits a few seconds that seem to make my heart drip with anguish, then croaks, "She was so broken. I'd never seen someone so black and blue. Her face." He closes his eyes. "Swollen, and her hair still matted with dried blood."

Fuck. My own eyes close, and I try to keep my shit together.

He continues in a rush as if he's afraid of the memory. "Her arm already had a cast when I met her, but she could hardly move, thanks to some broken ribs. Jake said it was a fucking miracle she survived, let alone Archie. She had some bleeding on her brain, which apparently came from a kick to the head."

I scoot the stool back, my coffee almost tipping over. "Down the hall, to the right," Warren says.

Stumbling into the washroom, I don't even make it to the toilet, but thankfully, I make it to the sink, retching and feeling like I couldn't hate myself any more than I do right now.

Getting my shit together, I rinse the sink and my mouth out, swallow my guilt and the mounting anger that's bursting to be set free, and return to my seat in the kitchen.

Warren's drinking his coffee, watching me with remorse-filled eyes.

I take a sip of my own, not trusting it to stay down but needing to fill my taste buds with anything other than the bitterness and sorrow currently residing there.

"Jake told me what he knew. Said she'd been found in an alleyway in the city. She remembers leaving work and stopping to buy some milk or something from the convenience store before she was cornered at her car. He'd overheard her parents arguing in the hall outside the hospital room, realized she was on her own, and called me."

Sniffing and trying to blink the tears back, I wrap my hands around my mug, staring at the liquid inside. "So that's it? You two just decided to be her knights in shining armor?"

Warren chuckles. "I worded it a bit differently than that, but yes. We had a chat and both agreed to help her out for a little while. Only, we had no idea of the struggles she'd yet to face, no idea about you, or that we'd grow to love her so much. And that boy …" Warren smiles at me, but it quickly turns into a menacing grin. "Whatever happens, don't even think about trying to keep them from us. You may be big, hulk man, but don't think that just because I married a guy I can't give you a run for your money."

Trying not to smirk, I simply nod my head and take another sip of coffee. "Noted. And thank you. For taking them in … for helping them."

He shrugs, as if it's nothing, and I stiffen when I hear the back door open behind me. "Warren?" Maggie's voice, soft and sweet, travels into my ears and helps to soothe some of the rage embedded in my heart.

She walks into the kitchen, Archie running in and smacking into Warren's legs. "There you are. Have you seen …" She trails off when she finally notices me sitting here.

"Ah, hey." She looks back and forth between Warren and me, her button nose scrunching in confusion, just asking for me to kiss it.

"He came to see me." Warren jabs his thumb at his chest, then leans down to pick up Archie. "Sorry, bunches."

She looks even more confused now, turning to me with questions filling her eyes.

"What did you need, bunches?" Warren puts Archie down when he starts squawking, and he runs over to me.

Smiling at his waddling, jean-clad legs, I reach down and scoop him up, smacking a loud kiss on his cheek. He giggles. "Bub, ba, bub."

Tiny fingers yank on my beard, which stings, but I let him do it anyway.

Maggie peels her eyes from me and finally answers Warren. "Have you got that pump? I was going to set up the mini jumping castle for Archie while the weather's still nice."

Warren exits the kitchen, and Maggie starts to fidget with her hands and bite her lip. She's nervous, which I hate, but I'm just glad to be setting my eyes on her. I can't stop looking, scanning every inch of her as if to reassure myself that she's all in

230 | ELLA FIELDS

one piece. That she's not that bruised and broken girl I'd been reading about, and that Warren was just telling me about.

Her auburn hair is up in a messy bun on top of her head, and she's wearing a green sundress, no shoes on her feet and her toenails painted yellow.

But I know beneath that beautiful exterior, the damage is still there. Healing, but still there.

Standing, I take the pump from Warren when he returns. "Where is it?" I ask Maggie.

Her teeth release their hold on her lip; her eyes bugging out in that way that still makes my dick jump and my heart inflate. "Oh, outside on the grass."

I follow her out, waving in thanks to Warren and closing the door on his grinning face.

She's already rolled it out, so I put Archie down and plug the pump in, holding it there and watching the brightly colored rubber fill with air and morph into a tiny castle. You couldn't fit many kids on it, but Archie loses his shit, squealing, crawling, jumping, and falling over as if it's the best thing that's ever happened to him.

I take a seat on the grass in front of it, ready in case he comes flying out, and watch him.

Maggie sits beside me, and it takes all my restraint not to reach over and tuck away a loose tendril of her hair that's escaped.

She does it herself as if she knows what I'm thinking. Maybe she does. "Why'd you come to see Warren?"

Shrugging, I simply say, "Guy talk. Nothing to worry about."

Maggie laughs, and my chest fills with triumph at hearing it. "Right," she says with a hint of sarcasm before sighing loudly. "Well, hopefully this will tire him out. He's supposed to be napping, but he had other ideas."

Archie rolls over, smiling and squinting at the sun, before rolling continuously around, making himself laugh. "I think it's a safe bet."

We're quiet for a while, but I don't want to force it, so I wait.

Finally, she says, "I didn't know when you might be back, not after …"

She doesn't finish, but I get what she's not saying. "I'll always be back. Whether you want me or not."

"Why?" She seems genuinely perplexed as if she thought I'd be angry. And I am, just not at her.

"Because you two are my heart, and I can't live without my heart."

I look over at her when she doesn't respond, finding glassy brown eyes staring back at me.

"Despite everything life tossed our way, we worked for a reason, Mags."

She blinks, her dark lashes drawing my eyes like fluttering sirens. "What reason is that?"

"Because at the very foundation of it all, we had a deep understanding of each other. We were friends."

"Friends who were in love," she murmurs, looking back at Archie.

"And that's the kind that lasts. No matter how much shit you throw at it. It endures; it survives."

"So much has happened, though, Felix."

"Yet we still love, and you've survived, and I'll endure whatever else I need to."

I grab her hand, bringing it to my lips and kissing the tops of her folded fingers.

"You're saying you want to be friends?"

"We already are, always have been. What I'm saying is that I'm here, and I'll continue to be, no matter what happens."

I let her take her hand back, returning my attention to Archie and hoping like hell that one day, she decides I'm worth forgiving and taking a chance on again.

CHAPTER THIRTY

Maggie

Folding the lids on the ice-cream containers, I put them back on the shelf in the storeroom before heading to the table and wiping up all the stray Play-Doh crumbs and globs.

"Hey, Maggie," one of the girls, Vanessa, I think, says on her way to the door. "Shouldn't you be heading out now?"

Chucking the wipes into the trash, I then tuck all the little chairs back under the table and move to the sink to wash my hands. "Yeah, I'm going now."

"'Kay, see you tomorrow." Vanessa waves, and I dry my hands, smiling and giving a small wave back.

Today's my first official day working at Bonnets Bay pre-school, and so far, so good. It probably helps that I still remember most of the employees from when I did my work experience here a few months ago. Still, it's new, kind of scary, but really not that hard. They've accepted me and welcomed

Archie with smiles and encouraging words, which makes me think I've ended up in the perfect place to start my transition back into the real world.

I clock out in the staff room, grab my bag, and make my way to the nursery, where I find Archie trying to stand on his head.

Belinda, the nursery teacher, smiles at me when I close the door behind me. "He's been trying to do that for the past five minutes. Laughs his head off when he stands back up and discovers he's all dizzy."

"That doesn't surprise me at all." I smirk.

Archie stands, indeed laughing and swaying, then notices me and toddles over, "Ma, ma!"

Kneeling, I wrap my arms around him. "Hey, baby boy." I kiss his head. "Ready to go?" Standing, I walk over to Belinda, signing him out and thanking her. "Say goodbye," I tell Archie.

He waves, and Belinda grins, waving back. "Bye, cutie."

I grab his stroller from the front entry and strap him in. Home is only a fifteen-minute walk away, and as much as it worries me, I want to make walking to and from work a habit. I'll save on gas and hopefully rebuild more of my confidence.

After shoving my bag under the stroller, I push the door open, surprised when someone holds it open for me. I glance up, about to thank them, and meet a pair of brown eyes I'd recognize in any life.

"What ...?" I laugh shakily, stunned he's standing in front of me. "What are you doing here?"

Warren was supposed to meet me, said he'd walk me the first few days or until I was okay doing it on my own. It's only just after five, which means Felix left work early to be here.

"Thought I'd see how things went today for you guys."

Oh. I move the stroller through the door and down the

ramp. He opens the gate for me and we walk out into the parking lot. "Aren't you busy, though? With work?"

He's come over every night this week when he's finished at the garage. We eat dinner together, then he baths Archie and puts him to bed before leaving. And even though I know he wants to stay, he never pushes it.

Felix shrugs, halting the stroller on the sidewalk out front and bending down to say hello to Archie. "This is more important. Isn't it, little man?" After kissing a gurgling Archie, he straightens, adjusting the canopy of the stroller and holds out a little box wrapped in brown paper. "I got you something."

Puzzled, I kick the brake down on the stroller and slowly reach out to take it. Unwrapping it, I find a white mug inside the box. I carefully tug it out, laughing softly at the picture of a green cat in a garden pot. It says 'Catcus' underneath.

After putting it back in the box, I tuck it in the storage under the stroller as Felix says, "It's not much, but I thought you could use it when you take a coffee break or whatever."

Without even thinking, I throw my arms around his shoulders, hugging him tightly. He freezes, then his arms slowly wind around me, squeezing me to him even tighter. "Thank you," I whisper, inhaling his scent and letting myself forget for just a few blissful moments.

He seems to be doing the same as his nose burrows into my hair.

Archie cries out behind me, and we break apart to continue walking down the sidewalk.

Turning onto the next street, Felix asks, "So how was it? Your first day?"

"Really good. I did my work experience there when I was studying, and so I knew most people and some of the kids already."

Felix kicks a rock with his booted foot. "I guess that would help, huh?"

"It does, a lot. But I don't know … it just feels good anyway. To be doing something normal."

"What? Working?" he asks.

"Yeah." We turn down the next street. "To feel like a functioning part of the world again, even if it is only in a small way."

Felix is silent for a long while, and I glance over at him while we wait for a car to pass before crossing the street. He's tucked his hands into his pockets, and his brows have lowered. "You aren't paying rent."

Blushing, I look away as we continue down the long road that runs parallel to the bay and leads to Warren and Jake's house. "No," I admit. "At first, I used to clean for them. Try to pay them back in any way I could. They humored me for a while, then they started getting pissed off about it. But I still help out when I can."

Felix huffs. "Like when they aren't around to catch you?"

He knows me too well, so I just shrug.

Sighing, he asks, "What about money, though? How do you get by?"

Yeah, this isn't something I'm proud of or necessarily want to have to tell him. But I think the time for keeping secrets, no matter how small, is over. "They made a separate account for me. It's got so much money in it, it's ridiculous. But I don't use it much. Only when we need groceries or medicine, stuff like that."

"Shit, Mags."

"I know." I chew my lip, feeling wretched.

"No." He stops me right out front of their house with a hand on my arm. "I mean, you need to start letting me do that stuff. I know they want to help, or they wouldn't be doing it, but it's my job, my responsibility." His eyes are hard, his jaw clenching.

I want to argue and tell him that now I've got a job—albeit with not a lot of money coming my way, but some—I can take care of myself. I don't say any of that, though. This is about more than just his pride. It's about more than him feeling jilted by two other males protecting me.

I know it's not that at all. He genuinely feels like he's not doing something he needs to. Like he's letting us down again. And I know that must make him feel like shit. "Okay," I say.

He blanches. "What, okay?"

I try not to laugh, moving the stroller over the grass to the side gate. "That's what I said, big guy."

The sound of his boots sinking into the grass follows me as he jogs over to open the gate for us to walk in. Once we reach the guest house, Warren comes outside, walking over to us with a huge smile on his face and his arms spread open wide. "She made it back alive! Huzzah!"

Archie, of course, thinks he's hilarious, kicking his legs and arms out and squealing in response. Warren gets him out of the stroller, holding him above his head then lowering him to his chest and adjusting Archie's blue shirt. "How was my little dude?"

"Good. Didn't miss any of us, not even a little bit." I push the stroller underneath the small awning near the door and kick the brake down.

Warren pouts at Archie. "She's lying, isn't she?" Archie grabs his nose, and Warren makes a honking sound, so Archie squeezes it again and again.

Rolling my eyes, I turn my own nose into the air. "Never mind me, I'll just be going then."

"Ohhh, somebody's jealous," Warren whispers loudly.

Laughing, I grab my bag and walk inside, gesturing for Felix to follow. He doesn't; instead, he talks to Warren for a minute while I unpack my bag then get some pasta, sauce, and meat out to get started on dinner.

I'm halfway through cooking when Felix steps inside with Archie, kicking off his boots and putting him down. Archie runs to the fridge, slapping it with his hand. "Mik! Ta, ta."

"Not yet, baby. Dinner soon, then milk."

He doesn't like that; his bottom lip bulges, and his pudgy little face scrunches. Felix scoops him up, roaring like a dinosaur and swinging him into the air as he walks off. He turns the TV on, and I listen to them play while I finish dinner.

Once it's ready, I place Felix's plate down on the coffee table and put Archie in his chair, getting his bowl of spaghetti and putting it on the tray.

"I'll do it. You eat." Felix goes to get up, but I shake my head and move the high chair closer to the couch as I sit down.

"It's okay; he'll feed himself most of this." Felix is always feeding Archie before he eats. I feed Archie some meat and eat my own while he demolishes his pasta.

I'm getting Archie's bath ready when I hear Felix let out a loud laugh. "He's even got pasta in his diaper."

"He's good at getting food in all sorts of random places. Couch cushions, beds, bags. One time, in a hurry, I put my bare foot into my sneaker, only to feel something squish between my toes."

Felix cringes, picking up naked Archie from the changing table and taking him to the bath. "A grape?"

I laugh, leaning against the bathroom door. "I wish."

He puts Archie in the water and starts cleaning the pasta residue from his hair. "Melon?"

"Nope."

Felix hums. "Cracker?"

"No. Though I do find those between the couch cushions a lot."

He snorts then pauses, looking over his shoulder at me with a look of disgust. "Oh, hell. Was it banana?"

Grinning, I nod, and he shakes his head, staring back at Archie. "Not cool, little man, not cool."

"It kind of reminded me of that time Jared came home after his twenty-first, ordered six pizzas, and forgot where he left one of them."

Felix tips onto his ass, laughing, and Archie stares at him in awe. "He woke up the next morning thinking he took some chick's virginity when he found pizza sauce all over his sheets."

We both laugh at the memory of Jared's hungover, horrified expression. "He was so worried, saying he didn't even remember bringing someone home, let alone taking their virginity," I say with my eyes watering. "And what did you say again?"

Felix rises back onto his knees, looking at me over his shoulder while Archie sucks on Felix's hand. "That the only thing he brought home was half a dozen pizzas."

Our eyes stay glued, Felix's lips slightly parted.

I break the moment by adding, "He was so relieved but also pissed off that he wasted a whole pizza he could've had for breakfast."

He shakes his head, laughing under his breath and turning back to Archie to finish washing him. "Should buy the kid a pizza as a joke for his wedding present."

"Not a bad idea." With my lip between my teeth, I leave the bathroom when Felix lifts Archie from the tub to the towel to dry him. I grab his pajamas, a pair of sleep shorts and a matching t-shirt with tools all over them.

Felix smiles when he sees them. "Is it weird that I want to

go shopping and buy him some more cool outfits?" He shakes his head, securing the tabs of Archie's diaper and squeezing his chunky thighs while grinning down at him. "Daddy hates shopping," he tells him. Archie tries to steal his legs back, but Felix gently shoves them into his shorts first.

"Not at all." I smirk. "Warren will happily take you."

Felix scowls at me, and I grin, leaving the room to get Archie's milk for him.

I'm cleaning up when Felix walks out of Archie's room ten minutes later. "Sound asleep. Barely got through half." He tips the rest of the milk out in the sink next to me. His arm touches mine for all of a second, but it feels like minutes as I try to concentrate on drying the plates and putting the last of the silverware away.

Clearing my throat, I mutter, "Big day, I guess."

I take the sippy cup and wash it out, putting it on the dish rack to dry and then wipe my hands. "I need to take a shower."

Felix's head snaps over to me from where he's standing behind the couch, watching the news on the TV. "Hmmm?"

Smirking, I repeat, "I'm going to take a shower."

"Shit, right. I'll catch you tomorrow then." He rubs his hand over the back of his head, moving to the door.

It's not a question but a statement. And I know with a certainty that both excites and troubles my heart that he will be back tomorrow and every day after.

"I was going to, ah, watch the newest Quentin Tarantino movie." I shift, stepping backward toward the bathroom, not sure why I said that.

Felix raises his brows. "Your roundabout way of saying I'm welcome to stay and watch, too, Little Doe?"

Trying not to let those two words sink too far under my skin, I shrug and head to the bedroom to get my pajamas out.

I can hear him chuckling quietly as I go and could almost kick myself as I step into the shower. I have no idea what I'm doing.

All I know is that I don't want him to go yet.

I never want him to go, but want and need are two different things, and I'm finding it almost impossible to stop them from blurring together.

After I'm done, I toss my hair up into a bun and take a seat beside Felix on the couch as he scrolls through the movie options and finds the one we're looking for.

We watch in silence, and when he moves my feet to his lap and starts rubbing, I don't protest or move them away. It feels too damn good, and my eyes are starting to feel too heavy.

"Will you go with me to the wedding?" Felix asks after a little while.

No preamble, no beating around the bush—that's not his style. I drag my eyes from the TV, blinking lazily at him. "Jared's?"

He's staring at me, his head resting against the couch. "Don't know anyone else who's getting married, unless you do?"

I nudge his thigh with my toes, and he groans. "Careful, Little Doe. Unless of course, you want a repeat of last week on this couch?" He tugs his bottom lip into his mouth, eyes heating.

My stomach quivers, and my thighs clench. I look away, knowing I'll be underneath him in two seconds flat if I don't. "You really want me to go to the wedding with you?"

He squeezes my foot. "Yeah. As friends."

"As friends," I repeat, still not looking at him. "Okay."

Sexual tension fills the small room—thick, heavy, and entirely unwelcome—but after five minutes, I'm finally able to concentrate on the movie.

I don't know how much of it I actually watch before I pass out, but sometime later, my eyes open, gazing up at Felix as he lays me down on my bed. He stares at me for a punishing heartbeat and smooths the tendrils of hair from my face. Whispering that he'll lock the door behind him, he leaves me with a tender kiss to my forehead before I have the chance to beg him to stay.

CHAPTER THIRTY-ONE

Felix

I lean forward to shake the man's hand. "Felix."

"Steve." His grip is firm, his eyes scanning.

Releasing his hand, I turn back to the small, wooden house. "How many bedrooms?"

He steps forward, gesturing for me to follow him inside. "Why don't I show you instead? It…" He pauses once he reaches the small porch. "Well, it needs a bit of work, as you can no doubt see."

I know that much, but I've been driving past this place for weeks on the way out of the Bay from Maggie's, so I couldn't help but notice the sign out front, advertising it for lease. The boards creak and groan when I reach the porch. They're weathered but not too bad. Just loose.

I follow Steve inside once he gets the door open, stopping in the doorway to take in the small, open plan living room, kitchen, and tiny nook for a dining table. The floorboards in here could do with some love, too, but the rustic look adds to the charm of the place.

"The bedrooms are down here," he says, standing by the end of the short hallway. "Bathroom and separate toilet."

I slide by him, continuing down the hall to take in the bathroom and toilet, which are old but not covered in mold, so that's a plus. Walking a few steps farther, I stop in front of a tiny room. "That's an office, but the last woman who lived here used it as a nursery."

"You can tell," I murmur absently, taking in the soft blue of the painted walls.

Moving on, I find another slightly bigger room with a closet, and lastly, the room at the end of the hallway. It's not much bigger than the one I have at home, but as I look around, I can see it. Our bed, Maggie's books and knickknacks on the deep window sill. My shoes tossed on the floor by the bed. The dresser and TV sitting at the end of the bed.

Peering out the window, I notice there's even a small shed and a fenced-in, level yard.

"How much?" I spin around and walk back out to the living room where we discuss numbers. The place is dirt cheap, considering it's across the street from the bay.

"I'll take it." I tuck my hand into my pocket, pulling out the envelope of cash I brought with me, the same one I'd tried to give Maggie.

Steve shakes his head. "It's got some issues, and for the price it is, I don't want to hear about it."

"Like what?"

He starts listing things. Leaky taps, rusted drain pipes, peeling paint on the back of the toilet door, missing screens on the windows, loose floorboards inside and on the deck, a couple of missing locks. He goes on a bit longer, but I cut him off because it's nothing too major.

"I'm an ex-con, but I'm willing to fix all that shit for you." His eyes widen, and I hurry to say, "I won't cause any trouble. I have a business to run and just want a place for my family to call our own."

Steve eyes me up and down, the lines on his face smoothing out when he shrugs, shoving his hands into his trouser pockets. "How about we give you a three-month trial of sorts, hmm? Any trouble, you're out, and I keep my deposit. Sound fair?"

Not exactly, but I agree and hand over a month's worth of rent before giving him my details and signing a contract that he grabs from his car.

He leaves ten minutes later, handing me the keys and speeding off down the street in his Porsche.

Taking my phone out of my pocket, I call Jared. "Yo."

"You using the truck this afternoon?" This truck sharing business should've ended years ago.

"Nah. Where are you?"

"Just about to leave Bonnets Bay. Gotta pick up some shit from the hardware store."

Jared pauses. "This got anything to do with why you left work early again? What are you doing?"

Something I should've done years ago. "You'll see. Meet me out front in twenty."

The sound of him dropping a tool reaches my ear. "Shit, you do remember I'm getting married next weekend, yeah?"

Fuck me, he's more obsessed with this wedding than his soon-to-be wife.

After locking the front door, I jump down the steps of the porch, walking to my bike. "Not like you'd let me forget."

He groans. "You can't get me into any shit. The timing's all wrong, man."

"Find your balls, kid, then meet me out front."

I hang up and swing a leg over my bike, taking one last look at the little brown cottage before leaving the Bay.

CHAPTER THIRTY-TWO

Maggie

"Cute mug," Vanessa says on our lunch break the next day.

I take a sip, putting it down on the coffee table in the staff room and stare at it. "Thanks. It was a gift."

Maybe it's the tenor of my voice, but something has her asking, "From that big, sexy bearded dude who showed up here yesterday afternoon?"

My eyes dart to her smug face. She shrugs, shoving a forkful of salad into her mouth before mumbling around it. "Can't help but notice." She swallows the food. "The guy's kind of hard to miss."

Chewing on the inside of my lip, I then let myself smile. "Yeah, it's from him."

"Baby daddy? Husband? Boyfriend?" she asks.

"Uh." I cough a bit. "He's Archie's dad, yes. It's a little hard to ex—"

The door to the staff room bursts open, thankfully stopping me from spilling any more information about my confusing life. "Ness, you're needed back. You'll have to take ten later," Belinda says.

"What?" Vanessa scowls. "How come?"

"Keira's just phoned through to our room. They need you to go help outside 'cause she's going home sick."

"She's always freaking sick," Vanessa grumbles, getting up and shoving her salad in the fridge. "Tell her to give me two minutes so I can at least use the dang toilet, and that maybe she needs to take a multivitamin or swallow some cement."

Trying not to laugh, I meet Belinda's gaze, and she mouths, "So dramatic."

Vanessa storms out a minute later, still grumbling, and I finish my tea before heading back to my room to start the afternoon activities.

Strapping Archie into the stroller, I try not to get my hopes up when it's time to go, but damn it, they are well and truly up because my shoulders almost slump down to the wooden ramp when I walk out and find no sign of Felix. He needs to work, I know that, and I need to sort out this mess called my feelings. I shouldn't be feeling this way. Except I am.

"Don't look too disappointed, bunches. One might think you don't love me the most anymore." Warren twists his lips into a pout as I approach him.

"I'm being stupid. Ignore me," I mutter.

We discuss how our days were on the way home, but I still can't curb this niggling feeling of disappointment that's unfurled in an unexpectedly big way.

"Jake's home. Come have a coffee with us. I know he wants to hear about how you've been doing."

"Okay, I'll just change Archie first."

Heading inside, my eyes flick over the money and note Felix left on my kitchen counter when I walk by it to Archie's room. It simply says to buy a dress, but I'm pretty sure I don't need five hundred dollars to do that.

When I'm done, I head over to the house and walk right inside, putting Archie on the floor and looking up to find Jake and Warren making out like they're completely alone and don't hear my son babbling.

I clear my throat and sit down on a stool. "Don't stop on our account or anything, sheesh."

Jake steps back, and Warren grins, puckering his lips at me. "Don't hate on him 'cause you ain't him."

Jake scowls at him. "You have that all backward."

"I could say many, many things in response to that, but"—Warren jumps down from the counter—"we're now in the presence of little baby ears and a blushing redhead." He shrugs, grabbing an apple from the fruit bowl and taking a bite.

Jake steps over to Archie, lifting him up and smiling when Archie smacks his stubble-coated cheek.

"Speaking of blushing." Jake arches a brow at me.

Warren gasps. "Yes! Do tell Miss Smile and Sulk a lot. What's the dish with the big, burly baby daddy?"

Trying not to laugh, I grumble, "I'm not sulking."

"Bullshit," Warren says with a cough and starts making coffee.

"Why would she be sulking?" Jake asks.

"She's sulking because the hulk didn't show up today. She got stuck with me instead."

Scowling at Warren's back, I hiss, "Am not."

Jake frowns. "He was going to pick you up from work?"

"No," Warren says, adding milk to my mug and bringing

it over. "He did yesterday, though. Being all sweet and stuff."

"Sweet?" Jake asks, perplexed, his eyes bouncing back and forth between Warren and me.

"It's nothing."

"Sure, sure." Warren waggles his brows.

Sighing, I admit, "Well, um, he did ask me to go to Jared's wedding with him."

"Shut the front door." Warren gasps, slapping Jake in the arm. "You said yes? You're giving him another chance?"

Jake glowers at me, and it's hard not to feel like a child scolded under his heavy gaze. "Not exactly ..."

"What does that mean?" Jake asks, tone firm.

Archie squeals and smacks his cheek again. Warren laughs under his breath.

"It means I said I'd go as friends."

"*Friends?*" Jake says the word like it's a foreign concept.

"Yes. *Friends.*"

Warren mutters what sounds like, "Bullshit," again, then walks over to me, undoing my ponytail and running his fingers through my hair as he asks, "When is it? We'll be here to babysit, of course, won't we?" His tone turns guttural on those last words. I can just picture him sending Jake a knowing look.

Jake sighs. "Of course. Always. But I don't know ..."

"Shush," Warren hisses. "She's a grown woman, and she can figure out what to do with all *that* ... on her own."

But can I? It's proving rather hard to figure out, or maybe it's too easy. All I know is the bruising to my confidence and heart feel like they're slowly fading and healing faster whenever Felix is around.

It's when he's gone that everything feels like it's on pause again.

And that's what unsettles me the most.

Later that night, I'm lying in bed, staring at the screen of my phone.

Felix never showed, and he didn't call.

I'm trying not to let that fact make waves out of puddles. But I've learned in order to feel in control, I need to take some control back in my life.

And so I'm pondering whether to text him.

The problem with that is, Felix isn't usually one for texting. He'd rather just call someone and get it over with.

I think in all the years we were together, after I'd moved in with him, I could count on one hand how many times he ever sent me a text.

And it was usually just to say he was pissed that I wasn't answering my phone.

I smirk at the memory, and my thumb hits call.

He answers after five rings. "Mags? Shit, what time is it?"

Something loud clangs in the background, and he curses again.

"It's almost ten o'clock. Everything okay?"

"Christ, I'm sorry. I was meant to call you but just got … side-tracked."

He sounds pissed off with himself, and my worry fades. "You're still at work?"

"Uh, yeah. I am." Pausing, he then asks, "How's the little man?"

"Good, he went to sleep pretty early. Another big day for him."

He hums. "And how was it? Your second day?"

"Great. I'm exhausted, yet strangely, I can't sleep."

"That a problem you normally have?" More noise reaches my ear, clattering and shuffling.

"Sometimes."

"Sometimes?" He huffs. "Be honest, Mags."

Hesitating for a few seconds, I then admit, "Okay, more often than not. It's getting better, though."

"Want me to come over?" He then rushes to say, "Vera and Jared are doing my head in with this wedding shit. You'd be doing me a favor."

That makes me suck back a laugh. He's never been any good at playing coy. I think about it for a moment, listening to the sounds he's continuing to make in the background.

"I'll unlock the door for you," I finally tell him, hanging up before I lose my nerve and getting up to make sure it is unlocked.

He shows up not even fifteen minutes later, but I don't question how quick he got here because I'm too busy watching him remove his shirt and jeans in the doorway.

"You're welcome to take a shower," I whisper, and he startles, obviously not realizing I was still awake. I can just make out his nod in the shadows of the room.

I listen as the water turns on, waiting with my breath quickening each minute until he walks back into the room in only a towel. "My clothes are filthy; I didn't even think about that."

"It's fine."

"I'll sleep on the couch." He drops the towel and tugs on his boxer briefs over his thick thighs, turning to go.

"You don't have to."

He freezes in the doorway then slowly turns around and walks over to the other side of the bed. Pulling the covers back, he climbs in, and I roll over to face the wall. Not wanting to be tempted to do something I'm not entirely sure I'm ready for again.

I can smell my soap on his skin, but I can also detect the faint smell of paint.

His arm moves around my waist, and he pulls me back into his hard body. I don't fuss, since it's where I want to be. And even though I can feel him hard against my ass, he doesn't do anything about it.

He just holds me and murmurs into my hair, "Sleep, Little Doe."

And for some reason, that makes me feel more at ease and closer to him than ever before.

Waking up to crying with a heavy arm wrapped tight around my waist, I hear Felix say, "Sleep, I've got him."

Archie's cries stop a few seconds later, and I happily welcome sleep's embrace again.

Later that morning, I take a shower and head out to the living room, finding Archie lying on Felix's bare chest on the couch, sucking his thumb while Felix stares at the TV.

He looks tired; they both do.

"Hey." I take a seat on the arm of the couch, trying to keep my eyes from staying locked on his chest. He's always been muscular, but now, well, it's all just rather distracting. Those huge arms and the wider chest that tapers to a slim, defined waist. And with him holding our baby? Yeah, I think my ovaries are singing.

"Hey." Felix smirks when he finds me watching.

"He been okay?" I nod my head at Archie.

"A little grumpy, but happy when I'm holding him. I think he's just tired. Lots of eye rubbing and thumb sucking."

I tilt my head, looking at our boy. His face is smooshed into Felix's pec, his brown eyes struggling to stay open. "It's only two days a week, but I suppose it's still quite an adjustment for him."

Felix gently smooths his hand over Archie's rump and back. Archie sucks his thumb and closes his eyes contentedly in response. "He's still so little. I'm guessing it'll take a while."

I agree and ask, "Coffee?"

He shakes his head. "I don't want to move him. Kind of tired myself, if I'm being honest."

"Then stay where you are; I'm going to get some laundry sorted."

Felix nods then says as I'm getting up, "You slept well last night?"

I'm glad my back is facing him, because yes, I did sleep well last night. He knows it, too. I'm saved from answering when Jake knocks on the door.

He opens it when he sees me standing here. "Maggie, some woman is at the house. Says her name is Elodie?" He pauses when he notices Felix behind me, then brings his gaze back to me. "I recognize her. From ah …"

"The hospital," I supply, smiling weakly. "It's okay, but what is she doing here?" I mumble more to myself than anyone else.

Jake answers anyway, "She's asking for you. I'd turn her away after all that's happened but…"

"What?" I breathe, worried now.

"She's got a black eye."

My next breath stalls. He presses a hand over my shoulder to halt my advance as I try to steamroll past him. "Let me just say that she's the happiest woman with a black eye that I've ever seen."

What the ...?

Needing to see what's going on for myself, I look back at Felix, who just waves a hand at me, his dark brows furrowed. "Go. I'll be here with him."

I find Warren sitting with my mom in their front living room, having tea and talking animatedly.

Right, okay.

"Mom?"

She gasps, her brown eyes glowing when they land on me. "Ma chérie, come to me, come to me." She gets up off the couch, rushing over to squeeze me in a hug, swaying me from side to side before taking my face in her hands. "Beautiful girl. The world has not changed that."

Stepping back, I ask, "What are you doing here?"

Hurt moves over her softly lined face, but then it's gone, and she's smiling again. I reach up hesitantly, about to touch her bruised eye, but then drop my hand back to my side. "What happened to you? Did Dad do this?" I point at it.

She sucks her lips for a moment, then looks at Warren. "Ah, there is lots to tell you, Magdaline."

Warren excuses himself, squeezing my arm on his way out of the room. Mom tugs me over to the couch, keeping my hand in hers. "Where is your boy?"

"He's sleeping," I say, not wanting to explain that right now when I want to know what's happened with her instead.

She nods. "I keep his picture with me everywhere I go."

"Your face, Mom. What's going on?"

She glances out the front window for a moment. "I've left your father. It was time."

I'd like to say I'm shocked except I'm not. Just relieved. "It was time years ago, but still, I'm glad." I squeeze her hand. "If you're okay?"

"Oh, I'll be fine. And I know you think that, but I just was not ready."

When I frown at her, she smiles softly. "It was something I needed to learn how to do in my own time. I was scared, yes, but I was also comfortable with the life we had made. Comfort brings strings that don't like to untie themselves just because you know something is wrong."

I blink, stunned; my heart hurting for her even though she has let me down significantly. "What made those strings finally come loose?"

She looks at me for a moment, then points at her face. "This is the second time. I'd always told myself that if he were to ever raise a hand to me, I'd finally leave. It had to happen twice before I did, which I'm not proud of, but …"

"You've done it now, though." I smile shakily at her. "That's the important part." I used to think this woman was weak. Now that I know what it is to try to be strong, to search for any crumb of strength at all, I realize that maybe I was wrong.

"Yes." She smiles, too, and I see the freedom dancing in her eyes. A spark that was never there before. "I've just moved into a filthy apartment south of the city. It has mice and roaches. And you know what? It still makes me very happy."

"What are you doing about the bakery?" I know my father; he's not the type to give anything away.

She waves her free hand dismissively. "He can have it. I've been saving ever since you moved out." She leans closer, whispering, "And I'll find a job by next week. I'm a fucking great cook."

I blanch, having never heard my mother swear before—not in English—then laugh. She laughs with me, and it's hard to remember the last time we were ever able to do so.

"Will he come for you?" My question sobers us as terror strikes my blood cold while I look at her bruised eye.

"Doubtful. He was more worried about his ego and his belongings." She sighs. "Enough about me. How are you doing?"

"Good. I've got a new job myself, and things have been a bit busy."

"I must admit, I was surprised when you finally told me you were here, living in the Bay. That nice man, Warren? He tells me that your Felix is back now?" She frowns with obvious concern.

"He is, yes."

She studies me for a long beat. "You're together still? He is treating you well?" She looks around. "Why are you still here then?"

"We're not together, not exactly." I don't know how to explain, or if I even should. "But he's been here, helping, and he loves Archie."

"Oh, I bet. But why are you not with him? What has happened?"

Swinging my gaze to the black entertainment unit, I rack my brain for what to say. "He wasn't happy. No." A laugh sputters out of me. "He was so mad that I didn't go see him when he was in jail. That I didn't take Archie to see him, mostly."

She hums quietly, and I look back at her. "Understandable. But did he know? What happened to you?"

I shake my head, and she hisses, "Magdaline. You did not tell him? Write him letters or call him?"

I don't know why I'm admitting all this to her, but despite how long it's been, my mom has always been able to get me to talk. One concerned look and all my troubles come rushing out of my mouth. Time moves on, but some things never change.

Drawing air in through my nose, I hold it in my lungs for a moment, then slowly release it. "I didn't know where he was, and when I found out ... I tried, Mom." I fall back into the couch cushions. "You have no idea how hard I tried. But once I felt like I might be able to do it ..."

"You were afraid for very different reasons," she finishes softly, and I nod.

She brings my hand to her mouth, kissing it then holding it in her lap. "So he forgives you now?"

"I'm not sure. I think so?" I run my other hand through my hair. "It took a few weeks for him to finally find out what happened. I didn't want to tell him and have him end up in trouble again with that temper of his. But ... before he found out, he hated me." I shake my head again, tears filling my eyes. "It was terrible. And I don't even blame him for feeling that way, which is what makes it so confusing."

"He hurt you?"

"No." My eyes widen. "At least, not physically."

She nods slowly, sadness filling her eyes as they look into mine. "I see. Now he's trying to make up for it?"

"I guess, yeah. I just don't know what I should do."

"What do you want to do?" she asks.

"I want to be strong on my own again. I want to live without feeling worried or afraid."

She doesn't say anything for a long minute, then pats my hand. "In you, I find strength. And it's perfectly okay to find your strength in other people. As long as you know you can find it without them, too."

CHAPTER THIRTY-THREE

Maggie

"You look …" Felix blows out a loud breath, his cheeks puffing out. "Fucking incredible."

I shift, my own cheeks burning, and adjust the green gown Warren took me shopping to buy yesterday. It was really last minute, but it was fun to try on all sorts of beautiful dresses.

"It was a hundred and twenty dollars. On sale." I give him a pointed look. "I've left the change for you inside."

He frowns, but before he can boss me around with his words, Warren calls out, "You're going to be late!"

Archie's sleeping at their place tonight. Felix jogs over the lawn to the back door, quickly kissing Archie's head before returning and taking my hand. I blow Warren and Archie a kiss, letting Felix lead me out the side gate to his truck.

"Not exactly the greatest mode of transportation when we're all dressed up," he huffs, opening the door for me to climb inside.

I try not to let the familiar interior bring forward any memories as he shuts the door and gets in on the driver's side. "Could have brought your bike?" I bite my lip, putting my seat belt on while he backs out.

He curses. "You'd have liked that, wouldn't you?"

Tilting a shoulder, I smile at him when he glances over at me, his brown eyes narrowing. His beard has grown even longer, thicker. And my imagination takes me on a ride where I'm sinking my fingers into it or feeling it between my thighs. Real life has my thighs clenching, and I cough, looking away.

We don't have to drive long, but that doesn't stop the nervousness from creeping in as we pull into the lot. The ceremony and reception are being held on the waterfront at the Bonnets Bay country club. After parking, Felix rounds the truck, and I grab my black clutch with one shaky hand, letting him take the other to help me down.

His touch soothes my jitters, but I still wobble a bit, grabbing his arm and laughing at myself. "It's been so long since I've worn heels."

He lifts my dress slightly, grinning at the black peep toe pumps before letting it drop and shutting the door. Looping my arm through his, we walk toward the entrance, where other guests are being ushered inside.

Felix is the best man, so we're quickly moved into position for photos before the ceremony begins.

Vera is a vision in her ivory lace gown. Elegant, breathtaking, and almost ethereal as she glides down the aisle on the sand, a twinkle in her blue eyes and an old man who's openly sniffling by her side.

The ceremony is beautiful. Their vows a simple yet powerful promise, and it's hard not to feel swept up by the happiness exuding from the evening's atmosphere.

Decorated in shades of ice blue and ivory, the ballroom has ribbon trim and glass vases with blue and cream flowers interspersed throughout. The chandeliers drip with crystal shards, creating miniature shapes of light that dance across the marble floor.

The happy couple twirls around the dance floor, Jared surprisingly great at waltzing. He whispers something into Vera's ear when he pulls her back to his chest, and she laughs with her head thrown back while he stares down at her with adoring eyes.

"They seem so happy," I remark, not meaning to out loud.

Felix's arm, which is around the back of my chair, shifts, his fingers playing with the loose curls in the ends of my hair. "They are. Total opposites with twin souls."

My head tilts, studying his contemplative face. His dark lashes bob when he brings those penetrating eyes to mine.

"Oh, my God, that's disgusting, Cleo. They're for decoration; they aren't edible!" someone shouts just as the music and the bridal waltz come to an end, turning the moment to dust.

Shifting in my chair, I find Cleo in a light blue gown, one of the bridesmaids, over by the cake. She giggles. "Shush, everyone can totally hear you."

"Why did we think it'd be a good idea to let the girls out to play?" Vera sighs, but she's smiling. The music starts up again, enticing other guests to the dance floor.

I turn back around, finding Felix smirking and rubbing his beard as he watches the women behind me. "Those chicks …"

"Crazy," Jared says, coming up behind us and squeezing our shoulders. "Vera's on it. Did you try the shrimp?"

Reaching up, I grip his hand. "Congratulations. You guys look amazing, and this place is beautiful."

He snorts. "Tell that to my savings account, on account of sending myself more broke and in more debt than ever before in my life." He's still smiling, though.

"Thought you said Vera was paying for it?" Felix frowns.

"Oh, she is." He winks, grabbing the flute of champagne sitting in front of Felix and downing it before depositing the glass back on the table. "She thinks she is, anyway."

With that, he bids us farewell, telling us not to do anything he wouldn't do, and returns to his bride.

The night wears on, but we sit and people watch, talking quietly about some of the strange guests. Like the man who'd been sitting by himself, then decided to leave early. Vera's dad, Felix informed me, before telling me about all the crap he put her and Jared through.

I'm surprised they even let him attend. But Jared would clearly do anything for Vera. And though she seems untouchable, encased in something colder than ice at times, there are moments when she's with Jared, her grandfather, and her friends when she allows herself to thaw radically.

"Want to dance?" Felix asks when everyone's starting to feel the effects of the open bar. I, myself, have had a few glasses, but I stopped when I realized Felix isn't drinking and remembered that he's not allowed to.

"Sure." I place my hand in his, and he directs me to the dance floor where only a few stragglers remain. Butch is there, trying to do something that looks like the moonwalk, which makes Jared boo and tell him not to quit his day job.

Felix laughs under his breath, wrapping his arms around me and swaying us gently until we're in the darkest corner of the room and it almost feels like we're alone.

My hands drift over his white dress shirt, up his neck, and fold until they're clasped together around it. "I don't think I've ever seen you in a suit before."

His lips tilt. "Get a good look, you probably won't again." He pauses. "Well, maybe again one day …" He trails off, and my heart skips at his unsaid words.

I lean forward, resting my head on his chest, and his arms tighten around me in response. "I think I prefer you in denim and boots anyway."

Warm breath hits my shoulder when he places a soft kiss there. "Strawberries."

It's a whisper, but the word strikes true, hitting me right in the chest. "My hair?"

He grunts, lips still resting against the skin of my shoulder, sending goose bumps racing over my body. "Sometimes," he whispers, "when I was away, I swear I could smell it. Thought that if I could locate the source, it would lead me to you. Used to drive me insane."

"I'm sorry," I croak, my eyes closing.

"Don't be. All roads in life … no matter where I've been or where I'm going … every single one will always lead me back to you. In this and every life after."

My head swims as I allow myself to absorb the conviction in those words.

So much has changed, and we've both changed so much.

Yet our hearts seem to recognize each other anyway.

Tears drip, escaping from my closed lids, and I lift my head at the same time Felix does, our eyes locking before I lean up, and our lips do, too. It's gentle, barely a touch, but it's also a question. He answers it by grazing his lips over my cheek, dipping down my neck and gently nipping my skin. My head tilts to the side, and a breathy sigh escapes me.

"God, the sounds you make," he whispers into my skin. "Especially when I touch you right here." His hand drifts between us, his fingers briefly skimming over my stomach, making it clench. "And here." He licks my pulse, which is thrumming in my ears. "And here." He softly runs his hands down my back, fingers following the curve of my ass and quickly squeezing.

A whimper falls past my lips, and his grin is evident in his voice. "There it is."

Lifting his hands to my face, he looks down at me before kissing my nose. "Let's get out of here."

Flames of unbearable heat unfurl in my belly, and I agree with a tremulous smile. We say our goodbyes before slipping out into the cool night, the breeze from the bay brushing over the skin of my exposed arms, yet doing nothing to soothe me as Felix helps me into the truck.

We're not even parked in the driveway properly before I'm climbing over the seat and into his lap.

Felix laughs as I grab his face, kissing his cheeks, his eyelids, his nose, and lastly, his lips.

He blindly puts the truck in park and grabs my arms, tilting me back. "I'm warning you now, Mags, you let me back inside you, and you'll let me inside again, night after night." He looks at my lips, then meets my gaze again. "Get what I'm saying?"

Puffing out a breath, I lean forward and whisper against his lips, "Loud and clear."

"Thank fucking Christ."

He yanks open the door, lifting me into his arms and slamming it closed behind him. We stumble down the moonlit grass and through the gate, my lips attached to his neck, my nose inhaling, and my fingers finally getting friendly with his beard.

"You're never getting rid of this," I pant, lifting my head as he closes the sliding door and heads to my room where he squeezes my ass then throws me on the bed. "Ever." I give him my best pointed look, which just makes him smirk while he flicks on the bedside lamp.

"Got it."

Stripping out of his jacket, he starts undoing the buttons of his dress shirt when I rise onto my knees, halting him. "Let me."

He drops his hands, his chest rising and falling faster beneath my unsteady hands while I undo the buttons. Once done, I drag the pads of my fingers over the dips and deep valleys of his abs, then up and over his firm pecs until they reach his shoulders. He groans deeply, twitching, and I shiver, loving the way he responds to my touch.

I smooth my hands over his shoulders, down his biceps and arms, dragging the white material with them. It falls to the floor, and I lift my gaze to his as my fingers land on his belt buckle next.

He watches me, nostrils flaring while I undo his belt and fly, then shove my hands down the sides of his pants, causing them and his briefs to fall to his knees.

He kicks off his dress shoes then shoves the pants the rest of the way off before gently grabbing the silken material of my gown. I lift my knees as he tugs, the dress gliding over my heated skin before hitting the floor and leaving me in my green bra and matching panties.

Gaining confidence from the way his breathing turns rough and the way his eyes are swallowing every inch of skin they can land on, I reach behind me and unclasp my bra.

His hands lift, calloused fingers trailing down my arms and taking the straps with them.

The bra lands on the bed, and my gaze stays on his as all the oxygen seems to vacate the small room.

"You're beautiful. Always so damn beautiful."

Flushing, I look away until his fingers turn my chin back to face him. "You don't believe me?" He puffs out a humorous breath. "You never did."

Shaking my head, I admit, "My body has changed, that's all."

"I'm aware of that." Strong hands smooth over my arms, moving slowly to my breasts and grabbing one in each hand. My stomach somersaults. He might be aware, but he hasn't seen it like this with any kind of light other than from the television.

He steps forward, thumbs gently circling my nipples before squeezing the hard peaks and making me gasp. "These tits are bigger, fuller, softer, and I'm rather fucking fond of them."

His fingers trail down over my stomach, finding some of the stretch marks near my belly button and hips. I hadn't realized he'd noticed them. "You are?"

"Fuck yes, I am. And these …" He groans, the sound reverberating through every inch of my body, making tiny hairs and goose bumps rise. "These little changes are my fucking favorite."

With my heart pounding its way up my throat and tears brimming my eyes, I rasp out, "Why?"

"Because." He grabs my hips, lifting me so that I'm standing on the bed for him to kiss my stomach, his thumbs gently rubbing over my C-section scar. "They're from our son growing inside you, and if I should be so god damned lucky …" His beard tickles as his tongue skates over the sensitive skin, his lips finding a small stretch mark and kissing it. "You're gonna get more of these after I put another baby in here."

I can't take anymore and grasp his head, dropping mine to kiss him. "I love you, big guy."

He curses, his tongue meeting mine in a slow rhythm of

surrender and familiarity.

We fall onto the bed, his cock grinding into my damp panties instantly when he spreads my thighs open. He growls, then yanks them off with so much impatience, I think I hear them tear. His lips return to mine, his tongue skims the roof of my mouth, and his hands roam everywhere.

He pulls away, his breathing heavy, then he's nipping and kissing a path down my neck, breasts, and stomach until he reaches my mound. Spreading me open, he shoves his nose right in, nudging my clit and making me moan. "Fuck, I've missed this sweet little pussy."

His tongue dives in, lapping at my entrance and making my hands fist the sheets.

Giving in, I let them do what they want and reach down to tug at his short strands of hair. His answering groan rumbles deliciously against me, making me tug harder and become more desperate.

A finger slips inside, and I begin rolling my hips into his face and finger as I start to feel myself drifting. His tongue flicks my clit hard, and my head flops back, my body succumbing to the overwhelming explosion of sensation.

He's inside me not even a second later, and I blink, eyes widening while I try to adjust to the intrusion. He stares down at me, his hand grabbing my thigh and hooking it over his arm as he sinks deeper. "Fucking hell," he whispers throatily. "I can still feel your orgasm."

"Yeah?" I whimper when he rocks his hips.

He nods, and I trail my fingers over the wet evidence in his beard, grinning then moaning when he ducks his head to suck on my nipple.

He removes his lips with a pop, still grinding but staying seated deep inside.

"Can you feel me stretching you, Little Doe?"

"Y-yes."

His eyes hood even more, arms lowering to hover his lips over mine. "Tell me how it feels."

When I don't answer right away, he nips my bottom lip. "It ... it burns, but it burns so good."

"Yeah?"

"Yeah."

His teeth then sink into my neck, sucking and biting gently. "How deep am I?"

"Too deep."

"Why's that?"

"Because I can feel you—"

"Everywhere?" he finishes for me.

I nod, swallowing a moan. "Everywhere."

With his lips fused to mine, and his hands digging into my hair, he starts to move, thrusting slowly and so deep.

And when he looks at me, right before we crest the edge together, it's then I realize he was absolutely right.

I finally feel like I've come home.

CHAPTER THIRTY-FOUR

Felix

Waking up with my heart encased within my arms felt like everything had finally shifted back into place. Hard dick or no, I get up and creep out of the room to get Archie, letting Maggie sleep. She needs it, and I'm just thrilled I'm able to help her get it.

"What, no walk of shame this time?" Jake asks when he opens the back door to their house, wearing a matching set of dark blue pajamas and holding a coffee mug.

Trying not to smirk, I shrug and ask, "How was he? He up yet?"

I'm answered by a, "Da, da, da!" as Archie comes barreling toward the back door, tripping over and looking around as if he's trying to figure out how that happened.

Grinning with my heart trying to punch a hole in my chest at hearing those words, I step past Jake and lift him up. His tiny fists grab my beard when I lean in to kiss his cheeks in rapid succession. "Were you good, little man?"

He answers me with a tug on my beard and, "Ma, ma."

"Sleeping," I tell him with another kiss.

When he spots one of his cars on the floor and starts shouting at it, I put him down, watching him run over to it before driving it across the floor.

"Coffee?" Jake asks, moving into the kitchen.

"Yeah, thanks."

"He was fine," he finally tells me with his back turned to me. "Slept all night. Warren got up three times just to make sure he was breathing."

I tug out a stool, positioning it so that I can watch Archie as he runs through the dining area with his car over his head like it's a plane. "He sleeps well."

Jake hums. "Milk?"

"Thanks, yeah."

He places it down in front of me, and I watch the steam rise into the air as the tension builds. "I read the letters," I admit.

He nods, leaning against the counter and watching me over the rim of his mug. "Haven't read them myself; I wouldn't do that to her," he says. "I can imagine that wouldn't have been easy, though."

Shaking my head, I sigh. "It wasn't, but it was necessary." After looking at him for a moment, I blurt out a quick, "Thank you."

He lowers his mug. "For betraying her trust and giving them to you?" He scoffs. "I wouldn't be that much of an asshole for no reason. I did it for her."

"I know," I say. "So thank you. Not just for that …" He waits while I glance over at Archie, trying to find the words. "I'll never be able to repay you, either of you, for what you've done for them both."

Jake looks mildly shocked, and Warren chooses then to walk into the kitchen. He claps me on the shoulder. "Just love her."

Jake nods, albeit grudgingly. "Through it all. You can repay us by loving her."

Feeling my throat clog with emotion, I take a sip of coffee and try to swallow it down. "I will. I always have. And I won't let her down again."

Warren takes his coffee from Jake, standing beside him and smiling. Jake still looks skeptical, but his jaw unclenches when Warren nudges him in the ribs. "Good," he says. "We're not going anywhere. We'll be watching."

I start to laugh, thinking he's joking, yet his hard, unflinching gaze tells me differently.

Shit. Okay then.

Scratching the back of my head as nerves tiptoe down my spine, I now wonder how they're going to take what I need to tell them next. "I've rented a place for us."

Jake raises both brows.

Warren looks horrified. "What? You're not taking our bunches or our little dude away." He stabs a finger at me. "I won't let you, tough guy."

Putting my hands up in supplication, I rush to say, "It's close by. Only a few streets away."

"Oh, and that makes it okay, does it?" Warren's easygoing demeanor disappears. He seems genuinely pissed off.

Jake wraps an arm around his shoulders, turning him to face him as they talk in hushed voices. Not knowing what the fuck else to do, I drink some more of my coffee and wait it out, grinning at Archie when he drops a car into my lap and says, "Bup!"

"That's a new one, little man." I pick him up, and he stands

272 | ELLA FIELDS

on my thighs, a little arm holding tight to my neck. I can hear him sucking on that thumb of his next to my ear.

"I know," Warren hisses, drawing my attention back to them. "Fine, whatever."

The two of them turn back around. "We've come to an agreement," Warren says stoically.

Jake legitimately rolls his eyes. "We have not."

"We have," Warren argues. "We get them Friday through Monday." He lifts his hands into the air. "Sound fair?"

"Uh …" I hold back a laugh because no way in hell am I sharing my woman and kid like that.

Jake sighs. "He's joking. We knew she'd move on eventually, didn't we?" He eyes Warren pointedly.

"Not joking. But yeah." Warren's shoulders slump. "I guess we did."

"Honestly, it really is only a few streets away. And I know Maggie; she's going to want to see you guys. You're both welcome whenever you want."

Warren steps closer, squinting at me as he surveys my face. "You mean that?"

Jake mumbles something like, "Oh, you've done it now."

Looking back and forth between them and suddenly feeling uncertain, I mutter, "Yeah, sure."

Warren claps his hands, turning back to Jake and laying a loud kiss on his lips before reaching for his coffee. "This is so exciting! I'm going to look for a housewarming gift online."

Jake smirks as Warren bounds out of the kitchen, coffee escaping his mug.

"Hey, wait. She doesn't know. I want to …" Too late. He's already gone. "Surprise her."

"Don't worry, I'll warn him." Jake straightens from the counter. "But are you sure surprising her is really the right way to go about it?"

I know what he's not saying. That after everything she's worked through in her head, she could probably do with being prepared. But I know Maggie, every version of her, and if I'm there, well, I just hope that's enough. So I nod and stand. "Yeah, I think she could do with some surprises. Especially good ones." I flick my head in goodbye, my hands full with Archie and my coffee as I use my ass to slide the back door open. "I'm going to let Archie play out here while she's sleeping."

Jake sounds intrigued when he asks, "She's sleeping okay?"

Putting Archie down, I actually smile at the guy. "Yeah, she is."

Looking at me for a moment, he chews his lip then nods slowly. "Good."

That's all he says before walking off, and I close the door.

Rubbing my tired eyes, I sit on a rock in the garden, sipping my coffee while I watch Archie try to do somersaults on the grass.

Kid's got energy today, much more than I do. I managed to slide back between Maggie's legs not long after the first round before she passed out. And while she slept, I just stared. Like some kind of fucking creeper. Not that I care, though. That woman has always made me do weird shit that I'd never thought myself capable of.

I smirk, taking a big mouthful of coffee as I think about all the times she's looked at me like I've made her heart soar by doing something simple for her. Things I wouldn't usually care about or bother doing much. Like putting laundry in the washer and turning it on. Can't even count how many times she ended up turned on from such a small thing.

And I'm not always stupid, so I kept doing it. I'll keep doing it.

My dick hardens even more, and I try to adjust it discreetly as I run through a mental list for future reference. These damn pants don't exactly help. I'm still wearing the same ones from last night. I need to get home and change.

Hands land on my shoulders, and the scent of strawberries fills my nose as Maggie leans down to whisper in my ear, "Got a bit of an issue, have you?"

"Nothing new there, Little Doe."

Her laughter tinkles into my ear, her warm breath hitting my cheek as she tilts my chin up to plant her soft lips on mine briefly. "Was he good?" she asks, stepping away.

I grab her hand, tugging her into my lap and putting my mug on the grass.

"He was. Jake said Warren got worried 'cause he slept all night."

She shakes her head with a smile, her finger trailing gentle circles over my upper back and doing nothing to help quell my now raging hard-on. "I can so picture that."

I grunt, wrapping my arms around her and lifting a hand to squeeze her tit through her pink t-shirt. She giggles, shoving my hand down and resting her head on mine.

I meet her brown eyes with my own and whisper, "I love you."

Her smile grows, and the world seems to right itself even more when she says, "Right back atcha, big guy."

Now, I'm not always a dickhead when it comes to my impulses. Oh, fuck it. Who am I kidding? I am. Some things don't change. But I'd like to think the fact I've put off this visit until now means that I've made *some* progress.

Even if that is mostly thanks to being so entangled with Maggie and Archie.

Baby steps, right?

"Hey, Phil." I tap the bar, trying to get his attention.

He turns around, putting a glass down that he was drying and grinning. "Hey, man. Long time, no see. Doing all right after your stint?"

"Yeah, good." I look around. "Sam in?" She's been living above the Westbrook for years.

"Nah, man. She left almost a few weeks ago now." He frowns. "Why's that?"

No fucking way. "She left?" I try not to growl, but well, I don't have much luck, and it happens anyway.

Phil startles. "Yeah, sorry. She pretty much just packed some bags, gave me back the key, and then left. Didn't say why or nothin.'"

God damn it. In trying to make shit right with Maggie, I've left it too late.

"Can I have it?" I ask.

Phil looks confused. "What? The apartment? Someone else is looking at it tonight. But I can—"

"No." I cut him off. "The key. Just need to check something out."

He shrugs, heading over to the back wall and returning with a small set of keys. I thank him and leave the bar, turning right as soon as I hit the sidewalk and unlocking the door at the bottom before jogging up the dirty, dust-covered stairs.

After unlocking the door to the apartment at the top, I stop in the doorway and look around, cursing and feeling like I could punch myself in the face for not thinking to pay her a visit sooner.

There's nothing. All her furniture is here, but as I yank open drawers and tear off the bed sheets, I find nothing of personal value left behind.

Nothing that would help me understand why the fuck she sent two thugs after my girlfriend.

Groaning and scrubbing my hands down my face, I take a deep breath and slowly let it out, hoping it takes some of my anger and frustration with it. It doesn't.

She's not here, and if I'm right, then she probably won't be back.

With nothing left to do, I lock the door behind me, pausing when something white catches my eye.

Reaching up to the top of the door, I find a piece of paper taped to it, and pull it down.

"Fucking letters," I grumble, unfolding it. Only, in this case, this one is from a woman I'd be happy never to set my eyes on again.

Dear Lix,

All I can say is I'm sorry. Not that it counts for much.

I saw an opportunity, and I took it. I wasn't thinking straight and didn't mean for it to go that far.

You're so much of my heart, and I've only ever wanted you to be happy.

But then I found out that she was pregnant. So when they were looking for you, well, I kind of lost it for a minute. I made a mistake. I knew it instantly, but it was already too late, and I know it's one that will stay with me for the rest of my life.

I know you probably hate me, and I deserve that.

And I know I'm a coward for leaving, but I couldn't bear to see you look at me with that kind of emotion.

It was good, though, being able to talk to you again, to hear you laugh and be there for you.

I just hope you don't let your hatred for me and what happened stop you from being happy.

All my love,
Sam.

Rage fills my heart, funneling through my body until my eyes and head start to swim with it.

Crumpling the note, I shove it in my pocket before storming down the stairs and blindly walking through the bar.

I drop the keys on the counter and flick my hand over my head when Phil yells out, "Bye, man!"

Out on the street, I stop for a second. Just a second to try to get my head functioning properly. All that goes to shit, though, when my eyes land on Hellsy, walking toward the bar.

I've got him pinned up against the brick wall before I even know what I'm doing. "Hey, Williams, shit …" he says nervously before my fist connects with his jaw. Someone gasps behind us.

He groans, spitting blood onto the sidewalk and grinning at me with blood-coated teeth. "Dude, I was just doing my job. It was nothin' personal."

"Nothing personal? You went after my fucking girlfriend for money, and it was nothing personal?"

"We gotta do what we gotta do, bro." He shrugs. *He fucking shrugs.* "Ain't anything special about her. Someone owes the boss man, they need to pay up. You know how it works."

I hit him again, growling into his face, "She was fucking pregnant and had nothing to do with it! *Nothing.*"

His eyes widen then fill with malice. "She's attached to you, motherfucker." He spits blood onto my cheek. "So that means she did."

Shoving him against the wall, I let go. Not just of him, but of the rage I've been desperately trying to contain. He drops to the ground after the fourth blow to his gut, groaning.

My foot rears back to connect with his jaw as visions of what he did to Maggie filter through my brain. The rage becomes everything I am. All I can see, feel, and hear.

Until a different sound penetrates my ears, and I see red and blue lights reflected through the window of the bar.

My heart stops.

Fuck.

CHAPTER THIRTY-FIVE

Maggie

My ringing phone startles me. It's only nine thirty, but I went to bed early even if I couldn't sleep, hoping that Felix would show. The empty space beside me on the bed glares back at me, tempting my conscience to go to terrible places.

"Hello?"

"Mags, hey." Jared's voice fills my ear, which has me sitting upright and panic clutching my throat. He should be on his honeymoon with Vera by now. "Can you by any chance get to the police station in Rayleigh?"

Breath escapes me in a rush, and I start to stammer, "W-what happened … is he?"

Jared rushes to say, "He's fine. He's okay. You just need to go to him, okay?"

I nod even though he can't see me and stare vacantly at the wall. "Maggie?"

"Yeah, yeah. I'll, uh … I'm going."

"Hey." His voice changes from rushed and worried to light and soothing. "Chill. Would I lie to you?" He curses. "Now I've got that song in my head. Want me to sing it to you, baby?"

He groans when Vera says something to him in the background. "Don't hit me, woman."

I start laughing, and he coos like I'm a freaking child. "There, go on then. Get your butt moving, he's waiting for you."

"Okay." I stand on shaky legs and grab my purse.

"Tell Felix to call me once you guys get out of there, yeah?"

"I will. Thanks." I hang up and drop my phone in my purse before pausing outside Archie's room. "Shit."

Digging my phone back out, I call Warren, hoping he hasn't gone to bed early for once.

"What, the Hulk not good enough to be your booty call tonight, bunches?"

Snorting, I hurry to tell him what Jared said.

He walks inside a minute later, waving a hand at the door. "Go. Need me to come with?"

"No, I'll be okay."

"You sure?"

Not entirely. "As sure as I can be." I grab my keys and walk out before I change my mind and tell him to come with me.

The drive to the city only takes just under thirty minutes, but it feels like hours before I finally pull in on the street outside the police station. Taking a few deep breaths, I push my hair back and open the door, looking around the darkened street warily before mentally kicking my butt to hurry up and get inside.

"Hi, I'm looking for Felix Williams." I stop at the front desk.

The attendant takes his time, looking me up and down

before shoving his pen into his mouth and glancing at a piece of paper.

"He's being questioned. Take a seat."

Questioned? What the hell is going on?

Nerves ignite low in my stomach as the minutes tick by on the old clock hanging above the front desk. The clerk continues to stare at me. Maybe it's because I'm wearing sleep shorts and a t-shirt, or maybe it's because he's got nothing better to do.

When I start to get too anxious, I almost shout across the room, "So when can I see him?"

He picks up a phone without taking his eyes from me and waits for someone to pick up on the other end. "Yeah, got a woman here for Felix Williams."

He nods slightly. "Mmmhmm, yep." He hangs up and stares at me for another full minute. God, he's starting to freak me out more than the situation is. I'm on my feet, about to scream or tear my hair out, when finally, an officer rounds the corner. "Miss?"

The officer looks familiar, but I only pause a second before saying, "Maggie. I'm here for Felix."

"Right. We're not done questioning him yet, but you're welcome to wait. Though, I'm going to be honest. The guy's on parole. Looks like he'll be going in lockup until he can appear before a judge at this stage."

I almost choke on my heart. "*What?*" His face crumples a bit with what seems to be remorse.

Fuck his remorse. They're not locking him up again. "What happened?"

"I'm not really at liberty to discuss all the details, but he's been arrested for disturbing the peace, physical assault, and—"

He stops when I hold my hand up and close my eyes, trying to think. I need a second to wrap my scattered brain around why the hell he'd do such a thing when ...

My eyes spring open. "Who did he assault?"

The officer shakes his head. "It's—"

"I know, but it's important."

"Why? He's committed a multitude of offenses, ma'am." He looks genuinely baffled, his kind eyes assessing my face before recognition sets in. "The hospital, you were beaten—"

"Yes, and this time, I'm ready to report an assault. Is there someone who can help me with that?"

His brows rise, and he glances back down the hall, likely to where Felix is, then back at me. "I'm Officer Marks, but I don't expect you'd remember that. This way." He holds an arm out, and I follow him down the hall, stopping by a door when I see Felix sitting there through the window.

He's in a chair, knees spread with his bent elbows on them, hands holding his head. Tears fill my eyes looking at him, but I don't know if it's because of what he's done, or what I'm about to do as a result of it.

"Ma'am?"

I tear my eyes away, leaving Felix just as his head shoots up and he sees me.

Officer Marks leads me into another room, holding a chair out for me to take a seat before he does the same on the other side. He flicks some switches on behind him and goes through the motions, before telling me to begin.

I sit there for a minute, feeling my pulse flooding my ears and head with its incessant racing. My palms start to sweat, and I tuck them under my legs as I try to compose myself.

But as the officer waits patiently, it hits me then. This is not just about wanting to get Felix out of this mess—though, it's the catalyst—it's about the anger that suddenly surges within me.

It's the injustice of not what was simply done to me, but to my mom and to many other women and people, that has me speaking.

"On March the second, 2015, I left work at nine thirty at night and stopped in at the convenience store down on Hamilton drive to grab some milk and bread. My friend who I was staying with at the time sent me a text asking if I would. I …." Stopping, I close my eyes, and the officer murmurs for me to take my time.

After a minute, I reopen them, steel my spine, and continue, "I got out of the car, got the milk and bread, and went back outside. But two guys were there waiting for me beside my car. They … they grabbed me. I remember the milk falling to the pavement and worrying about the wasted money." I laugh humorlessly, stopping when my breath hitches.

"In an alleyway nearby, they asked me for money. Money I didn't have. Money that my boyfriend apparently owed their, um, boss. I told them. I told them over and over I didn't have it. That I had no idea about it. And as they shoved me to the ground and kicked me, I told them again. When they grabbed handfuls of my hair before backhanding me in the face, I choked on the blood coating my mouth, telling them again …"

Officer Marks leaves the room to get the men's names and any other details he can on their whereabouts from Felix, before returning a while later with Felix trailing behind him.

"Mags." Felix rushes into the room, pulling me from the staring match I was having with the metal desk in front of me. His hands grip my face, brown eyes worried. "What did you do?"

"What I should've done a long time ago," I whisper, swiping my hands under my eyes then pushing him off me.

I ignore the hurt that passes over his handsome face and turn to Officer Marks. "He's free to go?"

He nods, his sad eyes turning hard when they land on Felix. "Count your lucky stars that these two men have been evading us for a damn long time and for a lot of shit, Williams."

Felix nods, and the officer sighs. "We were able to let you go this time based on the information you provided, but don't let us see you back in here again. No matter what those guys did, we've got what happened in your file, and your ass *will* land back in jail. That's not a threat. It's just the way the law works, so follow it."

"Yes, sir." Felix takes my hand, and I give the officer a wobbly smile.

"Ma'am?" I pause in the doorway. "Thank you for finally giving your statement. We'll be in touch if we need anything further."

Swallowing, I shove what might come from my head, telling myself I've done the right thing, and simply nod, before following Felix outside.

"Hey, look at me." He stops by my car, and I wiggle my hand out of his.

"Can we please just go?" I head to the driver's side, but he stops me, taking my hand again and gently prying my keys from my clenched fist then moving me around to the passenger side.

"You need to call your brother," I mumble when he pulls out onto the road.

My head feels like it's stuck in a steamy hot shower with the rest of my body cold and exposed.

Unsticking themselves from the blurring taillights of a car

in front of us on the highway, my eyes land on Felix's hand. It's clenching the steering wheel, and even in the dark of the car, I can make out the blood on it. My stomach turns, and I shift them away to stare back out the window.

Once home, Felix tries to help me out of the car, but I beat him to it and make my way to the side gate. "Maggie, please. Wait."

Spinning around, I glare at him. "You said you wouldn't leave me again, Felix."

He winces. "I know." Moving to touch me, he notices me looking at the blood on his hands and drops them to his sides. "But they hurt you." His voice breaks. "I couldn't … I can't."

"Stop, just stop," I almost yell. "You can stay, but you'll sleep on the couch."

He looks like he wants to argue again, but I turn away and walk through the backyard, assuring Warren that everything is okay before he leaves, looking at Felix with curious eyes.

Felix locks the door behind him, and I hear the shower turn on after I walk into my room. I climb into bed and stare at the ceiling, my heart bleeding tiny rivers that break the banks of my eyes and run down my cheeks, disappearing into my hair.

I stay silent when the shower shuts off, willing the tears to stop. They don't; they only come faster when Felix's weight makes the bed dip and he pulls me into his damp chest.

"I'm sorry. I wasn't thinking clearly. All I saw was you, broken and scared. And I'd just found this …"

I try to push away from him when he hands me a crumpled piece of paper. Frowning, I take it from him and roll over to switch on the lamp to read it.

It's from Sam. And none of it makes any sense to me besides her obvious love for the man lying behind me. I roll over, questions filling my gaze as he stares at me.

He tucks some hair behind my ear. "She told them that if anyone had the money Ryan paid me in advance to take on that job, it'd be his girlfriend."

Sniffling, I ask, "Ryan let them come after me?"

He shakes his head. "He told them to find me or Jared, but Sam overheard and told them they'd have no luck and to find you instead."

"What?" I gasp, my hand fisting the letter and scrunching it further. Letting it fall from my hand, I jump out of bed, pacing the floor beside it. Sam … *oh, my God.*

"Mags." He sits up, the comforter falling around his naked waist.

"She found me, Felix." I stop and look at him. "She's the one who found me. After what they did."

He curses hoarsely, glancing away. "Well, she's fucking disappeared."

"I know." He looks back at me then. "I saw her a few weeks ago while I was at the plaza as she was leaving." I laugh, feeling a little crazed. "This is all so insane. I don't understand … She never gave me any indication that she hated me. We weren't exactly friends, but she was nice to me."

"Come here." When I don't, he gets up, stark naked, and walks over to me to hold my face. "She was jealous. You didn't do anything wrong."

"Except love you and fall pregnant." My stomach lurches. "She wanted me to lose … oh, holy shit." I can't finish the thought, can't even fathom how anyone would do such a thing.

"Shhh." He drops his forehead to mine. "Jealousy can make people do some crazy shit. But she didn't succeed. They didn't either. It's over."

"But is it?" I step back, causing his hands to drop. "Is it ever really over?"

"It is, I promise."

"You can't do that, Felix. Didn't we figure out a long time ago that life doesn't give a shit about your promises?" He looks stunned. Good. He needs to understand that we can only control so much with our words. "And you're not doing a damn thing to help by trying to avenge your broken girlfriend."

"You're not broken, Mags."

"No," I admit. "Not like I was before. But life is going to keep happening, Felix. We've learned that the hard way; only now, after tonight, I'm not so sure you've learned anything at all."

"Don't say that; it's not true. You can't expect me to just watch one of those fuckers walk on by down the street after what they did to you."

He has a point there. And asking this giant, overprotective man who owns my heart not to be himself is like asking the rain not to wet you as it's already landing upon you. "I get that, I do. But did you even stop to think about what would happen? If you were sent back to prison?" My voice catches on those last words. "You got lucky tonight, Felix, but that won't happen again. How long would it be this time? And would it be worth missing out on even more time with Archie, with *me?*"

My eyes implore him to look outside his own anguish and, instead, to take notice of mine.

A choked sound leaves him, and then he's holding me. "I'm sorry. I didn't think; I was blinded by fury. But it won't happen again, I promise."

"Don't make promises, Felix." Planting my hands on his bare chest, I push away from him. "Live them."

His gaze burns into my back as I get in bed.

He remains there for a minute, and desperation becomes all I can feel when I hear him finally leave the room. But tonight's events have sobered me completely, flayed me open—even if I think it needed to happen—and I need time to process it all.

Hours later, as the sun changes shifts with the moon, I pad quietly out to the living room.

He's waiting for me, arms open and sleep softening his features.

I climb into them, laying on top of him with his arms around me and his breath stirring the top of my hair, and finally, I fall asleep.

CHAPTER THIRTY-SIX

Maggie

I watch as Archie dances in the living room, throwing plastic balls into the air and almost tripping over the ones below his little feet.

Felix left earlier this morning to head to work after kissing me on the forehead and saying he'd be back as soon as he could. Not long after, Officer Marks called me to let me know that Hellsy and Smith had already been arrested and were awaiting their bail hearing.

With the number of outstanding warrants and the horrible things they've done over the years, I don't predict them getting out of jail for quite some time.

I expected to feel relieved, and I am. But talking to Officer Marks about what happened is what's changed something. It's as if I've finally allowed myself to let it go. I've released it, put it out there for the universe to know, and doing so has settled something deep inside me that I can't quite pinpoint, but it's there, and it's no longer stirring or bubbling. It feels quiet. Peaceful, almost.

The door slides open. "Bunches, everything okay?" Warren asks, walking inside.

"Yeah." I blow out a breath. "Felix got into some trouble."

Warren tilts my chin to look at him, his eyes searching my face. "What happened?"

Putting my coffee mug down, I relay the events of last night to him. Every ugly detail.

"Well, damn." He runs his hand over his jaw. "Good on you. And good on him."

With my nose wrinkling, I almost shout, "*What?*"

He shrugs. "I'd have done the same thing if I ever saw those scumbags. *I* don't have a record, though, so I can see why you'd be upset."

"He could've gone back to jail, Warren. This is *exactly* what I was trying to prevent." I grumble, "And it happened anyway, didn't it?"

He chucks a few balls back into the living room. "You tried, bunches. Can't fault you for that. Just don't be too hard on him." He reaches up to tuck some hair back from my face. "You bring out the protective instinct in us men."

Snorting, I turn away. "He didn't need to do it."

"You might think so, and hell, maybe you're right. But look at what's happened because of it, hmm?" He picks up Archie when he comes toddling over, asking for milk. "That man loves you. We all do, but Felix feels like he's let you down enough times already. To him, he was doing what his guilt and his feelings for you demanded of him at that moment. Even if that meant he'd let you down again as a result."

"And men say women are confusing."

He scoffs. "You totally are. Why do you think I

married a guy?"

Laughing, I mutter, "Shut up. You'd have married a guy anyway."

"True. Anyway, work to do and all that lovely stuff."

Kissing Archie, he passes him to me. His chubby hand makes a grab for my lips, and I kiss it, causing him to smile. "Okay, I'll just be here." I look around. "Wondering what to do with this stubborn-ass man of mine."

Warren pauses at the door. "I think you've already figured it out, bunches."

"What?" I frown.

"*Your* man." He winks. "Think about what that means for a minute."

He leaves, and I raise a brow at Archie. "Your daddy is silly, isn't he?"

Archie babbles, "Da, da, dad." He pauses then asks, "Mik?"

Smiling, I kiss his nose and get him some milk.

The day drags as I stay in a silent battle with my own thoughts. But maybe it's a good thing. As the longing and the hope that seem to be smothering my dark worries have me realizing that maybe our fear doesn't always hold us back.

Sometimes, it's simply us. And in holding myself back, I could miss out on some of the best things this life of mine is offering.

Regardless of his mistakes and my own, we've already missed out on so much.

Time doesn't wait for anyone.

It's a wasted effort and often pointless trying to make it do so.

Felix shows up at around six thirty and takes over dinner and bath time for me, leaving me bereft of anything to do other than fidget and fuss while I wait for him to put Archie to bed.

While I'm wiping down the already clean counter, Warren and Jake knock on the door and walk inside.

"Hey." I toss the cloth to the side of the sink and dry my hands. "What's up?"

Jake looks around while Warren shrugs. "Just doing what's been requested of us."

Brows knitting, I mutter, "What's been requested of—"

"Hey." Felix walks out, rinses the sippy cup beside me at the sink, and then grabs his keys. I'm still trying to figure out what's going on when he says to Jake and Warren, "He's just passed out. We'll be back later."

Jake nods, and Warren bites his lip to hide his obvious grin.

I put my shoes on but don't have time to ask any more questions, thanks to Felix grabbing my hand and leading me out the door and to the front of the house.

His bike is here, two helmets sitting on the seat. When I just stand there, about to ask what's going on, he picks one up and puts it on my head. A squeak of excitement escapes me when he gets the bike started, and I right my pink dress as I climb on behind him, tucking it under my butt.

"Where are we going?" I yell.

He backs out of the driveway, yelling over the noise of the bike. "You'll see in a minute."

"A minute?" I want to pepper him with more questions, but he halts them by saying, "I love you, Magdaline."

He's good. Real good. My mouth shuts, my arms wrapping

around him tighter as he takes off. Sure enough, not even a minute later, he's pulling into the driveway of a small brown cottage a few streets away.

"Who lives here?"

He doesn't answer me until he's turned the bike off, grabbing my hand when I swing my leg over to stand. "We do."

My jaw drops, my eyes bug out, and my stomach dips. "We?"

Chuckling, he takes off my helmet and hangs it on the bike, then slides his hands into my hair. "We do, Little Doe. It's ours."

My mouth opens and closes sporadically, and I spin around to get a better look at the small house.

It's adorable. Kind of run down, but it looks like someone's given it a bit of love recently as we walk up the steps and I eye the fresh paint of the porch and windows.

Felix opens the door, but me? I'm still gaping at it all. The cute, white trim on the windows, the old rocker sitting on the porch, and a small pot of orange and pink flowers by the door.

He lifts me up, and I'm too dazed to let that startle me. As he carries me inside, my eyes scan the old wood floor, and he nudges the door closed behind us.

"This … is ours?" I breathe, my eyes dancing over the open plan room, still trying to catch up.

There's a three-seater couch, which looks new. A cute, rustic cabinet with a small flat-screen TV on it, and in the small kitchen, there are even a few appliances.

"All ours. Well, it's a rental. But still …" He sounds nervous, and my head tilts up to look at him. "Do you like it?"

"Do I like it?" I repeat, and the crease between his brows becomes more prominent with his increasing worry. His arms tense around me. "I don't. I *love* it."

His sigh of relief is loud and makes me giggle. He pinches

my ass, and I grab his face to smoosh my nose against his. "This is why you've stunk of paint? Why you didn't show up some nights?"

My heart swells painfully when he nods. He's been here. After working all day, he's been coming here and working again. I trail my finger down the side of his cheek. "You're a keeper, big guy."

He grins. "You plan on keeping me?"

I nod, brushing my lips over his and whispering, "Forever."

"Good, because you're stuck with me anyway, Little Doe."

He kisses me back, his teeth grazing my bottom lip and sucking it into his mouth, then he pulls away and walks down the hall. "Toilet's there, Archie's room there, there's another tiny ass room there, oh, and a bathroom. Laundry's near the kitchen." He walks into the room at the end and stops in front of a familiar looking bed. "But this is the most important room right now." He lowers my feet to the floor, ducking his head to my neck and inhaling before skimming his tongue over my collarbone.

Breath catching, I pull away, and he groans. "Is that my old CD collection?"

I walk over to the same bookshelf he had in his room at Darren's, running my fingers over them and finding even more things. My old books, some hair ties in a jar, and some photos of us. He's even taken the one I saw in a broken pile of glass in his room and put it into a new frame.

He jerks his head at the closet when I glance over my shoulder at him. "There's more stuff in there."

Rushing over to it, I slide the mirrored door open, swallowing when I find the rest of my clothes I'd left behind almost two years ago. Fingers brushing over the fabric, my eyes snag on a box below them on the floor, sitting next to some of my old shoes.

My letters.

Seeing that box knocks the air out of my lungs, and I sit on the floor, opening the lid to rummage through them.

Felix sits down beside me. "They're all there."

Tears fill my eyes when I catch a few of the words from those earlier days. The days before Archie arrived, and that fear, that turbulent force that controlled my every move, was both my sole companion and worst enemy.

"Mags." Felix pulls me onto his lap, and I drop the box. "Give me those doe eyes."

Lifting my gaze to him, I try to focus on him through the wall of tears. I blink, and they tumble down my cheeks. He catches them, thumbs stroking my cheeks, and his dark eyes, like melted chocolate, penetrate mine. "I know you don't want my promises. But I'm here, we're going to move on, and we're going to be happy."

I shake my head. "But …"

"What?" he asks softly.

"You weren't a witness to that." I glance at the letters. "To all my crazy. What if I have more setbacks? What if—"

He shushes me with a peck on my lips. "There are no setbacks, only stumbles. And I'm going to be here, ready and waiting to keep you steady, to keep you moving. Never doubt that, or yourself."

"I don't doubt you."

He gives me a sad, knowing smile. "But you don't believe me, either. Not entirely." Standing, he takes me with him as he moves to the bed. "That's okay because you will."

I know I will. Regardless of what this life brings, I can't walk away from my heart.

Sure, I might survive it again, but it wouldn't be living.

"Undress me, big guy." I tug his lip into my mouth then release it. "We have a home to christen."

He doesn't hesitate; our clothes and shoes land in a pile on the floor, right next to that little blue box. My back arches when he takes a nipple in his mouth and runs his hand over my stomach until it finds my entrance. He inserts a finger, and I roll into it, desperate to cling to the pleasure that surges within, but my need to do something else overrules it.

Panting, I squirm away, and he scowls, reaching for me. I smile and shove at his chest, which does nothing, but he tilts his head and humors me, lying down with his arms behind his head.

My fingers trail down over the hard ridges and tempting valleys of his torso before they drag gently along what they really want. I squeeze him, and he jerks, hissing and closing his eyes.

I watch them fly open as I take as much of him into my mouth as I can and suck, rubbing my hand up and down his shaft to make up for what can't fit.

He curses, his hands grabbing my hair as he gently starts thrusting. The salty taste of pre-cum hits the back of my throat, and I moan, my eyes closing.

"Fuck." He jerks hard and tugs my head off him. "Roll over, onto your knees."

Licking my lips and watching his eyes blaze, I hop onto all fours. His rough hand runs over my back, and it arches in response. "Perfect," he whispers, squeezing my ass.

Spreading my legs wider with his knee, his finger dips inside me, teasing at first, then he fucks me with it, knuckle deep until I'm trembling, thrusting, trying to get myself off.

He pulls out, and I swear I could almost cry until I feel his cock right there. He pushes in, groaning in the back of his throat and setting a punishing rhythm that has me so close to coming again.

He stops, and I almost growl. Chuckling in my ear, he murmurs, "Hold the headboard."

I grab it, whimpering at the new angle that has us almost upright and his cock resting over that magical spot. "Felix …" He's got me so worked up that I'm going to come, and he's barely even moving right now.

With one hand sprawled over my stomach, the other one reaches around to move my hair aside then grab my chin. Tilting my head to look at him, his eyes flare and he rasps, "Open."

I do, and he slips two fingers inside my mouth, watching as I wrap my lips around them. "That's it. Suck. Get them all nice and slick."

He pulls them out, and I shiver. "I'm going to come," I warn.

Pushing in and out of me again, he moves those fingers to my clit and rubs so softly I think I cease breathing for a moment too long. "Yeah?" He starts to rub harder, his cock sinking inside me in quick thrusts but dragging back out torturously slow.

My legs start to shake, and his teeth sink into my shoulder. "Do it," he hisses.

He moans roughly, holding me up and fucking me hard and fast as my orgasm rocks through me, rendering me a quivering, mewling mess.

He grunts, stilling and grinding his pelvis into my ass. "Fuck. Yes."

Lifting a hand, I shove some hair off my face. He pulls out, and I turn around, letting out a breathy laugh when he flops back onto the bed, taking me with him.

"This old bed is still pretty sturdy." I twist around to stare down at him, my breasts squishing into the side of his chest.

He huffs out a husky laugh. "It sure fucking is."

We're quiet for a minute, his fingers running through the tangled strands of my hair.

"I can't believe we've got our own place." My stomach curls with excitement. "It's amazing, thank you."

His hand freezes, brown eyes narrowing on mine. "Don't thank me for something I should've done long ago. I've failed us too many times, now, Mags. There's no room for any more what-ifs. Only doing ... living."

With my finger tracing the indent between his brows, I say, "You're my best friend, my heart; there's always room for error and forgiveness where the heart's concerned."

He kisses my finger when it reaches his lips, and smiles so wide that I feel a pang in my chest. "Marry me?"

My stomach drops, and I gasp, rearing back. "What did you just say?"

He laughs. "Those damn eyes. Come back here." Snatching my wrist, he tugs me back to his chest. "I know it's a bit unconventional, but I'm serious. I'm yours, always, and I know you're mine. So do something I probably don't deserve and become my wife?"

I'm still staring at him like he's grown an extra head when all his words finally sink in and cause my heart to burst. "You're serious?"

He smirks and tweaks my nose. "Is that a yes or a no?"

Dropping my forehead to his, I answer him. "It's an, *I thought you'd never ask.*"

EPILOGUE

Felix

Twenty-Two Months Later

"This ongoing feud is fucking dumb. Can't we just put it to rest?" Jared grumbles below the ladder, keeping it steady for me.

I step down, squinting up at the blue and green balloons then grab the ladder. "It's our cat. I don't know why it's such a big deal. Just give it back."

Jared follows me as I trudge across the grass to the small shed. Opening the door, I put the ladder away and dust my hands off.

"She'll kill me. You really want to see your only brother dead; is that it?"

He looks serious, which has me biting back a laugh. "Not my problem."

Groaning, he follows me again as I head toward the back porch where Maggie is fussing with the green and blue cupcakes, candy, and the birthday cake on the table.

"Can't you just get her another one?"

I stop then, turning to face him. "You know how women are; that shit's not the same."

"Problem, boys?" Maggie asks, her hand resting under the bottom of our baby boy, who's strapped to her chest.

"None at all. Just telling Jared here that we're still waiting for our cat to be given back." I jump up the three steps, leaning down to kiss Finn's head and inhaling that newborn scent before trying to take him from her.

She bats my hand away. "He's sleeping. And Toulouse is happy there. Vera and I have already spoken about this."

I grumble under my breath, feeling Jared's shit-eating grin on me. "How women are, huh?" He snickers.

Maggie rolls her eyes. "Where's the birthday boy?"

Glancing away from our eight-week-old's squishy, sleeping face, I look around the porch. "Uhh …"

Jared punches me in the back, and I spin around, cursing when he points at the piñata around the side of the house, hanging from the smaller of the two trees in the backyard.

We both run down there, finding Archie and a boy from his preschool—Theo? Christ, I don't know—beating the damn thing with sticks. "Hey, little man. Not time for that yet."

Theo drops the stick while Archie just grins at me as I take his, dumping it on the ground. "But dere's candies inside. We wants them."

"There's also candy up there on the table. Come on." I reach for his hand while Jared ushers the other kid along with us.

"Hulk candies?" the other kid asks.

"Yeah, maybe." I shrug and lead them back to the porch just as the back door opens and more people arrive.

"Tough guy, whose party is this anyway?" Warren says,

clapping me on the back when he and Jake walk outside.

"You're the one who got him into the giant green dude," I grumble.

Jake smirks at Warren. "Touché."

"Daddy!" Archie yanks on my hand. "Cake soon?"

"Soon, buddy." I pick him up, and we walk over to greet some of the women who work with Maggie at the preschool. She's on maternity leave right now, but she's adamant that she'll be returning for at least two days a week once Finn's six months old.

We'll see. I have my ways of convincing her to do what I want. And I'd like her to keep our baby at home until he's at least one. The shop's doing better than ever—with an influx of people buying Harleys and bringing them to us. So it's not like we're in desperate need of more money. But I get it; she's used to contributing in some way.

Despite her worries, she hasn't had any setbacks. She sleeps just fine, at least six nights out of seven. The only time I got concerned was when she was late into her pregnancy with Finn. She swore she was okay, but I was damn worried by the way she'd cry at random shit or get stressed out about stuff so easily.

Maggie doesn't know this, but I got her old therapist's number from Jake and gave her a call. Felt like a total dipshit after the woman reassured me it all sounds completely normal. That pregnant women get emotional and to just keep an eye on her.

The back door swings open again. "Archie, baby! Come to grandmamma." Elodie takes him from me, and her new boyfriend, Shane, shakes my hand. Well, not new exactly. They've been together for a year now, and she's come a long way from the quiet woman who was too scared to even help her own daughter. Now she smiles at everyone and everything like she's won a million dollars all the time.

I shouldn't gripe. I am happy for her. I'm just not used to the motherly affection she tries to pester me with. "Look at this beard." She tsks, pinching my cheek. "We should trim it, yes? Come on, we've got time."

"Mom." Maggie laughs when I look at her pleadingly. "Leave him be. Would you mind grabbing some of the sodas from the fridge for me?"

I send Maggie a grateful smile when Elodie bounds away with Archie on her hip. She tried to do the same thing when we got married. Came at me with the clippers ready to go and everything.

Unlike Vera and Jared, we didn't have a fancy wedding. We both agreed that we didn't need it. And so one Saturday morning, a month after we moved in here, we got dressed up and went to city hall in Rayleigh where we made our vows of forever. Archie, Warren, Jake, Elodie, Jared, and Vera were the only attendees. We had lunch with everyone after, and Warren and Jake took Archie for the night so we could celebrate all night at home. On our kitchen counter, over the back of the couch, and in our bed.

Archie comes running back outside a minute later—thankfully putting a stop to where my thoughts were going—wearing a cape and a party hat on his head.

"Looks like someone's ready to party." Jared walks over and scruffs his messy brown hair as he adjusts his hat for him. Archie grins and shakes his butt around, making Vera laugh as she walks outside.

"There's my princess." Jared grins.

Vera raises a brow. "Me or the baby?"

Jared chuckles. "My baby girl, duh." Taking their

five-month-old daughter from Vera, Jared smooches her chubby cheeks loudly then squats to the ground for Archie to say hello.

For someone who didn't want kids, Vera's never looked happier. She fusses over Mirabelle almost as much as Jared does. I see lots of dance classes and girly mother-daughter outings in their future.

Never know, though, she could be a tomboy and prefer to hang out at the garage. I stifle the urge to laugh, just thinking about how well that would go over with Vera.

Once everyone arrives, we start some games with the few kids here. Jared and Warren get stuck with the hilarious task of trying to stop them from whacking each other or falling over when it's time for the piñata.

After lunch, Archie thinks it's a great idea to smash his cake like he's the actual Hulk after blowing out the candles, resulting in tears from some of his friends.

"It's okay. It's fine." Maggie hurries to save some of it, slopping it into plastic bowls, shoving some spoons in, and handing them out. "See?" She licks her finger. "Mmm, yum. Tastes even better now."

They all seem appeased by that, snatching their cake and hustling into the yard to eat it.

"Holy crap." She laughs as I take Finn from her.

"Nice save." Once Finn's situated in the crook of my arm, I grab her chin with my free hand, bringing her lips to mine for a quick kiss. "Delicious."

She grins, and it has me trying to swoop in for one more when she swipes some cake on my nose. "Gonna lick that off, Little Doe?" I murmur. She looks like she's tempted, glancing around and biting her lip. I rub it off myself, and lick it from my finger, watching her teeth sink even further into that rosy, plump bottom lip before I tweak her nose, causing a beautiful smile to light up those eyes. With a smirk on my face and my dick twitching behind the confines of my jeans, I walk away before I'm tempted to say to hell with this party business.

We finish a bit of cleanup before I finally allow myself to grab a drink.

"Jesus Christ," Jared breathes. "I'm exhausted."

I hand him a beer, standing back against the kitchen sink after most of the guests have left.

"Right?" I take a deep pull on my own. "I hope we don't end up doing this shit every year."

"Amen. Vera's already planning Mirabelle's first birthday."

That makes me snort. "She's not even six months old."

"Right? Try telling her that." He pauses with his beer halfway to his mouth. "Better yet, don't."

I shake my head, laughing under my breath.

"And then he started yelling like a teenage girl about a floating turd in the bathtub. He scared the shit out of her and made her pee all over herself and in the water as he was lifting her out," Vera says, entering the kitchen with Maggie holding her stomach and going red in the face from laughing so hard.

"Talking about me again, beauty?" Jared smirks.

Vera shrugs. "Don't give me such great stories to tell then, Hero."

He grins, tugging her to him and gently taking their sleeping daughter from her arms. "I'll give you plenty more where that came from." He lowers his voice. "Much better quality, too." Vera runs her hand over Mirabelle's dark brown hair, smiling.

I turn to Maggie as she steps into my side.

"Tired?" I kiss her forehead.

"A little."

We soon say goodbye to Jared and Vera, leaving only

Warren and Jake, who are sitting outside on the back porch, watching Archie play with his new toys.

I'm about to steal Finn, who's asleep on Jake's chest, when Archie shouts, "Daddy! Uncle Wazza and Jake gots me a Hulk!"

Warren snickers, taking the toy from him. "Look, doesn't that scowl look familiar?" Warren holds it up, showing me.

"Very fu—dging funny." I catch myself as Jake gives me the stink eye and take a seat on the deck chair next to him.

Archie climbs into my lap, fiddling with a remote control car's antenna.

"Big day, mister three." I brush his hair off his face.

"I'm free," he mumbles.

Smiling I say, "I know. Hence the party, little man."

"Can we has another one tomorrow?"

Jake snorts, and I shake my head. "Maybe next year." Or the one after.

Archie pouts, but nods reluctantly before dropping his head and sticking that thumb in his mouth.

"Thought you guys were trying to break that habit," Jake says, looking at Archie with an affectionate smile.

"We are, but it's his birthday." Shrugging, I take another sip of my beer.

Warren chuckles. "Getting soft in your old age, Hulk man."

"Oh, shush." Maggie walks outside with some leftover food from the grill and scruffs Warren's hair, making him scowl.

She puts the food on the table and brings me a plate. Seeing my hands are full, she lifts a bite of steak to my mouth before sitting down next to Warren.

After they leave, I give Archie a bath. It takes ten minutes to get the green shit out of his hair from the cake. I think I find a piece of candy in there too. When his head starts lolling to the side, I quickly finish washing him and wrap him in a towel.

I laugh quietly as he falls asleep while I'm dressing him, then place him in his toddler bed and pull the covers up to his shoulders.

"Good night, buddy." I stare at him for a moment, so grateful that I can before kissing his cheek and standing up.

Maggie's in the doorway, a tiny smile playing on her lips.

"He fell asleep while I was dressing him." I smirk and gather her into my arms.

She wraps her own around my neck, standing on her toes to place a kiss on my cheek. "He had a big day. I can't believe he's three."

Sighing, I squeeze her hips. "I know. Finn okay?"

"Sound asleep."

I believe her but walk her backward down the hall a little to check for myself. He's on his back, tiny thumb in his mouth.

"What I can't believe is that we were lucky enough to get two thumb suckers."

"They'll grow out of it."

They will. And my chest hurts with the knowledge that I'll want to remember these moments. That I'll one day miss their little habits.

"Come on." Taking her hand, I lead her to the living room. "I'll finish cleaning up. You go sit down."

Maggie halts me with a tug on my hand.

"We have two sleeping children." She raises a brow. "Wouldn't you agree that cleaning up can wait?"

My dick stirs. "You've got the all clear?"

She frowns and tilts her head. "Were you not waiting for me in the clinic two days ago?"

Well, damn. "Had no idea that's what you were discussing in there."

Laughing, she drags me down the hall to our room. "And

pray tell, what did you think we were discussing?"

I strip her of her dress, throwing it to the floor and undoing my jeans as she shimmies her panties down her legs. Too impatient to get everything else off, I lay her down and climb over her. Humming against the swells of her breasts, I lick and suck a path to her lips. "No idea. Boobs, your ..." I pause then. "Maybe I should've come into this appointment after all."

She laughs again and grabs my dick, giving it a gentle tug. "Hurry up and get inside me, husband."

"Don't need to tell me twice." I test her entrance before sinking inside, stopping for us both to adjust once I'm fully seated. Fuck, who would've thought a few months would feel like an eternity, especially after we'd been apart for more than eighteen of them before?

Her legs wrap around me, her breathing picking up against my lips. "I love you, big guy."

"Right back atcha, Little Doe."

Slowly, I start to move, trying to savor every feeling that erupts within and has my blood pumping faster.

And as my heart runs her fingers over my cheeks, and her tongue sweetly dances with mine, I know that as long as I've got this—her, us, always—then I'll take whatever this life throws at me. The hard, the easy, and absolutely everything in-between.

Because life doesn't always need to be easy.

And I've come to discover that it shouldn't be.

It just needs to be lived.

THE END.

PLAYLIST

Little Black Submarines—The Black Keys

Ghost—Ella Henderson

Where the City Meets the Sea—The Getaway Plan

Clarity Acoustic Sessions—Foxes

Lightening Crashes—Live

Say You Won't Let Go—James Arthur

ACKNOWLEDGEMENTS

As always, my husband. Thank you.

My children—This journey has been an adjustment for us all, especially for the two of you. Thank you for saying yes to chicken nuggets or toasted sandwiches on those days or nights where I'm lucky if I even know what time it is.

Billie—No words or thank you's are enough. You've been with me since the start and I just know you'll be there, encouraging me to see everything through to the very end.

Amanda—Thank you for loving this story, beta reading, and making me laugh. I'm sorry for making you nauseous and the loss of sleep.

Just blame Felix.

Paige—Thank you for not only beta reading, but for the continuous support and the reminder to tell a story the way I want to. I can't wait to share more with you.

Michelle—My bad cop, butt-kicking, spreadsheet ninja. Your enthusiasm for my stories and your help in getting them into early readers hands makes all the difference.
I'm so fortunate to have you as a friend.

Jenny from Editing4Indies—Thank you for all your help in making my stories shine to their truest potential. Don't ever think you're allowed to leave me!

Stacey from Champagne Book Design—Thank you for all that you do, and for making my books beautiful.

Sarah from Okay Creations—Another new favorite cover. You're incredible!!

Readers—Whether you're new to me or I'm old news to you, thank you. Like a million, billion, trillion times, thank you for taking a chance on me.

Ella Fields' Tea Room—My biggest thank you of all goes to you guys. You're the light in what can be a very daunting and crushing industry. Sometimes I feel the need to pinch myself when I remember you've all joined a group due to a shared love of my books.

I'll forever be grateful for you all.

ABOUT THE AUTHOR

Ella Fields lives in Australia with her husband, children and two cats. While her children are in school, you might find her talking about her characters and books to her two cats.

She's a notorious chocolate and notebook hoarder who enjoys creating hard-won happily ever afters.

Find Ella here:

Facebook:
facebook.com/authorellafields

Website
www.ellafields.net

Instagram:
www.instagram.com/authorellafields

Goodreads:
www.goodreads.com/author/show/16851087.Ella_Fields

Made in the USA
Las Vegas, NV
15 January 2022

41279799R00189